AFTER- A CHRISTIAN INSPIRATIONAL SERIES (BOOK 1)

JOY OHAGWU

LifeFountainMedia

A CONTEMPORARY CHRISTIAN
INSPIRATIONAL ROMANCE SERIES

Click here to get Author Joy Ohagwu's starter Library for FREE.
Details are at the end of this book.

FOUNDATIONAL SCRIPTURE

* * *

"All that the Father gives ME will come to ME, and the one who
comes to ME I will by no means cast out."-*JESUS* (John 6:37)

AFTER 1

AFTER:

(AFTER- A CONTEMPORARY CHRISTIAN INSPIRATIONAL SERIES, (BOOK 1)

FOUNDATIONAL SCRIPTURE

"When men are cast down, then you shall say, there is lifting up;"- Job 22:29

* * *

CHAPTER 1

* * *

*F*ebruary 3.

"EXCUSE ME?" A woman with a colorful smile, and bright eyes, linked hands with a man equally middle-aged. Her brown leather purse hung off her other arm, its long handle dangling in the chill wind. Laugh lines creased the corners of both her eyes.

Yards ahead, the crowd roared. New Yankee Stadium at the Bronx came alive with noise. The XLVIII Super Bowl. Their excitement was palpable. Wow! I loved that sound. Flags blew in brilliant colors and fans chanted. The collective whistling almost deafened me. The mammoth crowd of about 60,000 people were celebrating. It took a football lover to grasp this moment's significance.

I threw a worried glance toward Matt, my brother, also my manager. He stood off beneath covered stands, and waved me over then disappeared onto the stage. Doors to the backstage entrance swung wide—waiting for me. Almost time. Five minutes to the "go" signal. I could tell this couple, "I have to be on stage in five minutes." The rest of the team was already up there, drummer and all, ready. I should be hovering in the flank by now.

I caught the view of a uniformed security guard, coming down the guarded entry tunnel, holding a radio in one hand. He entered the restrooms area, away from us. *Great.* The doors closed behind him.

The couple—rooted on one spot—faced me. They expected my help. I exhaled. *I can't turn them away.* They seemed truly lost. By the way, how did they get past security and enter through here? General entrances were the other way.

She held something out. Tickets.

"Yes? How can I help you, ma'am?" This cold breeze blew the heat right off my body, making for my bones. I shivered and rubbed my arms. That helped a little. I was quite relieved when I heard they placed a heating fan up on stage.

"My husband, Jim, and I have been coming here thirty years, from our second date—"

"Except the ten in between when we were abroad," her husband cut in.

She nodded. "Right. Now we're back, and this year, they changed everything. The seats, entrances, everything. I don't know the way to anything anymore. I can't find our seat. We want to be there from the start of the national anthem."

The one I'll be performing…

"Please, can you help us locate our seating area?"

Ha...Got to be kidding me...I'm crunched for time!

The couple adjusted their frame. It was just my luck for choosing to practice my voice routine outside, instead of the prep room. Something about this open air had drawn me but now the chill stuck to my skin like glue. I was supposed to move from heated prep room, onto heated stage, with nothing between.

I glanced from stage to tunnel, searching for assistants. There was not a soul. Just me and these two. Of course, everyone was seated—estimated 60,000 of them—waiting for me to take the stage and sing the national anthem to kick things off. In about three minutes.

Matt would lose his mind for this! If my personal assistant wasn't out sick, she'd take care of it.

With a drawn breath, and one more look at the couple, I made up my mind. Something about them, a genuine feel, melted my heart. I couldn't let them wander around looking for seats when this 30-degree chill wind conditions alone could make them faint.

They appeared worn already, with faces long. The lady leaned heavily on her husband's arm, her neck slightly bent toward him. His shoulder drooped as though he needed someone to lean on too.

"All right, ma'am. Please follow me. Let's get this figured out." I glanced at their tickets. Section A: Seats C34, C35. Honor tickets. *Ah, no wonder.* They were among attendees above fifty who'd been coming the past fifteen years. They received special seating close to the performance stage, only for this year.

I led them toward the arena but underneath an archway where you could walk to your seat. Wind came from behind, forcing hair onto my face. The chill turned my clothing cold, inducing shivers. I shrugged my sweater tighter. I should've worn a heavier jacket if I knew I was going to be out here this long.

A sign depicted Section A adjacent to the stage. It was not too far then. A group of *Seahawks* fans breezed past us brimming with enthusiasm as they hailed their team.

I quickened my pace, with the couple following close behind. *One more minute, Matt.*

The pattern here was the same as some new arenas I'd performed in recently. Newer places now prioritize aesthetics, making spaces narrower, and harder to find. That could certainly prove challenging for older persons. Matt had to be pulling his hair by now in frustration over my delay. My phone buzzed. I peered and read.

A text message from Matt. "Where are you, Candace? I saw you awhile back. Where'd you go? You're three minutes behind schedule. Hurry up. BTW, John said he's tuned to watch you."

I hastened my pace. "Coming," I muttered. I texted the same back, sliding the phone into my pocket. So far, no one had recognized me as

Candace "Wit" Rodriguez, the famous singer. Over the PA system, someone on stage told a joke to the crowd. Few laughed.

They're buying time.

I don't remember doing this much walking in a while, at least, not in recent memory. I was panting, and breathing heavier. I usually moved from a waiting car, to an elevator, to the dressing or rehearsal room a couple of doors down, double-checked makeup and outfit, and then headed straight to the stage.

There was no searching for anything. Chaperons were readily available to oblige my every need. Why was today different? Ugh. Well....There! Section A straight ahead, right beside the new detached stage extension where I'd be singing. They'd raised the extension after heavy snow caused damage. *I'll cut through from here onto the stage.*

I pointed ahead. "Ma'am, your seats are up the third row, right behind the stage area. From the numbers on the side of the rows, your seat should be somewhere in the middle." By now, I trembled, my voice included. How could I be so out of breath—and so cold? And I had to perform...It was only a couple—

"Thank you so much, dear." The strength of her tight hug surprised me. "Haven't missed this in the past twenty years. Thanks to you, we'll be seeing it from the best seats. God bless you." She laid a soft hand on my shoulder as we parted.

They began ascending the steps to their seats as I cut through the front row, squeezed through a circular demarcation, hopped down, and landed on stage, toward the rear. I straightened my shirt and brushed my hair back. I saw Matt and waved, his forehead crinkled as he scanned from side to side, searching, and looking every bit as worried as I expected. He'd give me an earful after this.

A few audience members I'd passed recognized me, and applause broke out close to the platform. I smiled broadly and waved.

Matt dashed over and swung to my side. "Where on earth were you? I looked everywhere. They were about to call someone else in. I told them you were here *somewhere.*"

There was only time for a one-word answer before they signaled me to ascend for my performance. "Sorry."

He stepped to the side as I walked forward. VIPs applauded, and the crowd cheered. Both teams lined up, ready, with hands placed on their chests. I heard a couple of jeers. Why would anyone jeer? Those jarred my nerves.

My phone buzzed. A new text message. From John Akum. The talent manager for Global Sound Records, where I'm signed. I frowned. John doesn't text me. In fact, he said he never watched my shows either. So I wonder why he promised he'd be watching today's? As the saying goes, wonders shall never end...

I stopped at the center of the new raised platform, at the middle of the main stage where VIPs flanked me. The extension before me, was small, circular, and shining as though made from glass. I scared a bit but climbed on anyway. It creaked a little then held. I exhaled in relief.

The heated fan above came on, blowing my hair carelessly. I wouldn't care, except I kept swatting it off my face. Everyone that was still seated rose to their feet. Some placed a hand to their chest. I pulled the cordless microphone off its hinge and clenched it tight.

Fancy smoke now billowed over the backstage. Flags flew high. Lights cascaded back and forth. Cheers bore loud then slowed at the MC's urge.

As the cheers subsided, I glanced at John's message, sent at the worst possible time. If he watched, then he saw me get on stage and could be observing right now. I read the text. It was one line—actually four words. "Your contract has ended."

What? My throat tightened.

One moment of hesitation was all it took. Fear set in. I second-guessed myself. My heart beat wildly, and my hands shook. My contract was over? I tried to focus but everywhere swayed. Dread sucked what little warmth I felt right off my body. My legs trembled when I steadied my stance. I pressed a hand to my queasy stomach to still it. *I can't do this! I'm not ready. My life's not ready.*

Nervous attack. Right now?

Sweat broke out on my forehead. If only I didn't have thousands of eyes pinned on me.

John purposely did this! Why?

Inside, the cold gripped me harder with steel hands. Outside, I couldn't bear the steady heat spraying my head from above, the heat I'd welcomed moments earlier.

I wished they'd turn it off. My hands grew clammy. I tried to hold onto an imaginary railing for support. That didn't work. Instead I stumbled, and took a wrong step forward. I flailed my arms to stabilize but couldn't catch myself in time. A loud crack groaned under my feet. My foot depressed backward on the edge. It creaked first, then split off and fell to the main lower platform. Another step back and my foot followed it down. It caved.

I fell through, beyond the gaping faux platform, and landed with a thud, knee first. The breath sucked right out my lungs as I slipped. My ankle burned.

My head still peered above the platform, but a wide circle beneath the main surface caught my leg, in empty space.

A security guard rushed forward. Half of me remained hinged on the slanted platform, not fully on the ground. He knelt and extended a hand to me. "Take it!"

I hesitated because I didn't want to slip off his hand and fall deeper. But I grabbed it and held.

He grunted hard, teeth baring. Clearly, he couldn't lift me alone.

I finally admitted it. If one fit man couldn't lift me, I was simply too big. Dirt clung to the foot of my pants. Sand on my feet, I attempted to climb over pressing the other hand. But I couldn't. So I stopped before I crashed through worse.

My brother appeared next to him. In a split second, he took my other hand, and they started to pull me up. Another gentleman, whom I'd seen among the VIPs, joined the effort.

"One, two, three!" They gave a hard tug, and I found myself atop the lower, more solid platform. The faux platform had been wooden, overcast with shiny silver coating. Some wood shavings splintered on my hair and arms.

Those around stood waiting. I pressed both hands on the floor and staggered to my feet, blowing wisps of disheveled hair off my face. I stumbled over the fallen mic then straightened. My gaze crossed from one crestfallen face to another. Humiliation washed through me as I shielded my face with a trembling hand.

The cameras clicked away. The crowd had quieted, but the security wouldn't take chances. The guard, who'd given me a hand up, spoke into his radio, then grasped my waist, and ushered me away. He held my arm protectively and led me off stage toward the backstage exit. My brother followed.

I stopped at the exit and shook his hands off momentarily. "The show hasn't started. I've not sang the anthem!"

The guard ignored me, and kept me moving until fully out of the arena to a private room. Leaving me and Matt inside, he shut the door and posted more security outside. I turned and faced the rest of the team. Anxious familiar faces peered back at me, waiting.

CHAPTER 2

"*W*hat in the world?" Kevin, my assistant manager, shouted as we walked in. "John's furious!"

I sat on a stool, trying to pick off the stubborn wood shavings I didn't shake away on our way in.

Everyone talked.

Matt raised his hand and called a hush. "One at a time, please."

I had one hand over my mouth, trying to wrap my mind around the chaos, head bent low.

Kevin spoke again, slower this time, his frustration controlled but arms akimbo. "What happened out there?"

I raised my head an inch, met his gaze, and then stared at the bruise behind my palm. I scanned the length of my legs for any other injuries I might have missed.

"Are you hurt?" Matt stooped, examining.

I twisted my ankle the other way, kicking off my heels. "Nothing major that I can see."

We were testing Kevin's patience. It showed in his grunted breathing.

The drummer—whose first name I always forgot until I arrived home—stepped forward. I called him his last name McCaulay twice.

He didn't like it, so I stopped. "I heard the crash. I didn't know it was you. I'm sorry." He always said something nice, even in despondence.

"Did someone push you?" Mark, our recorder-cum-assistant, asked. He never spoke out loud—unless he had to. Nods did his talking.

I rose, and tested my stance. My left ankle still hurt.

Speak the truth, Candace. "I fell. I was too heavy for the makeshift stage." The room went silent. I hadn't wrapped my mind around John's text yet. I took a couple of steps.

"Going back out there?" The drummer, McCaulay, approached from the backside, to right in my face.

I shrieked, then instinctively backed off, increasing my ankle pain.

"Wow, it's just me."

I walked over and slumped into a seat near our publicist who stayed silent, working his phone with both thumbs. Kevin hadn't spoken again.

Lord Jesus, what just happened to me?

"What now? Where does it go from here?" Mark asked.

I let out a nervous chuckle.

Ben, our publicist, stood. "The response online isn't good. It only gets worse. John wants answers."

Of course he does.

He never appeared at any of my prior concerts. When others praised my performance, he critiqued it—even though he said he never watched them. Then when I applied his critiques and improved performance, he stopped saying anything. Obviously, he watched. John...I can't deal with him right now.

Ben shuffled closer, his steps unsure. When he stopped yards away, I arched a questioning brow.

"John told us about your contract, Candace. We're sorry. He said you'll stay until this one runs out. Then it's over."

They already knew?

I sniffed, eyes brimming.

Amazing, how fast my world was crashing. *Slump in one go.*

My music career.

Weight struggles.

Obstacles.

Growing by the minute. Good thing I've still got Matt, my only immediate family. Our parents died when we were young. I got my fiancé, Ray Alford. That makes two. The rest? I don't know if they'll stand with me....

I laughed hysterically, perplexing those gathered. Done, I cradled my lungs, tired. "I can't teach. I can't dance. Music is my life. It's all I've ever known. To sing."

Now, my heavy weight took it from me. Why did I have to fall?

"You can always learn something new," my brother offered hopefully, but nervously swiped his tongue over his lips. He was scared. So was I.

"At thirty-one? Ha!" *Options?* I drew a blank.

"We'll figure this out. Don't worry."

I wished I could believe him. I didn't. Having faith wasn't my strongest suit.

What gave Matt faith for me?

I buried my face in my hands, trembling. "My life is over."

God, why did this happen to me?

I sobbed into my hands.

Matt stepped closer and touched my arm. "You're not regretting your decision, are you?" I waited a moment. He wasn't speaking of music nor of this failed performance. My sobs quieted, and I looked up. No. He was speaking of my faith, my decision to accept Christ seven months ago, which changed the direction of my music.

It took another moment to realize the room had fallen silent. All eyes were pinned on me.

This is it.

Everyone waited—for my decision.

The door creaked open.

I turned.

"Candace? Someone's here to see you."

The posted security guard. They knew to turn people away. After the snafu on stage? *Argh.* He must have seen the look on my face. "She insists. Said you helped her earlier. She wants to say thank you in person."

Oh, the couple. They were seated close enough. They must've seen what happened.

What now? I sighed. "Tell them this is not a good time," was on my tongue, but I stood.

It might go easier if they heard it from me.

* * *

I FOLLOWED the security staff out the door, shutting it behind. The man stood guard. There they were.

"Yes?" I spoke without smiling. If only they knew how I felt… not a good time. I would listen and politely turn them away.

The lady stepped forward. "I'm so sorry for what happened to you back there. I hope you weren't hurt."

More than my ego? No, not at all.

I smiled a little.

Her husband simply stood next to her, wide-rimmed glasses perched on his narrow nose. She—more petite—held out a card.

Okay, I was done. "Ma'am, I'm sorry, if you need more help, these gentlemen will be more than happy to assist you, please."

When I half-turned, she grasped my hand and halted me. I gave her a you-best-let-me-go side glance.

Security took one step but I held up a hand and he stopped.

She didn't budge. "I'm not asking for help this time. I'm offering it."

I faced her fully, impressed by her courage. "Go on."

She handed the card again. I took it.

"You were kind to help my husband and me. We didn't recognize you until you were on stage or we would have said something. It dawned on me you were famous. You weren't some random stranger. I couldn't have thought."

I let out a breath. *Famous? Not anymore. Infamous now. God, why?*

"We're Christians too. Despite your time crunch, you walked us to our seats. In appreciation, we'll offer you what we have." She glanced at her husband, smiling, then took his hand. He smiled back and stepped closer as though now sure I wouldn't bite.

"Jim and I thought you may need a place to get away for a while, with what you've got going on. We're inviting you to stay at our farm, Day Spring. Its twenty acres in Maryland. You can stay as long as you need to, until you figure out your next step. Our address and phone number are on the card."

A farm? Tad unbelievable! I can't accept it. Nope. Too much lay unresolved. It was mighty kind of them though. I'd give 'em that.

I smiled, and tucked the card in my pocket. "Thank you very much." If I didn't have too much going on, a farm sure sounded nice—for a day or two.

"I appreciate this. I have a lot to think about first. I'm sorry, I cannot accept your offer, but I'm grateful. Thank you both."

She patted my hand. Something about the sparkle of her eyes told me she'd seen quite a few unbelievable things in her days and remained unfazed by my response. "On the news a couple of months ago, we heard you'd become a Christian. Congratulations. We're praying for you. Good luck."

I nodded, and they slowly walked away, hands held together, like when they'd arrived before. He reached behind and with both hands, adjusted her coat over her shoulder.

I lowered my gaze to the white business card. An address, plus phone number followed Dr. and Dr. Mrs. Cantwell. Delicate blue print scrawled Ephesians 5:1-2 at the bottom. I tucked it in my pocket and reentered the private room, where I'd left my entire team in limbo.

* * *

BEN STOOD AFAR OFF, riled glare in his eyes, his feet tapping in staccato. His eyes traveled from mine to his phone where he typed furiously, stylus pen tucked behind his ear.

I tore my gaze from his face. Something was wrong—very wrong. I didn't ask. Didn't want to.

He'd done all the press statements seven months ago when the label announced my conversion to Christ and subsequent decision not to sing coercive songs. He'd taken the heated questions, the barrage of phone calls, e-mails, and social media upheaval. He did a great job.

Since then, I stopped being "Wit", as my fans called me, thanks to relationship navigation advice etched in my songs. Now, I was simply Candace. But a public torrent followed. He'd barely slept for two weeks.

I grabbed a stool nearby and sat, shoulders dropping. I had one more year on my contract. How could I fulfill the terms, without hurting my personal life and faith, and yet not frustrate the label?

Questions, questions, yet no answers. Ugh!

My brother rose and ran a hand over his shaved head. He might not be a Christian. But he was flesh and blood, so he stood by me. Gratitude for his solidarity welled in me.

But…what if he wanted to walk away from this chaos, to keep his rep intact? He'd stood in to manage my rise to the top. He'd also come along on a few tours so I wouldn't be alone on the road.

I looked at the entire room, occupied by my music team of four years. The past half a year had been as uncomfortable for them as it was for me.

So much change occurred in such little time…

I never really thought how my one decision to follow Christ affected all these lives. I simply knew I wanted, and needed to do it. So I did and let whatever happens happen.

Sitting in the middle of the back room, I couldn't help wondering what else might go wrong. I didn't regret my decision to follow Jesus. Not one bit. I wished I knew what I was supposed to do now, with everything crashing around me.

The audience of five before me represented every facet of my life. Both career and family, who waited to find out which way I'd go— back to my life as a popular worldly singer, or stay a Christian.

The two worlds do not blend—not with the type of rebel songs I typically sang. Songs like "Ignorant" or "Said Who?" were my trademarks.

My faith had changed *everything*. I was at crossroads. I had to speak as everyone yet waited. It was now or never. I shook my head and rose to my feet.

The room fell dead silent—waiting. Ben dangled his feet off the table he sat on, like he did when he was nervous about something.

Do it, Candace. Say it out now.

There was only one way for me. "I choose Jesus. I'm sticking with my faith—no matter what."

Ben sprang from the table and walked toward me, stopping a few feet away, hands slid into his pocket. "Final answer?"

My choice could mean his day was just getting started. I nodded. "Yes, final."

His lips tightened. "And if things get bumpy?"

He meant what if this "Jesus thing" was just a phase I was going through? What if I decided I wasn't good enough, never was? What if I did something I wasn't proud of down the road? Something incompatible with my faith? What then?

He was right. This was risky for me—very risky.

"If I mess up," my gaze met his, resolved, "so be it. I'll get back up and keep going. This is real. I'm not perfect, I'm still human, but now I look unto a perfect God for help."

Kevin ground his teeth. My sermonizing probably irritated his nerves. "John's not going to like that."

I know.

Ben chuckled, ran an impatient hand through his hair, turned his back, walked to the table, and sat.

Glancing at them one by one, my gaze settled on Kevin. "It's my decision. Anyone who feels uncomfortable with it, please feel free to walk away. I won't hold it against you. I brought all of you in, except Kevin, so you're free to quit." They'd hung on with me long enough. Now that the other shoe had dropped, it was their turn to choose.

No one spoke, but I knew their minds were frenzied.

"My personal faith decision shouldn't jeopardize your chosen careers. If you want to leave, please do so now." A strong wave of uncertainty hung over the room.

The guitarist stood up, then he nodded, "good luck", and walked out.

The drummer followed next, tilting his hat, and so leaving three people with me.

I swallowed. He'd be tough to replace, since he was the best on drums if you asked me.

"Anyone else?"

My brother jumped to his feet.

My heart skipped. *Not you too!*

But I waited.

"Time to face the real world, lil' sis. I told you it wasn't going to be easy—"

I shook my head for him to stop. He wasn't leaving—clearly just venting.

"Okay. Thanks for staying. Our limo back to the city leaves in fifteen minutes. Let's go." I rose with my feet shaking, while praying silently that no one else would quit on me. Coat in hand, I walked out without looking back.

CHAPTER 3

*A*fter unlocking the door into my apartment, I entered, partly dragging my feet. I shoved the door shut with my foot. Made my way to the living room, tossed my purse on the couch and keys on the center table, and exhaled. *The door.*

I forgot to double lock it. Sighing, I trudged back, and slid the locks shut. I'd been gone for one day and I forgot locking my doors! Maybe, I was simply preoccupied. My cellphone rang in my purse. So I rushed to pull it out, eyed the caller ID, and answered it.

I was relieved to see it was my fiancé, Raymond Alford.

Just the person I wanted to speak with. We hadn't talked in days and I couldn't wait to tell him what had happened—if he hadn't heard already.

Football kept him as busy as music did to me. Things between us have been a little rocky since I got saved. "Hey, Ray?" I held the phone tight to my ear, laid back, and raised my legs to the couch.

"Hey there. Howdy?" Uh-oh. He used "hey there" for strangers and people he didn't want to talk to.

I kept calm. "Um—its been a rough day, Ray."

He went silent. But Ray was never silent. I dropped my feet to the floor, and slid off the couch, while feeling the concern creasing my brow.

"Candy, I don't want to waste your time or make this more difficult than it needs to be, so I'm gonna say this quick."

"What do you mean?" But I was afraid. My fear was coming true. I thought it might happen someday. Someday might be today.

He paused again, as our breathing remained the only audible sound. The air crackled with tension—or was it just static?

"You and me. Don't think we're gonna work out. I mean, you can't mix oil and water, Candy. Things are different now. You're different."

The room spun in my eyes. I sank into the couch; and my insides sunk lower. "You mean because of my faith, or because I fell? Which one is it?"

Maybe he was just saving his career, like the others who walked out this afternoon. "I don't want to go into details. Ain't gonna help either of us. Just...move on." Either way, he was getting out of our relationship, is what he meant. How could I lose everything in one day? A wave of desperation pummeled me. *After four years through thick and thin?* "Why?" The hurt burned.

"I'm not going with you to church! All right? That's not my life. Now let's just do this like civilized people and move on. I thought to do ya a favor and tell ya myself. Goodbye, Candy."

Click.

Just like that. He hung up. I stared at the brilliant diamond engagement ring stuck on my ring finger. The day he proposed to me a year ago was a big event. A hundred people witnessed it. I was so happy. Now, it was all over with a phone call. Inside, I knew I should have ended things after becoming a Christian, but I loved him.

He said he was doing me a favor? A lie! He must've heard of what happened today. And bailed. I sat on the couch—head bowed, and with my soul rent—I cried. I removed the engagement ring, and threw it against the wall. An hour after, I sat on the carpet like an unfeeling robot, spent of tears, full of pain, heartbroken and confused.

Believing in Jesus was just one step I made. But it changed everything.

* * *

I HEADED into the bedroom for a box of tissue. Far to the wall, the voicemail blinked on my house phone next to the lamp. I assumed that it was probably Matt checking on me. Ten voicemails blipped as I neared. Ten? I rarely got an occasional missed call.

I pressed the Voicemail button and perched on the bed.

Message one: "Hi, Miss Candace, this is Randy from the city's most popular radio station, WNYS, here to get your thoughts on the viral video making the rounds online depicting your crash on stage. Please get back to me on 1-888—"

I slammed a hand down the Off button so hard I probably damaged it. Viral video? What viral video? My cellphone buzzed on my lap and I glanced at it. Matt's name appeared. "Hey?"

He panted like he just ran. "Candace, don't answer your phone! Don't turn on the TV or the internet."

Too late.

"I heard a voicemail from—"

"Lot more coming," he cut in. "We're all getting calls—me, Kevin, the crew. Also, don't leave your apartment." He halted, like he was thinking of something else to bar me from.

"Who put up the video?" I was curious.

He snuffed. "I don't know. Some kid close enough with a cell-phone, I guess. Thing is, it went viral and it's a problem. We can't contain it. I'm sorry."

I buried my head in my hands filled with anguish.

How much worse will this get, Jesus? One wreck was followed by another.

I tucked the phone against my ear. "I should tell you, that Ray and I broke up. He called me and said it was over."

Matt was quiet. "Why?"

A cry caught in my throat at first but I stemmed it. "He didn't say. Oh, he did say, 'you can't mix oil and water.' There you have it."

His quickening breath thundered through the speaker. "I'm going to call him."

"If you do, he'll feel indispensable. Leave him be. God's got me." As I said it out loud, I hoped my heart would believe it. Desperately. 'Cuz if I didn't...

"You have to look for a place to go and lay low, maybe at a female friend of yours." An angry tremor still overcast his voice. He exhaled long. But I knew that nothing he'd do would help. It was over.

What friends to stay with? The only ones I'd call could certainly pile the pressure on me about Ray, and would suggest to go back pleading. They weren't Christians so they wouldn't understand. They might remind me of the fame and fortune I lost for the sake of my faith, and fall. I'll pass on that offer. I can't risk losing my faith in Christ.

I sighed in frustration, rubbed my forehead where an ache radiated, and winced. The brown stain in my hand proved that I'd just mashed up my makeup but I didn't care.

"I don't know what to do, Matt. I'll pray and let you know." At the very least, I could do that.

"I don't know, Candace. This path of uncertainty...Hope you know what you're doing." He meant he didn't believe in what I was doing.

Fix this, Jesus!

"Good night, Candace." I noticed that he called me my full name. But he only did that when we're in life's trenches. And for our lives, those trenches didn't get worse than this. His wife called out to him in the background.

"G'night."

Ending this call felt like work. Like I'd lost my last lifeline, and crossed my point of desperation.

I wanted him to stay on with me, like he'd do when we were younger. Or when someone attacked me in school. Except that we were grown now, and everyone bore his and her own burden. Although absent, he cared about me. To me, that was enough.

I swung my legs up to the bed, and wrapped my arms around me. I trembled with cold and my life felt chiller. The freezing cold that was permeating my sweater felt much warmer than my inside. I sank deeper into the covers, wishing I could shrink into nonexistence. The pain squeezing my heart was surreal. I lifted my head and stared at the ceiling, wanting for words. Then my face fell for lack of what to say.

I opened my mouth, but instead of words, tears spilled freely down my cheeks. I cried until my voice went hoarse. I poured my soul out to my Maker while my heart shed its burden, painted in tears. I stayed there another full hour, not moving an inch.

When I was emotionally spent, I rose, returned to the living room, and searched for the ring. Finding it along the edge of the carpet, I picked it up. I retrieved an envelope from my desk drawer and slid it inside, sealed it up, and put it on top of the mailer.

I'd send it by express service tomorrow morning to the man who'd slid it into my finger. I don't need a sad reminder of my breakup with him. With the pestering voicemails and viral video, the storm was just starting. It was time to ready myself. I needed to lean on the Lord.

Returning to the bedroom, I began peeling off my clothing. Something fell out of the sweater pocket. I bent and picked it up.

Dr. and Dr. Mrs. Cantwell. Day Spring Farms, Beltsville, Maryland.

I dropped onto the edge of my bed.

Well…God certainly knew this storm was coming even if I didn't. What if…

I picked up my cell phone and dialed the number before thinking, wiping my dripping nostrils with the back of my hand.

I cleared my throat while pressing the phone to my ear. Hopefully, I didn't sound as bad as I felt….

It was ringing. "Hello?" The voice trembled a bit, but I recognized it. The lady from the game.

"Hi, Dr. Mrs. Cantwell. Um, this is Candace Rodriguez. You'd given me—"

She gasped. "Oh yes! Of course, I remember you. We got home an hour ago, thanks to Jim always forgetting to double-check our flights back."

Her laugh echoed through the phone. "I tell you, he has too much fun every single time we go down there. Talking 'bout how this team played and that team disappointed until he pretty much forgot our flight time—third year in a row. We caught the third flight back, two hours later."

She sighed. "It's a pity, I can't complain when I'm all toasty warm now. Oh is everything okay, Candace?" Her voice rang...so bright.

I desperately wished I could say yes. But I knew I couldn't. Not this time. "Actually, you might guess not. May I take you up on your offer for a place to stay for a while? I mean, if the offer still stands? I could crash for a few days, then—"

"Oh shush. Of course! Yes, you are welcome. Our home and farm are open to you. My husband, Jim, and I already prayed before we made you the offer. Feel free to come anytime."

How about right now?

That was too sudden.

I still got to figure out how to get there.

Maybe I'll use the airport? Media folks could corner me there. Not a good idea.

"How does tomorrow sound?"

Candace, only one day notice? Ha. It might also be too sudden.

"Perfect. We'll see you tomorrow. You'll be just in time for these casseroles I'm baking now. Come hungry. We've got lots of food so I promise you won't starve. After all, we're on a farm."

Thank You, Jesus!

But then I thought about it again. I was running away to—a farm. So? Who cares?

After all, there are people on farms too. "Thank you so much, Dr. Mrs. Cantwell. God bless you."

She laughed softly. "Call me Julie. Our pleasure, dear. We look forward to hosting you."

She came back stronger on the line. "Oh, they're predicting some showers tomorrow so hold an umbrella. We don't want you to get wet on your first day here. Wet soil could catch your shoes fast."

Freezing rain...just suited my glum mood.

A burning question pressed on my mind, one that had haunted me since the moment the stage caved, and it seared through me. "I got a quick question."

Something rustled where she was. Her repositioning the phone, maybe to her other ear? "Sure. Go on."

I'd thought about this long enough, that framing it couldn't be an issue. "If God loved me and wanted my good, why did I fall? I've lost everything."

I stopped. I wouldn't tell her about Ray just yet.

"Why?" I emphasized, hoping for some clarity.

Her exhale whooshed across the speaker. "After you fell, what went through your mind? What did you do?"

I thought about it, while absent-mindedly fiddling with a loose strand of thread on my blanket. "I cried out to God in my heart, and asked Him to remove the shame."

"Your music is your strength, Candace." Her deep breath rattled my ear. "It's your confidence. What you can do without God's help."

She coughed then continued in a moment. "As a matter of fact, it's your crutch. You lean on it when everything fails. Maybe inside, you don't even want His help. You just want Him around while you help yourself. He doesn't work that way. God wants our full trust. For you to develop that trust in Him, He'll have to break your crutches. It forces you to stand up in faith, and to quit trusting in yourself."

Her words pierced my heart, and their truth found hook in my soul. I knew she was right.

"Now, if He wanted to move you anywhere, you'd be more willing to go. You know why?"

With her thoughtful explanation, I did. "Because He broke my crutch."

"Exactly." She chuckled softly.

Wow, that was dead on. "Thank you very much. Good night." Not much else was left to say.

"Good night, Candace. Travel safe." She clicked, ending our call.

It's official.

I'm going to Maryland.

I just have to figure out how.

CHAPTER 4

*G*od planned an escape for me before my accident occurred. I could hardly believe it. Now I know meeting the Cantwells wasn't merely a coincidence. There I stood thinking I was helping them...when God was connecting me to grace. To help *me*. I smiled, for the first time in six hours. *God loves me.* I let that fact sink in to my battered heart.

I yawned, turning off my lamp. Light shone through my cellphone and I blinked.

Another call was coming through but I was exhausted.

I peered for the caller ID. Seeing that it was Ben, I groaned but accepted it.

"Hello?" He sounded half-asleep, yawning. "I got a phone call—"

Sadly, I knew where this was going. "Yeah, the viral video." I cut him off so he wouldn't become frantic. Chances were that's why he called. "I heard the news. I'll call you as soon as I figure things out. Please handle the press for me, okay?"

When silence trailed my request, I worried that I might have tasked him with more than he could handle this time around.

He yawned again, louder. "Okay. I got you covered."

He'd told me three months ago when his friend had offered him a job in LA handling press for a political campaign. He'd said he turned it down because he enjoyed working with me then. Only that I'm not sure about how long he would stay now.

If he left, I wouldn't stop him but I won't like it either. He always did a great job. "Good night, buddy."

I was half-relieved as he hung up.

I drew in a deep breath wishing for sleep. Too bad that I wasn't as sleepy as he was.

Going to the restroom, I sat there longer than I needed to, while making a mental checklist of things I needed to do—unplug my house phones, pack, and get to Maryland unnoticed.

I stood up and ran the tap until the water was quite warm, washing my hands.

Then I ran it cold.

I needed to cool my overworked brain. I splashed water on my face, shutting my eyes and letting its chill calm my nerves while I figured out my choice of travel.

I could drive. That would be a long drive—five to six hours from door to door.

I gripped the sides of the sink and stared into the mirror.

Use your imagination.

I grabbed a napkin, to wipe the remaining wetness off my eyes.

A Greyhound bus, maybe? It took too long, too.

Besides, someone could recognize me between stops and I couldn't risk such exposure.

I entered my bedroom and switched on the closet light. I began setting clothes on the bed to get ready when a light bulb went off in my mind.

Amtrak!

Yes. I could take Amtrak.

I sat slowly as I folded a shirt while ruminating. It was a great idea I stumbled on. The trip would take four hours tops. The train station had large enough crowd so no one would notice me.

Their train's coach cars gave enough privacy inside too. I smiled, picking up a blue jean.

I only needed a taxi from here to Penn Station and I'd be set.

Satisfied, I unlocked my phone and texted my brother, Matt. "Leaving for Maryland tomorrow. Taking Amtrak. Will send you details later. Oh, I'm mailing back Ray's ring."

Writing it to him sealed the decision for me. On second thought…I added "P.S. Don't tell anyone where I am. This stays between you and me. Send Lucy my love."

I strode to the opposite bedroom and opened the closet. Ray's stuff, from when we lived together until six months ago, caught my eye. They stayed in a neat stack at the foot of the spare bed where he'd left them.

He was meticulous. I'd give him that. One shirt, though, was strewn across atop the pile. He'd moved into this bedroom once I became a Christian and learned right. One week later, it got tough having him around and maintaining distance. We'd been too intimate before then.

So I asked him to get a place for himself. He didn't like it but obliged. He was supposed to come pick up these things but didn't.

I'll be adding them to the mail package for tomorrow…

With my mind made up, I lifted them off the bed and bore them to the living room, stacking them on the couch and placing the ring envelope atop.

There.

After returning to the bedroom, I pulled out my small luggage and began throwing random stuff in.

First my Bible, then my pair of black heels, followed by knee-length high winter socks, and hand gloves. For my choice of a coat, I debated. Black or striped? It was tough to choose. I crinkled my nose and bit a fingernail.

Oh yeah….It was going to be a long night.

* * *

RUNNING AROUND for one thing or another could bring stress to anyone. But fleeing your life, with pieces of your shattered heart falling along as you go? Nothing compared to the weariness and mental exhaustion it brought. Waking up at six a.m. was harder than I'd thought it would be. I rarely woke so early. But with me going to Maryland, today wasn't a regular day.

Last night, I'd planned to leave while it was still dark out. I still needed to send out Ray's stuff, ring included, first. So, I caught a cab to the post office and sent them Priority Mail. That delayed me until ten a.m.

By eleven, the taxi I'd hired had stayed with me, driving me from the Post Office to one block away from my apartment. I'd sat in the taxi, pleaded with him to assist me by picking up my luggage for me.

He agreed, after I promised him an extra twenty-dollar tip. I gave him my keys and told him to go up via the elevator to my apartment at the seventh floor. Then we resumed our trip to Penn Station.

My emotions were so wound up, that getting into the taxi this morning felt like a chore. There had been worse days, but none this emotionally exhausting. I threw my head back upon the headrest, and closed my eyes, feeling quite sapped.

Lord, please lead me.

Truth is, I was scared. Scared for where I was, even unsure where I headed. I was ignorant of where my life pointed with no visible future in sight.

If only I knew which way the dial of my life was turning, maybe I'd have some guarantee.

My attention drifted to Rosa, my best friend from college and that made me smile.

I bought my '03 Jeep Liberty from her when she moved abroad five years ago. I could've gotten a new one, but something about the way she took care of it, made me want to keep it in friendly hands.

She'd gladly sold it to me for five thousand dollars. She needed the money—every dollar—to start a small business in a village near Rome. Last I heard, she owned three coffee shops there. She was to be my maid of honor at the wedding.

How could I tell her now that there wouldn't be a wedding? A sigh escaped my lips.

The taxi stopped with a jerk and I peered—234 West 34th Street. Penn Station.

I put on my sunglasses just as the taxi navigated a sharp turn, arriving above the Amtrak station. People milled about in clusters. This was a typical New York City day—where the most arm space you got was an inch, if lucky. Pedestrians thronged despite the frosty weather. The wind which was blowing my hair messy didn't help matters.

I pulled my luggage, purse, and scarf out of the taxi, handing the driver a fifty-dollar bill. The trip cost twenty-five dollars, plus the twenty-dollar tip I'd promised, making forty-five. "Keep the change." He got five bucks extra. I figured that was worth the trip he'd saved me by trekking to my apartment for my luggage.

The clothing layers covering me created a perfect disguise. Only my family would recognize me. Even they'd have to look hard at first.

I descended the steps, with a hat on my head, wearing sunglasses, and then a scarf covering my mouth and part of my face. I wasn't just cold from the weather; I was cold from the world.

I couldn't fathom how God pulled things together.

What if I didn't help the couple yesterday? I swallowed.

I'm here now. Focus.

Broken crutches. I'm trusting God alone.

I navigated the crowd, arrived, and queued up at the Amtrak ticket counter awaiting my turn. "One ticket, please."

The clerk looked up. Her eyes were puffy as if she hadn't really woken up. And this was at noontime. I huffed a little. That made two of us. I wished I'd wake up to find the past twenty-four hours hadn't occurred.

"Where?"

I blinked, returning to her. "Maryland."

She hissed. In impatience? She leaned purposefully into the mic, and spoke slowly. "Where. In. Maryland?"

I stayed calm and scanned the area map locator behind her. Then I saw it. "New Carrollton Station?" Hoping I got the station's name right.

She twisted her mouth and pressed some buttons. With a quick jerk on the slip and pull of the glass slider, she handed me a ticket. "Just one?"

Need I more? "Yes. One."

I paid, accepted the ticket, and walked away to confirm my departure time. It showed a half hour wait. Not bad.

Sanders, a coffee shop, beckoned a couple of yards down. I rolled my luggage over.

Upon arriving, there was another queue.

I needed to grab a quick breakfast and be ready to go. A young man sat on a medium height stool, holding up tracts. A song played on a radio hugged close to his feet.

Gotta be one of those... Not sure what they're called. Street performers?

I turned when I recognized a song. A Christian song. Our eyes met. He smiled. I listened more and took one slow step toward him.

"Who sang that?"

He pointed to a leaflet. "Michael Arden Smith. He'll be performing live next weekend. Wanna come?" He held out one tract.

I hesitated. "Are you playing a CD?"

He shook his head. "No. It's a Christian radio station—95.1 FM. There's an app for it. You can tune in online anytime you want."

Wow. I nodded, taking the tract from him.

He rose and showed me the app on my phone. We searched first, then I selected the Christian radio station, same one he listened to. It began playing, syncing with the music on his radio.

I paused the play. "Thank you."

Now, I was glad that I got some company for the road.

He nodded, glancing at my luggage. "Wherever you're at, you can search for a local Christian radio station, there'll likely be one there. And then listen to it using the app."

I thanked him again and quickly got back in line for breakfast. Fifteen minutes to go.

I ruminated on the song I'd heard, "Joy in the Morning", as the radio moved on to play another song.

While I was growing up, Christian songs weren't my thing. Except, "Amazing Grace", which they played when my late Aunt Trina got married. I was six then. I don't recall another occasion where I listened to anything Christian by intent.

I had silenced my phone before leaving my apartment and turned it off later. But I knew some calls would still be coming in, so I disabled all incoming calls. If anyone needed to reach me, they had my brother as their point of contact. I felt sorry for him, imagining the barrage he was dealing with.

Being my manager was tough, but I'd rather have him in that role than anyone else. Sometimes, the blood relationship made it harder to talk businesslike, but he had my best interest at heart so that mattered most.

"Yes, ma'am." It was my turn to order. I stepped up to the counter. "Double cheeseburger, french fries, and one large drink—to go. Oh, make that two orders."

Better to have more food than less.

They might serve something inside the train, but I quit counting on that since last summer. I'd caught a commuter rail ride in Santa Cruz with no stops for twelve consecutive stations, thanks to a mechanical malfunction. Two hours passed before I got to eat.

My stomach snarled with hunger again. It growled while I bought the ticket earlier on.

The waiter smiled in reaction to the sound. "Here you go, ma'am."

I'd have to scarf this down pretty fast judging the time I had to board the train.

I accepted the food but frowned. Usually, you paid first and then got your order.

"Wait. Here's my card." I handed it to him.

But he gave it back. "No need. The customer in front of you paid for your order." What? A complete stranger paid for my meal? I craned my neck to the door to see who it was.

They were already gone.

I glanced behind, had an idea, and lowered my voice to a whisper, "I'll pay for the person behind, please." He nodded, took my card and swiped it, then gave it back.

* * *

STRETCHED out on my forward-facing aisle seat, I sipped a drink, slipped some fries into my mouth, and leaned back. Something about the freedom of the rails made me forget my troubles and munch while the train pushed ahead.

I was born here in the city, grew up here too. Maybe it was time for me to be somewhere new.

Thanks to my career in music, I've traveled even farther, closer the Canadian border, but this was my home.

Always.

I'd changed my mind on eating first and gone ahead to board the train before eating my meal. It was later a good decision because people piled onto the train fast, and within seconds, seats were scarce. I'd snagged my preferred aisle seat, next to a young man about half my age, a teen. His face was glued to a video game. I was almost sure he'd play it through the entire trip.

The weather was frigid, lingering in the high 20s. Yet for some reason, I felt stuffy. Could it be because I just ate, or was it the speed of the train? Undecided, I turned on the fan above my seat. My teen neighbor squirmed. So I whispered, "sorry," to him. I turned it off as soon as I felt better.

Three hours later, we'd passed New Jersey, gotten close to...Pennsylvania? I didn't want to strain my eyes figuring it out. I scanned for Christian radio on the app in my phone instead. Every state we passed, I searched for a new one and listened until we were out of coverage.

I listened to everything from Christian rock, contemporary Christian, to hymns that made my eyes grow moist, Christian rap that made me jump to my feet at crescendo—and drew a worried glance from a man across who looked like everything bothered him, with his nose turned up.

Four hours in, my feet felt heavy as lead. I shifted in my seat. Those in seats around me dozed off, appearing relaxed. I lifted my feet and swung them back and forth to stop muscle cramps.

The motorman announced, "New Carrollton Station, next stop."

Relief calmed my worn nerves. *Almost there.*

I made a mental note to call Rosa while I was in Maryland. She always supported me. Having crossed international borders, she may appreciate my venture cross-country.

We neared my destination at 5:45 p.m. Lack of sleep the night before caused my lids to droop heavy. The train pulled up at the New Carrollton station, its wheels sighing, horns blaring, and then the announcements came on. "Arrived at the New Carrollton station. Please check your seats..."

Tired to the bone, I dangled between options. I could check into a hotel for a couple of hours to sleep before heading to the Cantwells. I don't want to get there looking and sounding unenthusiastic.

Then again, it was too late in the day already.

I sighed and bowed my head, leaning it fully on my knees where no one could see. I opened my heart, with my eyes closed.

Lord Jesus, I'm here. I've never been in Maryland before. I'm very far from home, family, friends, and everything I know. I need a new beginning, a fresh start. I don't know where this road heads. Show me. Lead me. Comfort me.

I paused.

Lord, just change me. Make me new, and I will praise You.

That 'bout summed up my whole heart. I glanced up at the almost empty cabin. Many had disembarked at every stop, including the teen boy who got off at the Philadelphia Station stop.

Why did I have to journey approximately two hundred miles to pour out my heart to God? Maybe a new environment made it easier to see my past from a distance...and embrace something new.

I looked around to gather my stuff.

A second sweep of eyes later showed that there was nothing I was forgetting.

After alighting from the train car, with my purse and coat in hand, and my luggage close behind, I walked toward the door marked Exit. The sun was setting on the horizon, but my day had just begun. The sunset could very well be my sunrise.

CHAPTER 5

 B PATRICKSON

I THREW the last set of cedars into my truck and began my ride home. Nothing short of a miracle would make these logs sufficient to complete the Makings' house. Good thing it was almost finished. Only part of the roofing, gating, and cementing the driveway remained. And that shouldn't take more than two weeks...give or take.

Driving through Kentucky streets was always a sight to behold. Farm trucks mingled with posh rides and vintage bikes, plus pedestrians on their daily hustle. A mix of all professions were featured in the daily life of Louisville.

Lord, why am I back here?

I exhaled, with my patience running thin. Seven years later and I was back to the start. I thought I'd be long moved on from here. Well...I did have some success—until the 2008 housing market collapse did me in.

Turning into the store owned by my childhood best friend, Dan, I pulled into the lot and opened the truck door. I rested my arm on the headrest and retrieved the precious package—steamed lobsters in a bowl, then got out of the truck. Dan loved seafood. Any variety, grilled or steamed, he'd eat it up.

Slamming the truck door, I glanced at my feet and saw the dried dusty sand that hugged my boots. Something told me I should've shed them a long time ago. Problem was, they were rugged and served me just fine.

I approached the Kentucky Family Store on Bridge Avenue. On second thought, I pressed the Lock button on my keys. The Ford F150 remained the sole survivor of my life's storm, which had swept me back to Louisville. The truck responded with a flicker of bright lights and a happy beep to confirm the lock.

Dan's eyes lit up the moment he spied me from behind the safety glass. He stepped out and gave me a bear hug. "JB, my man! Good to see you."

We laughed. I patted his back, handing him the steamed lobsters.

He scanned me as he accepted it. "You look good, man. Been a while I haven't seen you."

I nodded. "Thanks. So do you. I see Catherine's been cooking up some good grub for ya."

He smiled, ushering me to the lone table and chair closer to the register after locking the safety bar. When we sat, he opened the bowl, releasing aromatic steam. He set it on the desk and retrieved the disposable fork beneath. Judging from his beaming smile, I may just have made his day.

"Hmmm. Thank you, my friend. You remembered my favorite. Catherine is good. We're doing fine. How's the construction business? I hear some homes are going up around Garden Park?"

But I didn't want to speak of construction. Or even think about it. "Someone's always building something, buddy. Glad to hear you're all okay."

He raised his head from the food he'd already dug into. "What can

I get ya? I got a few things here. Couple of snacks to tide you over till you get home."

I shook my head. "Don't worry about it. Moreover, I'm not going home. I need to pass by the funeral home to pay the final bill for my mom's expenses."

He stopped his fork midair and caught my gaze, his face awash with a compassionate look. He knew how much she meant to me. How much she'd been through—we'd been through. "I'm so sorry, man. Sad not to see her again."

I shrugged, not wanting to raise the matter. Grief had almost taken me with her nine months ago. I hadn't realized we hadn't seen each other since her funeral. But then time seemed to run short when you're hit with an emergency.

"Thank you. Folks like you helped me. I'm lucky to have you as a friend." We shook hands, his non-lobster occupied hand.

The phone rang behind the counter. He raised his head and wiped his hands with a napkin. He rushed over the secure bar, hopping.

"Hello? Yes. Hi, Mr. Patrickson."

My dad? I frowned and waited. He waved his hand like, "what do I do?"

I rose to my feet, unsure what to tell him to do.

"Yeah, he just got here. Give me one minute." He put the phone down.

I scratched my head. Before I became a Christian, I would simply tell him to say I wasn't here. This time I walked over, bracing.

"He said something about your grandma?" Dan's eyebrows curved in uncertainty as he handed over the phone.

I nodded to Dan, then accepted the phone. "Dad?" I didn't know why he would call me considering that we didn't have conversations. He gave orders. If it wasn't rightly carried out, there was hell to pay. Very simple. These days, we avoided each other all day, and muttered good night at night. Since mom died.

It was easier that way.

He asked about my plans the day after the funeral. I told him I was still thinking about it. He hadn't asked again since then. And now he was calling me in the middle of the day?

"Your grandma is on the line. Hold on for her." His gruff voice echoed.

I waited.

Grandma Patty, my maternal grandparent, was every inch the alternative parent I needed. Except she lived far away.

"Hi, Grandma. Are you okay?" I was afraid because I knew that she wouldn't call and insist to speak with me if all was well.

"Yes, honey. Everything's fine, praise God." Despite her verbal assurance, her voice sounded frail.

We bonded over Christianity for many years. She helped me grow in my faith. Years back, we'd talk on the phone for hours before I went to Wall Street. Then, I became busy. Now, I had much time to spare, but her energy only carried a half hour, not like before.

"Listen, JB. I wouldn't ask for this if it wasn't important."

I swallowed, more anxious for her sake than mine. "Okay, Grandma. I'm listening."

Her breath came in heavy spurts.

My apprehension grew. I pressed a hand against my forehead and leaned my back on the wall.

"I need your help. I'm moving to a senior care facility. I need someone I trust to take over my farm. You're the only one I know can."

What? Take over a farm? I gripped the phone tighter. I simply couldn't.

"But Mr. Winifred is there, isn't he?" He'd been running the farm for ages, maybe since I was ten. I couldn't remember.

"He's old too. He's moving in with his son and daughter-in-law in Mexico. He leaves in one week."

One week? I swallowed hard and tried to continue listening. This was more than I could handle. Way more.

To begin with, I hadn't completed the Makings' house. I needed more time. Moreover, I prayed to go back to New York—not Maryland. Bile rose to my mouth. I threw my head back to the wall as confusion swirled. I loved my Grandma, but I couldn't do this. The thoughts rushing through my head traveled faster than my apprehension to accept.

Lord, I asked for New York, not a farm.

Most of her following words flew over my head. I avoided glancing in Dan's direction as I struggled with her request. Yet, I knew that I also couldn't turn her down. Not with the inner peace settling in my heart with the prospect of acceptance, even though it didn't make sense to me.

One week…

Lord, I accept Your will.

"All right. I'll wrap up what I got going on here. I'll see you in a week." I didn't like it but I wouldn't debate God's will.

She let out held breath. "See you, son."

As I hung up, my eyes met Dan's. His hand went up on his waist. "You're leaving?"

I nodded. "For Maryland."

Last time I visited Grandma was fifteen years ago, for my eighteenth birthday.

"Wow," Dan exclaimed, jaw dropping. He seemed lost for words after that.

That was a fitting reaction.

Because I wasn't excited either.

* * *

CANDACE

"Welcome to Maryland!" Mrs. Cantwell threw her arms around me and squeezed me tight. I hugged her back and smiled, noting the industrial grade truck she'd driven to pick me up at the Amtrak station. I'd called to let her know I'd arrived and would grab a taxi to the farm.

She insisted on picking me up instead. Maryland didn't quite appear as I'd imagined it. It felt more like Long Island, and moved at regular pace, but felt a little less chilly.

I liked the much of it I'd seen.

"Here. Let me get that for you." She pressed open the doors, and I dumped my luggage inside, watching my steps for ice.

It had indeed rained. Leftover snow slickened the ground and could easily slip me.

"How was your trip?"

I slid in after her, reached my hands toward the hot air, glad for the warmth. "Good. It wasn't too hectic."

She nodded, driving off the passenger pickup lot and merging into the I-95 Highway after a few miles.

As we sped by, I wondered how she could maneuver a huge farm truck so expertly. "How long have you owned the farm?"

She curved her shoulder. "Not long. It would be two years this summer. But we farmed in India on our medical mission a long time ago." She laughed. "We practically turned the clinic grounds to a farm plot. Parents wondered why their kids loved coming to the clinic. Until they found the free food drew them. And, of course, we would then provide health care in addition."

This lady was charming, and easily likeable. I smiled as my own nerves settled.

We arrived at a large farmland one hour later. Year-round crops fanned out in all directions as we drove deeper. A large house sat in the middle of the land, appearing taller as we neared.

I glanced at her. Spiral curls hung low on her shoulder. Wrinkles lined both sides of her eyes, the first thing I'd noticed in New York. She seemed…content.

"How long have you both lived in the area?"

Mrs. Cantwell turned briefly. "Ten years. Since we returned from Spain, that was our last pit stop. When you've raised two kids abroad and they have no idea what the American experience feels like, it's time to come home. And I've been married to Jim for thirty years."

She seemed lost in the memory of it all, ruminating, until a smile spread across her face. "When we first bought this farm, people thought we were crazy and didn't know what we were doing. Why would a medical doctor and his wife, a PhD in physical therapy, live on a farm instead of a posh town home? A farm out in the middle of nowhere? But God gave us a vision, a goal."

I prodded her on. "What goal?"

She glanced my way. "To save lives."

I scanned the field whizzing by. "Out here in the middle of nowhere?"

She smiled, shooting up an eyelid. "We save lives preventively. A few years ago, when my husband opened his family practice down-town, which he still runs, we realized that even prevention wasn't enough."

She made a left turn, followed by a quick right, into Hope Lane.

"Too many people were already very sick. There were too few treatment solutions beyond pills in a bottle and injections in a syringe. Hardly any illustration of practical proper diet and exercise, lack of which caused most of those conditions in the first place. So we taught them to begin exercising. And to eat healthier foods. Showed them how to choose healthier options even when far from home. We advanced how to live off the land naturally and eat and live a healthy life through adopting holistic lifestyles.

"In a nutshell, we gave them hope. They responded in gratitude. Remarkable change happened for most of them. They'd always heard bad news—'you're not going to get better, sorry' or 'this is a lifelong illness, we can only manage it'....Yes, sometimes, that was true, but changing their lifestyles bought them some more time with their loved ones."

She nodded, tossing those spiral curls springing. "Hope changes things, Candace. You can't take away someone's hope. Ever." She swerved to avoid what looked like cow dung in the middle of the now-one-car lane.

"How many people patronize the clinic?" Maybe their goals to prevent illness were lofty, I opined inwardly.

She grinned and tapped a finger on the steering wheel. "To date? More than five thousand. Weekly? About fifty, and only because he can't do more than one day in-person clinic days nowadays. Most times, he leaves at the crack of dawn that day. His staff take visitor

JOY OHAGWU

appointments all week, gather medical histories and charts, and send them here. He sits in his study and reads each one, seeking remedies. A few times, I've caught him praying for them before he leaves in the morning. He saves lives with dedication."

I glanced at the land, imagining how vibrant it would look in springtime with green leaves swaying in the wind.

"What do you do with all the food?" The crops' value could be huge when harvested.

"That depends. We stock up for the year, and we gift our patients, and friends. We exchange produce with neighbors. What's left, we donate to homeless shelters."

I hadn't realized, until now, how much my diet would change just by coming here. I was going from drive-thru to farm food.

Wow. Call that a transition. It shook me inside.

No more, "give me number five on the menu, with a side of fries and one drink". On bad days, I made two orders—of everything.

"You'll soon find out time runs short around here." Mrs. Cantwell turned. "You're the first person we're bringing home to help. I believe in divine leading, and in divine purpose. If you approach your time here with an open heart, you'll grow. Otherwise, nothing changes. The choice remains yours."

She rode into the driveway. A smaller, extended residence appeared next to the house. It stretched long off the side, with its own flagstone path connecting it to a garden on the right and to the main home.

It was beautiful. It seemed more modern than the main home. Glass windows ran from top to bottom out front, giving the feel of a sunroom. The edge I could see had regular cement walls.

The garden spread next to it, a bit separate from the main house and surrounded by a low decorative wall. A small white wooden gate opened at the front, likely designed to keep animals or plants in rather than humans out.

A sense of peace radiated here.

It felt like home, surprisingly.

Mrs. Cantwell killed the engine and alighted. "We're here. Home sweet home."

I opened the car door and stepped onto tarred ground.

Cool wind blew across my face and whisked my hair backwards. Mrs. Cantwell swept around the car onto the sidewalk, toward the front door. She detoured, heading to the garden. There, she pulled a pin off the gate's hook. The gate creaked, swung wide, and stopped at a cement-elevated hinge on the side.

"You go through the front and let me see if Jim is out back, all right? Sometimes, I can't get him away from chasing those stubborn rodents." She pointed toward the front door and disappeared to the back.

I lingered for a moment, wondering how anything grew in such a season. Then I lifted my bag from the truck, set it down, and yanked the pull. I dragged it along, stopping at the three-step platform to the front door. On the left lawn, a tree stood in the middle, as its branches swung wide, with well-trimmed green grass beneath. A red toy car secured by short rope dangled on a branch, twirling with the wind.

I walked up the stairs, lifted my luggage, and stopped short at the door.

The lion head-shaped doorknocker read "Burpees For Breakfast". The words, imprinted on a circular ring, hung off the lion's mouth.

I looked back and forth, bewildered.

Burpees for breakfast?

Was that what I'd walk into? I let go of the box, set it to the ground, and stared at the door.

So I left my normal life for this…farm? I inhaled a deep breath.

Maybe that was the problem. My norm didn't work anymore.

I certainly can't keep going in that direction. The day I gave my life to Christ, everything changed.

I could no longer enjoy the same music, nor dance to the same songs. A few generic things stayed the same but most changed. I yearned for something new, something clean, something to satisfy my soul. I longed for more of God. My own songs were not what I wanted anymore.

Singing national anthems was my way to transition, and to carry my fans along. But now, half measures no longer worked for me, and apparently for God, concerning my life.

It's time for change. God led me here. Easy or not, I'm ready for this.

Burpees for breakfast? Oh yeah! How 'bout for lunch and dinner too, served with a side of squats? I smiled and took determined first steps up into my future.

CHAPTER 6

"**F**ather God, we thank You for today. We give You praise. You are faithful and kind; Your mercy is everlasting...." Dr. Cantwell paused the prayers and exhaled.

Steam rose off the breakfast plate, teased my nostrils, sparking my mouth to water. I inhaled the enticing aroma.

Feeling guilty, I turned my focus from food to the mealtime prayers again. Dr. Cantwell and his wife were quite the couple. The farmhouse, ordinary from the outside, was exquisite inside. Painted art lined the wall all the way to the staircase leading to the bedrooms. The living room, quite large—larger than standard, appeared even bigger with the huge space between it and the dining section cut off with light lace curtain partitions.

They flapped at my glare, as though a rebuke. I shut my eyes again.

"Lord, as we partake in this bountiful meal may we not simply ingest food, but good measure of Your loving-kindness. In Jesus' name we pray." A chorus of "amen" wrapped it up.

Eyes officially opened, we each drew a plate from the stack Dr. Mrs. Cantwell graciously provided.

She'd insisted on setting the table for our first breakfast together without my help. I dished from a bowl of hot mashed potatoes, scooped up some scrambled eggs, and pushed aside the broccoli. From the corner of my eye, I caught her exchanged glance with her husband. I didn't bother looking up. When I did, they both smiled at me.

I conceded then. "I hate broccoli." In fact, I hated anything green, but I couldn't say so. I had to be polite. After all, she did tell me she rose at six a.m. and cooked this meal to have it ready at seven thirty. This was early breakfast to me, but when in Rome…

"How was your trip yesterday?" Dr. Cantwell asked. The good doctor was actually away when we arrived. Mrs. Cantwell said he'd responded to an urgent medical request at a farm seven miles away, to help deliver a baby after the midwife faced a breeched birth. Luckily, he'd said, farm roads don't typically have speed limits so he got there quickly. When paramedics arrived, he'd already successfully delivered the healthy baby. He stated it was one of his profession's joys. Later, he'd proceeded to a nearby farm to pick up milk and eggs.

I took my first bite, savoring a burst of flavor that slid down my throat too quickly. "These scrambled eggs are delicious! What kind of spice did you use?" I meant it. I couldn't figure out the tasty spices but I liked it. I scooped more eggs when neither of them took a second helping. I'd skipped dinner last night, as I told Mrs. Cantwell I'd like to turn in early. To be honest to myself, I felt weighed down. Plus, I needed time to think. So I woke up at six thirty this morning famished.

Her lips curved into a smile. "Indian curry. Direct import. Plus a little Mrs. Dash, unsalted, and some raw pepper."

I did notice there was virtually no salt in the food, but didn't complain. My hosts were practically senior citizens so I doubted they'd eat much salt. The pepper tingled on my tongue a little. I sipped some water. "How did you discover the combo?"

She pointed her fork to her husband. He waved a dismissive hand, probably knew what she was about to say. She kept her fork trained on him. "He's got more wanderlust than I do—I can tell you that."

He rolled his eyes, wiped his lips with a napkin, and arched his eyebrows. "Nope. I only wanted to climb the mountains in India, but no. You had to test out the food, the spices, the local herbs and such. You said at the time it was because they were presumed to be awesome for physiotherapy." He mimicked her voice.

I laughed at the couple's sweetness.

She retorted, "You could not wait for one more day to climb those mountains and got us stuck in a waterlogged town."

He waved his hands. "It was going to rain in two days. I had no choice."

She pressed her lips. "I suffered a fever for three days."

They sobered and grew silent. My laughter died.

He slid off his seat. "Excuse me." His half-eaten plate remained on the table.

She shook her head, and twisted her fork around an empty spot.

"You okay?" Something had clearly changed in the atmosphere.

But she didn't respond immediately, she just stared in the direction he went. "It was a bad time for us. I was pregnant and almost due. Long story." She exhaled, putting her fork down. "We have two sons. One's in college in California, reading physical therapy, his name is Tim. He's on a Study Abroad program right now. He won't be back until next year. Our second son is also in college. In Boston, studying psychiatry, James. Like his dad, he volunteered for Teach America and will also be gone for the next year. They're not perfect, but both are wonderful boys."

I stood up when she stopped speaking, grabbing my emptied plate. I doubted anyone was still hungry. "I can clean these up if you want."

She sighed and rose too. "I need the distraction. You go on ahead and unpack. I'll give you a tour much later. Get to know your room. Pray. About why you're here, what God has for you. Believe it or not, that's a greater priority for us. Jim was going to tell you after breakfast but well... feel free to come to us if you need anything. Our home is open to you."

She nodded toward the back door, which also doubled as a side exit. "I'm always out in the garden fixing up some loose fence or something else. Once the weather warms up a bit, that's where I'll be. You'll find me inside or out there."

We loaded the leftover meals onto the wide trays, and carried them to the kitchen. We walked past a wall library stacked full. A reading chair nestled next to it had a throw over the side, hung off the cuff. Scriptures in small plaques adorned the wall from where we entered the kitchen.

After clearing my plate, I returned to the residence. It could easily be a one-bedroom apartment, if it had more solid inside walls instead of log and higher roofing, plus a kitchen. It was more like a modern cabin. Nevertheless, I was grateful for the privacy. The Cantwells were nice. But I needed a personal space, and they knew it. There must be more bedrooms up at the house, but they chose this detachment for me.

Perfect.

I strode along the hallway to the front, enjoying the stream of sunshine bathing the entire area. A chaise lounge chair stretched out at the center, facing the sunshine. A wide mat covered part of the wooden floor. The windows ran glass top to bottom, shielded by light lace curtains—curtains like the ones inside the main home. Steam from the indoor heat turned the glass translucent.

I sank into the brown leather, chaise lounge sofa, covering my feet with a light blanket. I leaned against the soft pillow in its curve, and closed my eyes.

What am I here for, Lord God?

Professionally, I had nothing. No future in music or anything else. But God brought me here for a purpose. Maybe to write a new song. Or finally to lose weight since my diet would change. Whatever the reason, I needed to find out soon. Time wasn't waiting for me.

I rose, and wrapped the blanket around my shoulders to ward off the winter chill. I went toward the bedroom, intent to put my stuff into the bedroom closet after I saw whether it needed emptying first.

* * *

JB

I steered my truck into the Makings' driveway barely twenty-four hours after I accepted Grandma Patty's request and my life went haywire.

"Hey! You can't leave that there." I stopped the truck, door ajar, jumped out, and strode to the man whose back was to me.

He straightened upon my approach. Oh, it was the older gentleman I'd hired last week. A day laborer.

This was the fourth time he made this mistake in two days. "Señor, you put it in the mixer first, and stir it. If not, it won't turn out well."

It goes bad, and I lose this contract. I didn't say it to him though. Communication was a language barrier between us, but he seemed teachable.

"Here. Let me show you." I'd hired him for a day, seven days in a row. "See?" I demonstrated what I'd said to him.

He nodded, taking the tool. "Gracias." Gladly, he began replicating my action.

Sometimes, showing taught faster. The man obviously had problems drawing his attention away. He appeared troubled whenever I gave instructions. I knew this because I'd been there. I wondered if he had anyone in his life. Maybe a wife, or children, or a brother, sister...

Experience taught me sometimes you have people, but in reality, you got no one except God. Worrying never solved a thing either. I'd tell Carlos to make sure we retained this man. At least, daily meals would be off his list of concerns.

I, on the other hand, had more issues since last night.

Candace Rodriguez, the singer.

I shook my head and sighed, entering the mansion through the open back door.

I was busy searching for videos on farm management, like Dan had suggested that I did. A viral video began automatically playing.

I wasn't even sure what I was looking at until I saw the lady fall. My hand shot to my mouth. That had to be painful. Then I read the caption and info beneath the video.

It said that she received Christ months ago—which was none of my business. I had pressing concerns. Getting back to my stock market career topped them.

Then God seized me.

Pray for her, welled deep in my heart.

God had to be kidding me. I had one thousand problems, and she wasn't one of them.

But no, the Holy Spirit didn't let me sleep.

I swung a curve to the fancy stairwell, made with steel handles and marble flooring as the Maskings had requested. Going down the basement to do a final check on the completed work, I rubbed my swollen eyes. I'd resisted God until eleven last night. I finally gave in and prayed for her.

This was supposed to be a simple prayer. I chuckled. Thing was—I couldn't stop.

Everything about her, I prayed for. I cried to God for her soul to stay, for her life to follow His ways, for her face to focus on the Savior, not on her problems. It wasn't until five a.m. before I caught a wink of sleep.

Then here I was at eight trying to work. Satisfied that our work in the basement was done, I headed back up and out toward the front.

Praying for Ms. Candace Rodriguez was harder than I'd prayed—even for myself. Why God would ask me to pray for someone I didn't know, would not care to meet, and was not part of my life, I couldn't guess. Two days gone and I was still praying for her. So much need surrounded me; I'd love to focus on those. Or get my prayers for myself answered some.

Striding through the Maskings' house, I knew our work was finished inside. I made my way out front where, standing on a high ladder, Carlos shouted instructions across the lawn.

I stopped, smiled inwardly. He hadn't changed since high school football days. Still yelled at the top of his lungs even when he need not. What would he do when I left in five days? He'd bring the new rooftop down. I chuckled.

"Hey, Carlos!"

He waved, climbing down from the ladder. "JB! Glad you're here. We got to get—"

I ushered him forward, strolling to a shaded area. "I need to talk to you first, man."

He dropped the hand shovel when we reached and stopped.

"Listen, I'm going to be moving to Maryland. Next week. My grandma called me. She needs my help."

He scratched his head. The crease on his forehead saying he didn't like it. "How long you going to be gone for?"

That's the thing, Carlos. "I might not be coming back anytime soon. I'm going to hand everything for this project over to you. You got a lot more experience than anyone else here. Thank God, we're almost finished. I hired more hands a couple of days ago. So by next week, we should complete the finishing touches for roofing right before I leave."

He pointed forward. "I'll do the driveway. It's the only other thing that's left."

Thank God. I was relieved.

He patted my shoulder. "Ah, man, I'm going to miss you."

I shook his left hand. He had a slight limp on his right, since we were kids, so he became left-handed.

I pointed toward the garage. "The elderly man over there mixing for the fancy stones? I need you to let him keep his job."

He glanced over, and then patted my arm. "You got it, JB. Thanks for everything. For this job."

We hugged.

"Hey, what are friends for?" In truth, he was overqualified with his degree. There were no jobs, so I hired him to assist me. Hopefully, when this ended, he'd find another contract or a better job.

He followed me toward my truck. "Let's go talk numbers so the accounts are straightened up before I leave." Inside my heart though, I was being frank with God.

God, I don't want to move to Maryland. Take me back to New York, please, God. But I'll follow where Your will leads.

In my heart, the prod sounded again, *"Pray for her."*

CHAPTER 7

 ANDACE

MY EYES FLUTTERED OPEN. *Oh, right. I'm in Maryland.* The morning sun filtered through the window. The bed creaked as I rose a bit, leaning on my arm to check the time. Eight twenty a.m.

Strangely though, Burpees For Breakfast knocker at the main house came to mind.

I'd grown to like it. Not the burpees, since I'd never done one. The residence I meant—it was a home away from home. A hotel on a farm. It was beautiful. And the natural lighting added to its appeal. Greenery and fresh air abounded.

Maybe this was what I needed. It gave me privacy. Oh, and then the sunroom. I loved it.

Dr. Cantwell quit dinner last night and rushed to his clinic to aid an emergency patient. Mrs. Cantwell gave me a tour of the residence yesterday after dinner.

Soon after, I retired to bed early. The bed creaked again as I shifted my weight to sit, shuffling the comforter closer. If the freeze wasn't snapping my toes, I'd venture outside.

Instead, I curled up, pulling its warmth to my chin. I yawned and wondered what I'd have been doing in New York right now.

But I can't afford such thought. I'm here. My heart needs to be here too.

New York was a safe, predictable environment for me. This—is not. Best not to think of anywhere else right now.

Determined to start my day, I peeled away the comforter and slid to my feet, the lush carpet blocking the chill from racing up my legs. I picked my phone up and pressed the On button. The battery symbol flashed—phone's dead. I'd forgotten to plug it to charge the night before because I'd taken off my shoes, slipped beneath the covers, and fallen asleep.

"Ugh." I put it down on the side desk.

I had to use the bathroom first.

I dragged my feet to the bathroom and sat there for a couple of minutes—thinking.

This whole trip was crazy, wasn't it? Why travel all the way to Maryland? What about Aunt Emma's place in California? I could've gone there and stayed for a bit. Her kids would love to see me after three years. Aunt Emma would too. We haven't seen her since our parents' funeral. Matt and I have been on our own.

We were already doing well. We didn't need much support. Now, with my music directionless, there's no saying how things might turn.

Was coming here foolish? I could go back now.

Trust God. Leave your crutches. Aunt Emma and all.

Mrs. Cantwell's words hit me at the most unpredictable times. I sighed in agreement.

Okay, God. You win. First, I got to get myself together.

I stood at the sink and stared at the wall mirror.

What would I even be rushing back to in New York? Performing music? Wolves in human clothing lurked out there, ready to tear me apart if I dared show up on any stage in the country.

No thanks. I wasn't ready.

I have to find my reason, and my strength before gaining courage to face the world again.

There lay my purpose in Maryland. Finding strength to face the world again. I flushed, even though I didn't use the toilet. Just sat there and cleared my head. I washed my hands, and returned to the room.

The spacious bedroom joined a living area, which extended down a hallway, then led to the sunroom. The sunroom was just as wide, if not wider than the bedroom. Every time out there, I was grateful those light lace curtains provided certain shade though far from the street view. I noticed how well arranged the residence was. Not a thing was out of place.

Whoever cleaned this room was thorough. Most likely Mrs. Cantwell.

I sat on the bed and rummaged through my purse. There it was. My charger. I figured Matt might be trying to reach me.

I jerked straight at the thought. "Oh no!" I hadn't thought of that last night.

Hurrying to the living area, I found a socket next to the gray couch.

I bent over, plugged the line into the wall, and connected it to my phone. The word *Charging* flashed in red lights so I stood.

It would be another ten to fifteen minutes before I could call. I was supposed to call him before going to sleep. I groaned. I slipped my feet into my slippers, pulled my hair into a bun, and hand-brushed stray strands. I slid on a pair of jeans, my new XXXL t-shirt, and a sweater. I remembered the size because I liked it and had it custom-ordered to fit me.

Minutes later, I made my way to the phone, which I'd placed on a desk beside the couch.

Picking it up, I dialed his number.

"Hello?"

Relief washed through me. "Matt? Sorry. It's me."

He let out a loud breath. I could imagine the relief on his face. "I was worried, Candace. You were supposed to call. You all right?" He had reason to be angry. The alarm in his voice was unmistakable.

"Yeah, I'm fine. Sorry, I was tired. I went straight to bed. I tried to call you this morning then saw my battery was dead so I had to charge it first."

"Okay."

"I'm at the farm. I'll text you the address like we discussed. My hosts, they're both doctors. They're a nice couple. Last night, they said I could stay as long as I needed to. They just want to help me so I'm really grateful."

I wanted to ask if he was okay or busy worried about me but now was not the time.

Sometimes, his words stung when he was angry. I sure didn't want a taste of it today with me at fault.

"Glad to know you're all right. Next time, you better text or something. Are you comfortable? Have you eaten?" Okay, he was more worried than angry.

"Matt, I'm fine, okay. Stop worrying. How are you and everyone?" Everyone, meaning his wife and the team.

"They're fine. They all say hello. Listen, I spoke to Ray."

I gasped in shock. "You what?! I told you not to call him. C'mon, Matt!" I rolled my eyes. "He's going to think he's my entire world. That without him, I'm done for."

But Matt wasn't having it. "Candace, what he did was wrong. Someone had to tell him that. For you."

I understood, but seriously, I needed him to just go away since he'd made his choice clear. Ugh.

"Well, thank you, I guess." He'd stood up for me and that meant a lot. Though uncertain about my life, I kept a calm voice to allay his fears. "I'm all right, Matt. I just need some space and time. That's why I'm here at the farm."

He sighed. "I know. The phones have been ringing, calls coming in, e-mails, you name it. I'm holding the fort for ya. You focus on you down there, all right?"

I was so glad that he understood. "Thank you, Matt. I will."

He paused, like there was something else he would've said, but then he offered. "Okay. Take care of yourself. Let me know how you are doing so I don't get worried."

With nothing else left to say, I agreed. "Sure, I will. Take care of you."

I hung up, returned the phone atop the desk, and plugged it back in. Some sport magazine, and workout schedules lay carelessly underneath the desk. I ignored them. Beside the desk, on the other side, something tall stood covered. I walked over and raised the flap. Then I fully unveiled it, scattering loose dust.

An elliptical machine. "Um—wow."

Whoever stayed here before me was really into fitness. Maybe one of the Cantwell sons. I replaced the flap and covered it properly, dusting off my sweater from any residue.

Burpees, now an elliptical machine…what next?

* * *

JB

"JB, did you call your grandma yet? You should let her know you're on your way."

I rummaged through my bags in the truck searching, as he spoke. "Dan, did you see the little—there it is."

I glanced up while picking the bag with my study materials in them. My books, Bible, study journal, and personal items nestled inside it. I laid them up against the front seat, next to me. "Yeah, I called her and told her I'd arrive tonight. She's almost ready to move. I also told her you helped me get things taken care of. She says hi."

Dan had visited her once with me. During my eighteenth birthday. He and two other friends. We'd all traveled down as they'd never been on a farm, so it fascinated them. That was my second visit—and last until now.

I closed the back of the truck and checked to make sure the gas tank was shut. Then I turned to him. "This is it, man. You take care of things around here."

We fist bumped. "Your old man, I guess he's not coming out."

"You know he's not coming. It's all right, buddy. God is in control."

We hugged, and I opened the driver's door.

"Stay in touch, JB. Let me know what's going on."

I nodded. "I will."

As I shut the door, a lump formed in my throat. Dan was the closest to family I'd had in a long time, aside from my pastor who doubled as my mentor. Dan gave solace since my return a few years back. He helped me get into construction, much as I detested going that route since Dad said it was all I'd ever do in life. Construction. Or nothing.

I started the truck, and it boomed in response, ready. I pushed it into gear, and waved to Dan.

He waved back.

I swallowed hard, backed out of his parking lot, and joined traffic.

This morning came with an air of freedom. Not just because I was leaving Kentucky. No. Because the burden to pray for Ms. Rodriguez finally lifted.

I was glad that I prayed for her. I'd actually begun enjoying interceding for someone whom I'd never meet just because God wanted me to. For now, I was happy to be burden-free. I smiled inwardly.

With a full day's drive ahead, I could make good use of my time on the road. I pressed Play on the tape from church I'd bought, titled, "Walk By Faith"—my favorite topic. After all, I'd need a huge dose of faith on this trip.

There was no turning back.

"I walk by faith not by sight," I muttered. My favorite Scripture too. It got me all the way to Wall Street. It would get me through whatever waited ahead.

Three hours into driving through the I-64 East corridor, and road construction slowed me down. The temperature read 37 degrees, which was warmer the past couple of days than the twenties we had in Louisville all last week. It was still frigid, so I turned on the heater.

I spotted a driver come to a slow stop beside me when traffic slowed. A young lady, wearing a sleeveless shirt. In winter? I faced the road again. I guessed everyone's internal temperature's different.

Once past the construction zone, traffic sped up. I drove forward, not looking at any other driver. This would not just be a long drive for me. It was a time to think and pray. I needed divine guidance. I knew nothing about farming except that seeds go into the ground and animals eat grass. Here I was about to go take over a farm!

After another hour, I sped past the city limits and into the 1-68 East, crossing West Virginia, and headed for Maryland.

* * *

CANDACE

"There is a connection. Then there is a God-connection." Dr. Cantwell adjusted his lenses, too big for me to actually see his eyes. They were huge, like magnifying glasses. "You know the difference between the two?"

I withdrew my hands into my sweater pockets and raised a brow. I'd copped a spot on the steps of the main home earlier, wanting some fresh air when Dr. Cantwell spotted me on his way home late from the clinic.

He'd stopped and sat with me for a quick chat.

"What?" I asked.

He smiled. "When God Himself brings people together," he nodded like a teacher in a classroom with an attentive pupil, "he pulls purposes together. See, God has a plan for every life. Sometimes, the plan for one life may depend on that of another."

Dependency...

"So, if one fails—"

I didn't want to complete it. I had yet to begin my journey, whatever it was.

I was afraid to fail before I started.

He continued, "All those whose destinies are linked to one purpose, could get affected. Of course, God could change all that and do a redirect." He looked me in the eye. "But how do you think you'll feel being the reason God had to redirect someone else's life, because you failed Him in His purpose and plan for your life—which He provided you adequate resources for? Don't answer. Ruminate on it. I'll see you tomorrow."

I rose, walked to the door, and then stopped. "How does one start losing weight?"

He removed his glasses. "You have to want it badly enough. The tools are at your disposal."

Right.

I saw it already. The elliptical machine. "Good night, Dr. Cantwell."

He rose too and opened the door to their home as I strode to the residence. "Good night, Candace."

* * *

JB

Arriving in Maryland at evening time meant getting caught in the I-95 rush hour traffic. Or so the weather radio station I'd tuned into had warned.

But it was too late. Rookie error.

Since I was already caught in it, with no faster route, I stuck with it, crawling at snail speed.

One hour later, I veered off the I-95 South, cutting through Exit 25 and entering Beltsville. I'd called my grandma to let her know.

She said it had been great timing as we were having dinner with friends tonight. They wanted to say goodbye to her before she left.

I was too tired for a party but I agreed, knowing that it would make her happy. Moving to an assisted living facility from your own home cannot be an easy transition. But she sounded like she was handling it well.

* * *

CANDACE

This morning, I went into town with Mrs. Cantwell. I wanted

workout gear. Everything I could find—tops, shorts, tights, sweat scarves, sneakers. I'd searched online, and I found lots of suggestions. By the time we got back, it was midday. She said we were hosting some neighbors for dinner. One of them was leaving for an assisted living facility and she owned the farm next to theirs.

They'd like to honor her with a family-style dinner. She'd said that the woman's grandson was coming into town and would join as well.

I said okay and offered to assist with the preparations.

But my mind was occupied.

Lord, songs, please. I need songs. I need to lose weight too.

"We need to steam veggies. Everything else, I've made already. Baked, grilled, you name it."

I shook my head. The woman was a walking ball of energy. She had the agility of a twenty-year-old. "No problem. I can take care of that."

As we prepared for the party, in my heart, I cried my deepest needs to the Lord.

Songs.

Weight loss.

In that order.

* * *

"THANK YOU ALL FOR COMING."

People of different ages, and races filled the dining room. One commonality bound them—they were farmers or lived with a farmer.

It was incredible to me. I walked to the kitchen and put away some of the already-used dishes as Mrs. Cantwell offered her welcome. After that, I needed some air.

I made my way to the back door directly facing the flagstone path to the residence. Then I sat on the steps. She said they rarely used this door unless they had a large gathering like today.

Though outside it was a little chilly, I savored the fresh air.

"You know the temperatures are freezing. You can catch a cold out here."

I jerked to my feet, as my eyes tracked the voice.

The man stood by the corner reading, with one hand slid into his pocket, and the other holding an open book. He leaned on the wall, appearing unperturbed by my scanning gaze. He was tall. I'd give him that. At least taller than me. Our eyes met.

"I'm sorry. What are you doing out here too?"

His lips arched to a partial grin. "Smart lady. Same as you, I presume. I was searching for a minute of quiet."

He was that type, huh? Armed with a witty tongue. Well, I had no time for that. My schedule was full. Burpees, anyone?

"Great then. I'll go back inside now." I turned and opened the door.

"Wait. You dropped something."

I spun to see what he meant. It was my music notepad. Must've fallen from my back pocket when I sat down.

He picked it up, and handed it to me. "You sing." I'd sketched a music note atop my pad.

He said it more as a statement.

I nodded, accepting it. Our hands touched briefly but I drew mine back. "Yes. Well, I used to. I don't know. It's complicated."

He chuckled, flipped around, and faced his book again, one hand shoved back into his pocket. "Great."

The word stopped me short. "Great?"

He twisted his head slightly above his shoulder, meeting my gaze and holding it. "The best songs emerge from axis of uncertainty, and from difficult places. You might be on to something." He faced his book again while I returned to the party, his words lingering on my mind.

CHAPTER 8

"*Ms.* Patty, please rise." Mrs. Cantwell raised her hand.

The elderly lady, who appeared to be in her mid to late seventies, rose gingerly, holding a walking cane, leaning on it slightly. A smile lit her face, shaving years off her age.

"I've known you for two years as my neighbor. Every one of those days has been an absolute pleasure and honor. Not only have you enlightened my faith, you've taught me to hold onto my anchor in Jesus when tough times roll in. You are the best neighbor, friend, and sister I could've asked for."

Applause rang through the room of about ten people.

Mrs. Cantwell stretched her hand to me on one side, and to the person standing to her right on the other.

We took them.

"Let's join hands as we pray for her journey into a new life."

Everyone stood, formed a circle, and joined hands.

To my right was Mrs. Cantwell, then the guy I'd met outside, then Ms. Patty, Dr. Cantwell, the manager of Ms. Patty's farm, Mr. Winifred, his wife, and their daughter, all eight.

Ms. Patty slowly took the center.

Head bowed low, Mrs. Cantwell prayed, "Lord, Maker of all things, we come before You today, presenting Your daughter, Ms. Patty..."

As she prayed, I sensed more than one person's life was being changed here.

Tonight felt charged, as though it was much a farewell to Ms. Patty —obviously endeared to all—as a welcome to new beginnings for me at least. I'd only been here one week, but it felt longer, and they felt closer, like I'd found another family.

"Amen," we chorused at the end.

Each took turns to hug her, and wished her well as she found her seat again.

When it was my turn, I stepped forward, bent low, and hugged her lightly, while being gentle with her frail frame.

"Candace, welcome! It's good to have fresh faces around here. Have you met my grandson, JB?" She pointed ahead.

My eyes followed her hand, and landed on someone equally looking back at us, smiling.

It was the guy I met earlier.

"He just arrived tonight. He'll be taking over the farm for me. I hope you two get along since you're the only young folk for three miles in either direction." The wink in her eye implied more than simply getting along. I pretended not to notice.

I rose to full height as he approached, extending his hand. I took it, and shook it firmly, but his grip was firm too.

"JB Patrickson here." He offered a broad smile.

"Candace. Candace Rodriguez."

He began to nod, then froze as though recognition sparked, with his eyes pinned on mine.

I stared at him, confused by the sudden change in reaction.

Then as fast as it came, it vanished. I wasn't sure what had happened.

He quietly withdrew his grip and slid his hands in his pockets, like he'd done earlier outside. He offered a formal, teeth-baring smile. "Nice to meet you, ma'am."

"Ma'am? I'm hardly that old," I blurted before thinking.

He continued smiling. "It's how we show respect. I'm from Kentucky."

He just arrived…but he was already getting on my nerves.

"Candace is fine, JB. Pleasure is mine as well, mister."

His grandma stared from him to me. "Okay then." Her narrowed eyes spoke more than her lips. She winked to him and smiled toward me. "Aren't you going to ask her for her phone number? I thought that's how you kids do it these days."

He blushed all the way to his fingertips, cast me a quick glance, then averted his gaze. "Grandma, um—we just met."

Stuttering a bit, shifted him from the confidence he'd shown the second we met until a minute ago, as he looked up at me. "I'm sorry, Ms. Candace." He changed it up…I'm now Ms.

"No offense taken. It was nice meeting you, Ms. Patty. I wish you well, JB."

As I turned, partly amused by his discomfort, I heard her say, "Now you made her upset."

He ushered her toward the living room where guests were now seated, chatting away.

In the kitchen, I found Mrs. Cantwell, knee deep in clearing dirty dishes, and trashing leftover food.

"I can help."

She pointed toward the deep baking pan. "Great. Hand me that, please."

I picked it up, and handed it over. "The party was nice."

She must have worked hard to put it together on her own.

I could've helped if I'd known earlier.

She smiled. "So is the cleanup after-party." She accepted the pan, then slipped it into the warm water-filled sink.

Laughing, I rolled up my sleeves and bent to stack in more dishes to soak. "It sure is."

As we worked between sink and dishwasher, I pondered on the man I met. He seemed wise for life's challenges, but unsure about women.

Hmmm. There was some kindness about him that I admired…

some depth. My mind stayed on JB, as my problems took second place.

* * *

JB

The time was eleven p.m and I still laid awake hours after the party, unable to sleep a wink. It wasn't jet-lag. It was something worse. Today has been the most bizarre day of my life. I met Candace Rodriguez, the famous singer. Her fame wasn't the point—at least not to me. I'd just met the person God laid in my heart to intercede for, even when I'd never met her and never expected to.

I remembered the video of her fall, and then the following commentary. They were vicious to say the least. They probably built the stage with smaller-sized people in mind. But no one considered that possibility.

I was in Kentucky. She was in New York. The chances of our paths crossing? Nil.

Yet I obeyed God and prayed for her. The most recent news was of her fiancé jilting her and finding another lady—in one week.

When I was glad to have my life back, no more prayers for a random stranger, then she hit me between the eyes—no longer a stranger.

As I looked into her eyes at the dinner, the omniscience of God awed me. I couldn't wrap my head around the fact that we stood face to face, shaking hands. Impossible! So impossible to comprehend.

I turned to the other side of the bed, laying on my arm. Something blipped close. I raised my phone and checked the time—11:58 p.m.

JB, time to sleep. You got a farm to run. I sighed, put the device down, and slipped my hand back under the comforter.

I was here to assist my grandma. No more worries about Ms. Rodriguez. Yes. That's what I'd call her, to widen the distance. It would keep me focused on my task. Satisfied, I shut my eyes and, within moments, sleep came.

* * *

CANDACE

The next day, I rose early with enthusiasm, and felt refocused.

My goals took center stage again.

I threw my feet off the bed onto the floor. The plush carpet welcomed my wiggling toes, a contrast to the hardwood floors on the rest of the residence, except for the throw rug in the living area.

The main home's living room was carpeted too. I'd never gone up to the bedrooms, so I wasn't sure what they looked like. I wasn't curious either. I had so much on my mind. First on my agenda, was a change of clothing from my pajamas, then to the reason I made myself rise early.

My best friend, Rosa.

As I rummaged in the closet, I recalled the last time we talked… almost a year ago. Things were different then.

I wasn't a Christian yet.

Everything was as it used to be.

Our chat centered on me telling her how high my albums rose on the charts. She was happy for me.

I do recall there was an edge in her voice. But I was too caught up in spilling the news of my success to ask.

Guilt thinned my lips out now. I couldn't change the past, but I could be a better friend.

Found it.

A dress long enough to keep the chills off. I stretched it over my head, and it fell to my ankles. I swung a sweater over it, buttoning it up. My teeth chattered as I crossed to increase the heat, pumping the fan from a one to a five.

Rosa had been on my mind since before I left New York. I walked to the living area of the residence, leaving the bedroom door open for additional heat to seep through.

A second seat rested against the far wall to the left. It was smaller though and piled high with long shoeboxes and empty bags.

The residence had three sections—the bedroom, the spacious

living area, and the sunroom out front. An indoor hallway linked them all, and a narrow open garage stretched wide outside, as it snaked right to join that of the main house.

Last night, I'd moved the elliptical machine from the corner of the living area, and dragged it across the throw rug to the center of the room. With the blessing of the Cantwells, I could begin using it. I'd dusted it up with a towel, and plugged its cord into the wall. Today I'd chosen to start my day on it going forward. Nothing stopped me from exercising.

I lost all my excuses. I had equipment, convenience, and time. Nothing stood in my way—except my will.

Inside, I wanted to lose weight, but I didn't want to exercise. I thought about it, I even rationalized it. But it was time to do it.

I sidestepped the elliptical, walked to the couch, and sat, unplugging my phone from its charger on the side desk.

Music is a very competitive field. No one's place is secure. You have to work for your place every day. Frankly, people put in more work than I did. The crowd just always liked me—until now.

As I sat there, I was deeply aware of the passage of time. Every day I wasn't engaged with music, drove it further away—both for support, enthusiasm, and yes, money. The stakes were high, time was the currency, and I felt as though I was burning through it carelessly, while writing no new songs.

I needed help and trusted counsel.

I picked up my phone. The time showed as seven forty-five. That's…one forty-five in Rome.

Perfect. I pressed Dial.

The line sounded coarse at first. Then she picked up.

"Candace! Where on earth have you been?"

"Planet Earth! So good to hear your voice, Rosa. How are you, girlie?"

She sighed. "If the flight tickets were cheaper, I could hop on the plane just to give you a hug. I miss you seriously. Our coffee on your birthday mornings, I miss terribly. That by the way, used to be the only free time you ever had open all year round. Busy bee."

The guilt went up a notch. I resisted telling her my calendar was now clear, twenty-four hours, every day. "I'm so sorry, Rosa. I'll make time to call more."

But the clock was ticking on both ends…and I hadn't said why I called. Time to get down to the main reason I called her. "How is your business doing?"

"Oh, you won't believe it." She laughed. "No one would believe it. I've only been here a couple of years, yet it feels like I've been here twenty years. Remember when I first came and told you how hard things were? Competing coffee shops sprung up on every corner. I would even give out free coffee once a week to get people to enter my shop."

Her voice beamed. "Scratch all that, Candace. Now, people queue up for breakfast here. I not only serve coffee, I serve breakfast meals until noon, when I can close the shop if I want to. Sometimes, I leave it open for another hour or so with my staff running things. It's simply ah-mazing! Of course, on weekends, I stay open for my loyal all-day coffee drinkers."

I laughed, feeling so glad to know she was doing well. I'd been worried.

"Ah, gone are the days. Back in college I lived on the stuff, remember? Sometimes ten cups a day." The memory came to the fore.

"Until the headaches started, then you stopped."

"Yeah." She did recall.

"Soda took over." She was listing my addictions as they happened.

I sighed. "About that, I'm still a work in progress."

I hated to admit that I still consumed so much of it.

"You need to lay off soda. I tell you, the sugar alone is incredible. What'd they say? Like ten teaspoons in each can? It's just too much."

Need I tell her that I've gained another fifty pounds since she last saw me, partly thanks to high sugar intake?

Working in the studio was tasking, and fast food got me through the long days.

No, I'd keep that info out. I wasn't going to make excuses either.

"Rosa, I need to lose weight. I'm also working on new songs as a Christian now."

I'd told her when I accepted Christ.

It didn't change our friendship because she wasn't bothered.

"I got a question. I need your candid experience for this." I clutched my sweater closer.

Winter....Grrr.

"Sure. Go ahead."

I knew how sensitive this was. I'd pondered it a few times last night when I'd chosen that she'd advice me best.

"Why did you move—to Italy? I mean, you could've stayed here. Or you could've moved to a different city, and state maybe. Started up somewhere else. Instead, you moved halfway across the world, to another country?"

Like I'd just traveled 200 miles for a fresh start, yet not knowing what it looked like, I reminded myself inwardly.

"You're in a country where they look different from you, don't speak the same language per se, and you had no guarantee of success. How did you do it, Rosa?"

I could imagine her in her short black, curly hair walking amidst brown and black straight haired people, standing out.

She hesitated. "You just have to have faith in people. Believe that looking different is no big deal once you've realized all human beings are alike. God made us all, so why bother because someone else appears to be from a different race?"

She was taking it kindly. She had such a stellar perspective. One of the many reasons I liked her.

"Moreover, you know I fit in everywhere I go. How did I succeed in business? I lost my fear. I chose to believe without a doubt that I would succeed here. Yes, I knew no one. I couldn't even speak one word of Italian, and there were no guarantees."

She chuckled. "Come to think of it, Candace, there are no guarantees in life anyway. Everything we do stems from faith. You believe you'll succeed, just like you believe everything will work out when you rise every morning. Does it always go that way? Of course not.

But you tell yourself that anyway, because you know what? For the most part, everything is fine, except for the few occasions when it's not. Why live in fear of those occasional moments of disappointment and miss out on the overwhelming times of appointment? It wouldn't make sense, right? It's simple math. More positive, less negative. "

She sounded so optimistic. It had contagion effect on me.

"When I arrived, I focused on the opportunity to succeed. Sure, no one else here starting up a new business looked like me, but I turned it into a good thing. Once a week, I added a free croissant to go with the coffee. I did a few things others weren't doing and it worked. I was courteous to my customers. I gave each a smile. It's free. We talked about their kids, school runs, their stress of the day. My coffee shop became a second home to them. They'd come and buy a cup, just to chat. Now, they're not just here for the coffee. They're here for the experience. That is how you win, Candace. Make your music an unforgettable experience. At least, it's how I won. It's hard work, and a struggle especially when you had a bad day and don't feel like being friendly and nice. But remember, the customer standing in front of you does not know that. They only know what they receive within those few moments of interaction."

I already began thinking of how to apply that in my music. Maybe I'd add some non-music benefit to it. But, what?

"So, as an entrepreneur or business woman, it's your job to not drag your past moment into your future opportunity. In a nutshell, that's it. Of course, I skipped the parts about sleepless nights, and days when shipments arrive late thanks to weather, yada yada yada."

We both laughed on the light note.

"You mean the fun stuff, huh?" I pulled a blanket over my feet when shivers ran across my skin.

"Honestly, whatever you do, you have to believe in yourself. Say you can do it. Then go do it and watch what happens."

She'd given me far more than I expected.

"I'll tell you, Candace. There were two months when I made no sale. Not one. I wrote on a sheet and posted it to my wall in my bedroom. 'Rosa, you'll outsell yesterday today.' I said it to myself every morning. I went out there and worked to realize it."

God just provided me with the inspiration that I needed.

"Thank you so much, Rosa. I appreciate you sharing this with me."

I was grateful she didn't ask me why all these questions. She just gave me hope. And help.

"Sorry, a beeline of customers is due to arrive in an hour for a special birthday event. I have to get set up for them. Candace, you made my day! I'm giving out a free cup of coffee plus breakfast to one customer, courtesy of you, lady."

I laughed softly, feeling honored and missing her already. "Me too! Great talking to you."

It was time for me to get some hot tea. The chill was reaching bone deep.

"Can't wait to see you when I come Stateside next summer."

I hoped I lost the weight by then.

"Me too. Thank you, Rosa. Have a good day."

She was starting to sound far. "Sure thing."

We hung up.

Mission accomplished.

Thank You, Jesus. I'm ready now.

CHAPTER 9

*A*fter my chat with Rosa, I sprang into action. I'd start afresh on my music. I knew that already. I just didn't have the courage to take the first step. This afternoon during lunch, I'd ask my hosts how long was too long for me to stay with them. But first, I wanted to do something, learning from Rosa's experience.

I went into the bedroom, with a sense of hope rising. I wandered to the mirror, phone in my hand, and stood there. I admired every curve on me, however imperfect.

God made me. I am beautifully and wonderfully made. I know I'm a beautiful person.

With closed eyes, I imagined myself in a small-sized dress. I chuckled, opened my eyes, and snapped a photo, fully clothed with the sweater, long dress and all. This was nothing more than a keepsake picture.

Hearing laughter outside, I headed out to see the cause. A boom echoed off the residence walls. I gripped the side of the door, scared. I'd just finished helping Mrs. Cantwell order plant seeds. We'd hoped they'd arrive in time to plant the garden in a matter of weeks. Spring is said to start soon. But with this frigid cold burning my toes, I found that hard to believe. I slipped my feet into warm pink slippers and ventured out.

A tractor idled before the main entrance in the wide driveway, its engine roaring. Black soot billowed off the top of the exhaust pipe, on the side.

A farm tractor.

Dr. Cantwell stood beside a male figure leaning over the hood. When he saw me, Dr. Cantwell waved me over.

I began to approach. Then the man straightened. His brown hair tumbled, resting on his nape and I recognized him.

JB.

I paused, tempted to turn. *You should've just gone back inside, Candace.* But my feet kept moving toward them.

"Good morning, Candace! Look who we've got here helping me fix this truck-of-a-kind. I could never even get it started before. He's already made strides with it."

JB held the side of the truck, with his gloved hands darkened with grease. "Good morning."

No Ms. Candace this time? Good. The brown leather coat he wore was long, and it stopped at his knee. Tall brown boots met the coat there. Waves of deep-brown arm hair peeped from the sleeve of his coat.

He pulled something from beneath the open hood, laid it on the side of the truck, and then bent over again.

"Morning, JB." I stopped close enough to Dr. Cantwell. "Good morning, Dr. Cantwell."

JB tugged at some cord again, and the engine roared, letting off more soot. He braced his waist against the truck and straightened up.

Our eyes met. His steeled, mine, I guessed, curious. We held for a moment, too long if you asked me.

"How's the music coming?"

I faced the tree with the toy car. Frost dripped off a few bare branches.

Some scattered white still dotted the landscape. Far in the

75

distance, a surprising spread of crops survived winter, still blooming green. Maybe the sloping topography shielded them? I wondered.

"Good."

Dr. Cantwell turned, screwdriver in hand, clad in overalls. "I'm going to go get my special toolbox. I think we'll need it. I'll be back."

Fleeing the scene? Ugh.

"That wasn't what I expected to hear."

I spun.

Looking me straight in the eye, JB dropped a towel he'd used to clean his hand. There was something about him. Something unsettling. His eyes appeared resolute, like someone who knew exactly what he wanted. So sure of himself, yet not proud. I felt almost like he'd sized me up all in one moment.

Cool wind whistled past my ear. I shivered a little and tried my warmest relaxed smile to ward off his stare. "Really?" Suddenly feeling small in my five-feet-ten-inch frame.

"Focus. It's what drives everything we do, who we are, what we pursue. Focus is everything. That is, after faith in Christ."

I glanced away, quite sure now. "You recognized me. You've heard."

He surveyed the open hood then me again. "Man wants to toss you aside after one mistake. But God holds you after ten thousand."

The words pierced my heart. *Who is this guy?*

He straightened and turned to the tractor's hood. "The only thing that matters is where your heart is."

His attention settled on me again, full brows narrowing. "Focus drives performance. Find out what you want most, then keep your attention on it."

Fascinated, I wouldn't let him stop there. "What matters to you most, JB?" I was curious.

Mr. Philosopher.

Even this guy, must have something he was working towards.

The shadow of a smile crossed his face. He slipped off the gloves, laid them on the side of the hood, and began filing something blunted like a rugged pin. "Oh. Simple."

I crossed my arms, and studied his reaction.

"It's not a what: it's a who." He continued filing.

The front door swung open and Dr. Cantwell emerged.

Yet, I wanted the answer. "So who is it?"

JB locked eyes with me, seemingly also aware of the pending interruption. "Jesus. Jesus Christ."

I swallowed.

"He's my everything."

I tore my eyes away. "He's mine too."

He took a step. "Then pursue Him and Him alone."

Music filtered from inside the main house where Dr. Cantwell still stood, door ajar, struggling with something. It sounded like someone was playing a piano.

I'd no idea there was a piano in there.

"Close the door, Jim! We're losing precious heat," Mrs. Cantwell called.

He stepped out of it and toward us as the door gently shut.

I turned to JB, now bent over the hood again. I bit my lip and gazed at this man who seemed only a few inches taller than me, about the same age range, but so much wiser. How did he become that way?

"JB, I think this is what you needed, right?" Dr. Cantwell offered him the tool.

It was time for me to leave. "I'm going to go get some stuff done. See you later."

I wasn't sure which one of them I referred to as I took off.

I wanted to talk more but feared his words might go deeper than the surface. Having come out of a break-up one week ago, I needed some time. I strode to the residence. It was time to think.

* * *

REENTERING THE RESIDENCE, I grabbed a towel and dusted the bedside stand, placing a pen, notepad, and gum on it. That was the only part of this residence I'd found untouched. Mrs. Cantwell wiped and dusted down the entire place before I got here. She'd shared that she only had a few hours to do so, prior to picking me up. She'd mentioned that her younger son had stayed there for a couple of months one year ago before he moved to Boston. I unpacked the remaining items from my luggage and settled in.

With my choice made, I was going to be here for a while.

CHAPTER 10

* * *

"**C**ome. Let's go for a milk-and-meat run. We're actually swapping some fruits and veggies for milk and meat with JB's farm. It's not far. I'll meet you out front in say, an hour. Sound okay?" Mrs. Cantwell called me.

"Sure. I'll be happy to. I'll be there in one hour. I need to shower first."

It had been three weeks since I saw JB. He'd mostly been off my mind.

I'd lazed around, gone up to the main house for meals, and prayed a lot. Somehow, the privacy, peace, and quiet afforded my life much needed calm.

In the past, everything moved at a fast pace for me. All I did was catch up to it. If only I took a few minutes each day to reflect, maybe things could've been different.

Being in concert year round didn't help at all. I feared that if I took time off, I could easily get replaced.

I entered the bathroom and sat on the edge of the bathtub. My hosts had been so kind since my arrival. There were more than enough supplies in this portion of the house. The bath soap here could last an entire year. The towels were stacked high in a basket, and some slippers waited by the door the first night.

Last night, I'd asked again how long I could stay. They'd said however long I wished to, they didn't mind as long as I left feeling whole and set for success.

I bent my head, and stooped low to grab my nail clippers, while trying to figure out what I'd be moving forward to.

I should be in the shower now.

But instead, I headed to the bedroom. I felt the desperation for change within me. I continued to the shower, exhaling.

A bath sounded best right now. I was about to get a headache, and someone was waiting for me.

* * *

"I'M READY, MRS. CANTWELL," I called out.

She emerged from the side of the house clad in farm overalls, which she peeled off and hung by a tall wooden hook knocked into the ground by the garden's small gate. Placing her rubber gloves beside the front steps, she dusted off her hands, and began slipping on woolen gloves.

She waved me on. "Let's walk. It's about one mile up the hill from us. Those tomato vines are impossible! I've tried to curl them to the sticks I planted for them. But guess what? No! They follow the sun, chasing it like a kid after the ice cream truck."

We laughed. "But isn't that how we long for God and how God chases us?" She nodded and put up a warning finger, her laughter still lighthearted. "You always stick close to your source, Candace. Never stray. I guess I'll move the sticks to where the sun faces for good measure. I probably should've put them there in the first place."

I wondered if she ever had any problems since she always wore a smile.

"I already had one of the boys who's here to till the land for plant-ing, send up payment for the items we're picking up. Veggies are running short this time, so I changed my mind. We paid in cash instead."

I shrugged my hands deeper into my sweater thinking that I should have worn thicker gloves. "So, have you always enjoyed farm life?"

She shook her head. "I never knew the first thing about farming. My dad was a soldier, my mom a housewife. I grew up in different cities before I turned eighteen. But I also made friends from varying backgrounds, and my love for travel was born. I wasn't afraid of other cultures, in fact, I loved them, and was intrigued by them. As an adult, I made it a learning experience. You can learn from anybody if you allow yourself to open up a little."

I was running out of breath. Her pace was that of a teenager. She was already noticeably slowing down just for me. Even that was too fast. I struggled to lift my body weight off each foot as we went. Then I began to sweat.

"I can slow down if you want me to."

She'd noticed my heavy breathing, plus the supportive hand that I had on my waist. I wanted to politely decline. But I couldn't. "Yes, please. Thank you."

She slowed to a stroll.

It was better that I acknowledged it, than faint and have her call 911.

"I married my husband when I wasn't sure what I wanted to do, but I was sure I loved him. Our parents gave their consent, and we moved to Europe for a few months, after he completed his medical education. We prayed then moved to India. We located a mission in Central India where new doctors got to put their skills to work, in exchange for room, board, and a stipend. We loved it. I began learning how to assist the medical team but noticed my strongest skill was in the recovery ward. I helped injured people get back on their feet. We returned to the US temporarily, and I enrolled in college for physical therapy while my husband worked in the hospital. After two years, we packed up and left again."

Fields stretched out on both sides of the road. Some withered corn stalks swayed afar off.

"Armed with my new degree, I headed recovery clinics, and direct care for a few small outpost clinics in cooperation with the doctors-in-charge. I continued my Bachelors and Doctoral degrees by distance learning through the University of Maryland. I also took up interest in preventive care, to reduce the incidence of disease. You see, a lot of the patients we catered for were very poor. They lived in shantytowns, with poor drainage systems, unclean water supply, and lack of food variety. All these factors heightened the incidence of disease and high mortality rates. Plus, some of those cultures encouraged early marriages, so girls were married and pregnant before their bodies were ready to nurture a child. This brought significant complications, which we had to deal with. The girls were also having too many pregnancies too close together because they began having children early in their teens. Yet, some kept bearing children into their forties."

We reached a fork in the road. Even in flat shoes, my heels were already killing me. We took the left, came to a bend and an uphill climb. I was almost done with the bottle of water I'd brought. This walk was taking more out of me than I anticipated. Mrs. Cantwell? She looked like she just stepped out of a car. No sweating, no panting. And she was far older than me. I was still listening to her but increasingly distracted. *Can we get there already?*

"So when we realized that we needed to solve the issue at its source, we called together the community leaders. We explained how their culture, economic challenges, and environmental condition contributed to their health."

I slowed even more as we began to ascend the hilly terrain. So did she. I was glad she paid attention to me even though she was speaking.

"What did they say?"

She chuckled. "They asked us if we had a solution."

I held firm to the empty water bottle as my knees began to weaken. How much farther was JB's farm?

"So what did you tell them?" I would not tell this woman, almost twice my age, that I couldn't walk up a hill. So I swallowed hard but kept going.

A car drove past us, honked, and she waved. "We said yes. We had a solution."

She laughed again, stopping for good measure. She pointed to me. "You know people want to hear you got a solution, until you tell them they are their own solution." She turned, and we continued.

The break wasn't enough to catch my breath, but it did me some good.

"We said, 'You are the solution. Stop giving out your daughters in marriage before nineteen, at least. Clean up your drainage system and start a weekly garbage collection schedule. Close the drainage so flies don't go from there to perch on the food in your hand, transmitting toxins. Net your homes, if you can afford it. If not, keep all water in your home covered until use and throw out dirty water as soon as possible."

She paused again. "If you do all this, your disease incidences will certainly be cut in half. Your health will improve. Your girls will live and not die in childbirth. On our part, we will plant a garden at the clinic, a community garden. Everyone will farm it, and when it produces, we all share the fruits and vegetables. This will improve the health of your children significantly. Men, cut down your alcohol intake and smoking to see health improvements."

We both stood next to a street lamppost.

"What was their reaction?"

She raised a finger. "That's when it got interesting. The town hall went silent. Soon as they realized there was no magic pill—that everyone was going to have to change to solve the problem—they turned their searchlight inward. There were a few dissenters. Surprisingly, most were on board. They formed an action group. They agreed not to give their daughters in marriage until eighteen. We said, fair enough, much better than thirteen and in some cases twelve. We started the community garden. The gentleman, who owned some plots of land next to the clinic, donated it to us for farmland. By the next year, we had huge acres of land, purely as farmland. Everyone pitched in. Kids went there to farm after school in the evening. Adults went in the morning before they went to their own jobs, businesses, or even farms. I didn't know the first thing about farming, but I wanted to save lives. So I bought some books to help me learn so I can help them. Then I joined the effort."

She chuckled. "The first day, I was trying to yank an overgrown weed off the ground. It was so hard it snapped off in my hands, and I landed with my butt on the ground, and my fingers were blistered. The women all laughed at me. From then on, they began to show me how to do it. I was supposed to wet the ground first, and then it would come out easily."

I laughed loud at the story.

"Safe to say, I don't land on my behind anymore."

We crested the hill, and I'd barely noticed when we reached the top. I was so absorbed with the story, my body grew accustomed to the journey. The initial difficulty was gone! I was breathing a little easier. It was still tough on my lungs and my feet burned, but I'd live.

She pulled her gray sweater closer to her body. "At the end of eighteen months, the drainage system, mostly handmade, was finished and fully covered. We took donations to help net the schools and dormitories for the children and for some of the poorer families, especially those with lots of kids. They implemented everything—well, almost everything we told them. The men didn't give up their drinking or smoking, but they did change their ways when it came to their wives, daughters, and other children. The girls stayed in school longer, permitting them to pursue more dreams. Some enrolled in college, while getting married. Others traveled to the West for higher education. Within two years, the entire community was seventy percent healthier than when we arrived. More doctors from the US, Europe, Africa, and the Middle East joined our team. We were quite fortunate."

She took a swipe at her hair. "But I became unhappy. We had one child. I was pregnant with our second. My husband had taken some time off to train for his mountain trek, like you heard the other day. I wanted to support him, but my overwhelming desire for him to be present when our second baby was born made it tough. We fought a lot. It got really bad. I even thought of ending the marriage. We could barely stand each other in the same house. I would stay at the clinic long after it closed, until I was sure he was asleep. I had asked him to cancel the climb, but he refused. He said he would only be gone a couple of days. But it was enough time for me to come down with a fever. I spent three days in the clinic fighting for my life. He was too far up in the mountains for anyone to send him a message. It wasn't these days when you have cell phones, radios, and the like."

She drank from her water bottle. "They sent someone on foot. By the time he returned, I'd given birth one week prematurely. I was scared for my child. I was grateful that our son survived, thank God. Our marriage almost didn't. It was heartbreaking. We grew apart for another year. Then we chose to return to the US. A decade in India was sufficient. Our marriage was on the brink of destruction. I'd lost interest in the work we were doing. My faith in God was in jeopardy as well. A friend of ours invited us to Europe for the summer. We accepted, scraped up our little savings, and moved there. We were supposed to stay three months; we stayed eight. And God did some major work in us during that time. I was so bitter, and the bitterness was crushing everything good inside me. Jim buried himself in his work, but I knew he was hurting too."

She smiled sadly, inching up a shoulder. "God has a sense of humor, you know. I'm almost sure of that. One day, Jim returned home, and he carried this basket, it was wrapped. I glanced over absent-mindedly, asked him what was in it. He shrugged, and said he didn't know. Someone at work had given it to him for his birthday. I'd forgotten completely. My mind raced, searching for a reason why I forgot, how to make it up to him and remedy the fight I was sure was about to happen. He rushed to me, dropped the basket on the ground, grabbed me, and kissed me. Then he said. 'No worries, I still love you.' He walked away and went to sleep. I didn't sleep a wink. We were supposed to fight it out—as usual. It was to turn nasty, and then we'd each go sleep elsewhere. I had gotten so accustomed to the negatively charged atmosphere—peace and forgiveness were alien. He shocked my system, shocked me into the right path. I cried all that night, coming to God in repentance. I shed all my bitterness at the foot of the Cross, realizing I was about to lose the most important thing in my life due to something that happened long ago. I didn't see how it was also a painful experience to him. He hurt too. I was too blinded by my own pain to see it."

The tip of a house emerged above another hill in the distance.

We were almost there…

But now, I was too engrossed in the story to care. My feet were barely moving, but I dragged them along.

"Early the next morning, I went up to our room. I'd not been there in a while. I usually crashed on the adjustable bed in our other room. That way I could get in late and leave in the morning without crossing paths with him. So the room looked and felt new to me. He'd organized my stuff and left them right beside my side of the bed. But I didn't go there. My heart was so torn. I went to his feet. Just like Ruth in Scripture, I uncovered his feet and lay across the bed and slept. When I woke, I was laying on his side of the bed without knowing how I got there. Later, he told me when he'd woken and found me at his feet, he'd cried, lifted me, and laid me down properly then covered me up. He said I'd slept like a baby. Then he made us breakfast. We ate happily for the first time. Our marriage was new all over again. We talked freely without judgment, about what hurt us. Apologized for things we'd said in anger and moved forward. We began to make plans for returning to the States. Our sons are the best things that ever happened to us. We are grateful to have them in our lives. But without that day when things turned around, I bet they wouldn't have had the good foundation they did. Now they're grown and gone to live their own lives. We are alone again but this time, content. We are now doing what we did in Asia, but in a different manner—still saving lives."

We arrived at a green colored doorstep and rapped the door-knocker.

"Let's see if someone's out back."

Animals sounded around the back. Some chicken cluck, cattle

moo, and other sounds mixed with noise of a feed tractor. One goat sauntered around, peered at me eyeball-to-eyeball then decided against it and returned the way it came.

A live goat! I only knew it was a goat because in fifth grade, the teacher gave us a homework assignment to identify animals. I didn't know any of them so I went to the local library. They look a bit different in reality though. The one in the textbook had the same color of hair all over. Multiple shades of brown, lighter in the middle and darker at its extremities, covered this fella. And a patch of white sprouted along its ear.

I chuckled in delight.

"Never seen one before, have you?" JB's voice startled me. He wore black plastic boots splattered with mud, and a sky-blue colored long sleeve formal shirt with black pants. He grinned. "Hello, Mrs. Cantwell."

She smiled back. "Hello, JB. I see the animals are doing well. Good job taking care of things."

A short distance away, a lady seemed absorbed with her task, serving out items to buyers under a zinc-shaded roof.

A few cars parked off the street's curb. People alighted from them and headed to the shade.

"How are you holding up?" Mrs. Cantwell handed him a list.

"Good." He accepted it. "I'm learning as I go."

He tilted his head slightly. "Please come with me." He spun on his heel, and we followed. Underneath the shade, he pointed to the list, handing it to the lady. "Betsy, I need you to fill this order, please."

She wiped her hands with a towel and took it, running a finger down. She looked up, face expressionless. "No problem, ma'am. They will be ready to pick up in fifteen minutes if you can wait."

Mrs. Cantwell nodded. "We'll wait."

JB led us toward the house, shedding the boots at the base of the steps and slipping on regular shoes. "If you would come inside, I can make some tea."

Mrs. Cantwell hesitated. My guess was she only had tea with his grandma.

He was too young.

"Please. I insist."

She couldn't say no. Neither could I.

"All right, JB. Plus I'd like to hear how Ms. Patty is adjusting to where she is."

We walked up to the house, turned a corner, and entered. The warmth indoors pleasantly contrasted the cold outside.

"I'll get us all something to drink. I know I could use something hot right about now."

After he disappeared, she muttered, "He's so kind. Just like his Grandma Patty."

I nodded, lacking words. Was I supposed to endorse him? I was working hard to keep him off my mind. A compliment was not in my immediate plans. But I had to admit, he was making strides in impressing me.

Pictures lined the wall, like at the home of the Cantwells. Two photos. One of a man who appeared to be in his forties with his hands in his pocket, a black-and-white photo. A second of a young boy with big curly hair and a wide grin, probably in his teens. His eyes showed brilliance, but his smile bordered sad. I presumed that it was JB most likely.

He returned carrying a tray with three mugs of tea on it.

I didn't care much for tea, but I was cold. I received one from him. "Thank you."

So did Mrs. Cantwell.

He served himself last. He took a seat, forming us literally in a semicircle then looked right into my eyes. "Are you enjoying the farm life yet?" A straight shooter.

I cleared my throat. "Sure. I came here because I—um—needed a place to gather my thoughts, to plan a way forward after what happened. You?"

He scratched his head, setting some brown curls loose. "Ah, I'm learning. A lot."

Mrs. Cantwell sipped. "Like?"

A frown lined his forehead. "I'd like this to be a modern farm, using natural feed as much as possible, and it's just a start. There's a lot of work. Grandma did so much, but I need to continue where she stopped."

Some frustration colored his tone.

"One step at a time, JB." Mrs. Cantwell lowered her cup and nodded. "It can't all be done in one day. You take it in stride." She cautioned.

I downed the rest of my tea, placing the cup on a table.

Mrs. Cantwell did likewise. "Your grandma always said, 'You can't eat what you don't feed.'"

We chuckled as JB rose, and collected our cups. "You sit. Let me check on your order. One minute."

As he strode off, I began to appreciate how much he bore on his shoulders. The fate of this entire farm rested on him. His decisions, day in and out, forged paths for those who worked here. It decided whether they fed their families or not. What a huge responsibility!

When the only thing I cared about was my music. I was so short-sighted to see my blessings. My only responsibility was me.

As he returned, we stood, and followed him out. "I've got my truck right outside. It's too cold so I can easily drop you both off at the farm."

I wanted to jump on the offer.

Mrs. Cantwell shook her head. "No, we'll walk. Thanks for the offer."

I mumbled inaudibly.

"All right, thank you very much for coming. See you again soon." He shook hands with both of us.

We split the load between us and began the trek back.

I felt my shoulders droop, as my lips pressed together. I stifled a coming frown and kept my face plain. I wanted the ride back. But I stayed quiet and stared right ahead as we walked home.

The downhill trod got easier, the air lighter, and a pep in her step showed our little visit had cheered her up.

"Thank you. I'm glad you brought me here."

She shot me a quick glance. "I know we could have taken the ride from JB."

I arched a brow. She'd read my mind.

"A beeline line of customers waited underneath that tent. I doubted the young lady he hired could handle it alone. She needed help. If he left with us, he'd lose some customers. He needs all the funds he can get. So I didn't want us to cause him lost sales."

That had been mighty kind of her. I was too engrossed about my comfort to see his apparent need. "Sorry. I didn't see the line."

She was thinking about his progress.

"How did you and Ms. Patty become friends?"

She smiled then raised a finger. "Since the day her two goats wandered into my field and ate up a good chunk of corn."

We laughed and her voice lightened. "I was livid. For days, it had been war against rodents and eager birds feasting on the corn, and also on some fruits too. Then here came these goats devouring what was left. I went up there and confronted her. She listened to me calmly. She called one of her gardeners, and he went to redirect the goats. But it wasn't what got me. Her reaction afterward got me. She apologized profusely. I didn't want to seem like a weakling so I told her to tell her husband to see my husband for damages. She quietly said he was gone a long time ago. Just like that, all the anger and pent up frustration disappeared. I didn't ask what happened. I simply told her not to worry about the damages. It was just food crops, not a biggie. She broke down and began to cry. Like I'd lured past pain to the fore. I hated myself. I wondered why I'd reacted that way. I apologized. We became friends that day, and we're still friends. It's a good thing when your neighbor is your friend. You avoid a whole lotta trouble."

"Wow!" was all I could say.

CHAPTER 11

*W*hen we neared Cantwell farm grounds, we approached bare land toward the back, overgrown with weed and brushes.

"What's that land used for?"

She glanced at it. "Oh, we let some land lie fallow for a year. Next year, we'll crop it and let this outer one lie fallow."

A worn footpath started from beside the road's edge and cut straight to the center of the bare land. Some grass grew on the path, but it was clearly worn. Probably used by the farmhands.

Soon, we arrived home. My feet felt like melted rubber, but I stood strong.

"You achieved a milestone, Candace. I'd bet you've not walked such distance in a while. You probably wouldn't have believed you could do it, except you got up and did it without contemplation. Contemplation is a thief of goals. Three miles in your pocket now. Who would've thought, huh?" She gave me a thumbs-up. "Remember that next time you face an obstacle."

We split up.

I took the flagstone path to the residence, walking on air. I was in pain, but I'd pushed my boundaries three miles farther today.

I entered to the sound of my phone buzzing. I'd not gotten even a text in days.

I rushed to pick up the call. It was Matt. "Hey, bro. What's up?" I panted as I spoke.

"You okay? You don't sound right." Concern tinged his voice.

"Yeah, I'd gone for a walk. Three miles. Just got back."

He was quiet a little.

"Tell her about the YouTube video," someone shouted through the background.

"What YouTube video?" I frowned. "Another one?"

He sighed. "No, it's the same one. He thinks you haven't seen it or heard about it yet."

Well, really I hadn't seen it. I'd left my home because of it, yet I hadn't even viewed it. I should. I figured that it couldn't be worse than living the actual experience.

"How are you holding up there?"

I surveyed my surroundings. Plush couch surrounded by a well-lit house, with calm and quiet. "I've got food, shelter, light, and peace. What else do I need?"

He paused long. There was something he wasn't saying.

"Write. A song. You need a new song, sis."

But I knew that already.

"The label says there's one more song required for your contract. They're willing to part ways and let you off the rest of your time, if you could do one more song. They recognized that you would prefer working with a Christian label, but would like you to make one more song. To wrap things up with your fans."

I had one concern though.

"What type of song? Those I used to sing? 'Cuz I told them, I'm not—"

"They know that," he cut in, his breath coming in heavy.

Of course, he wasn't on my side on this.

"They said sing whatever you like, about God, you, whatever. Just let it be you singing it, and them recording and getting paid for it."

My shoulders loosened. *One more song, God.*

"Okay. I'll do it."

He wasn't done. I felt it.

"You haven't written any new songs. For a while."

The silence hung heavy.

What could I say? I sighed. "I know, Matt."

He exhaled. "Do you really think you can handle this?"

A million-dollar question. Desperation crept in. I just wanted to crawl under a rock.

Trust God, Candace. Out of nowhere, that came.

I swallowed. "Yes. By God's grace, I can. Thanks for the call." I hung up quickly. I didn't want my heart overcast with the doubt ringing clear in his voice.

I can't lose faith in my ability or God's. That's the only reason I was still standing tall. He may be my brother, but he wasn't a Christian. So he might not stick with me if this soured. Since he was my manager, economic interest was his paramount focus. He could leave my side whenever.

I feared that he might be closer to that decision than ever.

It's me and You, Jesus. Just me and You in this.

I dropped into the seat slowly, closed my eyes, and stilled my thoughts from imagining all that could go wrong.

This reminder from him was just what I needed...In addition to figuring out which way my life was headed, I needed a new song too.

I rose to get some water, suddenly thirsty. It was incredible that *I'd* be finding it hard to write a song. I shook my head.

I used to release albums twice a year. Now I can't even write one song.

I chugged down the contents of my glass, letting the water cool my nervous insides. Many moons ago, I'd thought you could write on just about anything.

But Christian music was different. I can't write for someone I don't know well enough.

I shuffled back to the couch. I needed to learn who God is, and key into Him. Only then could I write songs for or about Him. I picked up my Bible, and turned on the Christian radio.

Time to get to work.

First book I'll read? Matthew. I walked to the sunroom, with music playing on my phone, a Bible in my other hand, blanket hung on my shoulders, and sun streaming in from a distance, arraying colors on my feet.

I sank into the lounge, feet swung up. Opening the book of Matthew, I read, "The book of the genealogy of Jesus Christ, the Son of David, the Son of Abraham…"

* * *

TWO WEEKS LATER, I had five books of the New Testament fully read and digested, and the Christian radio hammering away all day long, leaving me feeling accomplished. Reading continuously instead of in bits has its reward.

I hadn't written a song, but something else haunted me—Mrs. Cantwell's words the day we went for the milk run. She'd said I'd accomplished a milestone walking three miles. I hadn't repeated it since. The weather had thawed significantly. Spring was here, and the snow had mostly melted. The weather was clear, give or take a few days when it rained. For the most part, I could walk outside again if I wanted to.

I just didn't. I stayed cooped up indoors, waiting to write a song. I'd walked back and forth the hallway, formulated something that didn't seem to rhyme, or touch the heart, or even make a difference.

I'd done voice practice for hours, and stretched myself to increase oxygen flow to the brain. I'd done it all. And yet, no song. Then, I'd prayed. Nothing.

My frustration had reached its peak. I avoided my phone. Each occasion I saw the time, reminded me that—the clock was ticking, and time running out. I didn't want the pressure. So I turned my phone face down unless I had a call.

Weight loss? Well, that became secondary. There'd be time for it later. First, I wanted a song.

I walked over and sat on the bed, head bent, brooding. I needed something to take this edge off.

My head shot up.

The online video.

What better time to see it than now?

I picked up my phone, opened a search bar and typed my name. The video popped up. First in my search result. I huffed. *First thing people see about me is this?*

I pressed Play, rolled up my feet on the bed, and laid back.

It started when I took the podium, ran all the way until the moment after my fall. I pressed Pause. It was too real, and much harder to watch than I'd thought. I saw myself in video, unedited for the first time. I was big! I looked down at my body, and it didn't seem so. But the video didn't lie. It was right there.

I pressed Play again. It played past my rescue and being led off stage then ended. The video had been viewed three million times. I could only imagine what those viewers thought.

I scrolled down to the Comments. First one read, "She is a mess!" Air caught in my throat.

I lowered the phone.

Next comment, "Where is she? Probably somewhere choking on cake, cookies, and ice cream!"

Tightness closed my throat, and I pressed a hand against it. I scrolled down, all the way to the end.

"Such wasted talent!" The next one read. "Is she even seeing herself in the mirror?"

The last on my screen caught. "She'll never lose the weight! Forget her. Her career? Press delete." A cry escaped my mouth. My lips trembled, and I used my hand to try to still them. I turned the phone back down.

But it began ringing. I thought twice, and then picked the call.

Mrs. Cantwell was on the line. "Candace, aren't you coming down to join us? It's time to eat."

I calmed my voice. "Be right there."

Click.

* * *

SPLASHING some water on my face had done me some good. As I sat at the table, eating with the Cantwells, my mind worked at fever pitch. I had to tell them. I lowered my fork. "I want to lose weight. But I need your help."

I'd dropped my heavy load on the table, waiting for their reaction.

Their forks stopped midair. They simply stared.

Dr. Cantwell spoke first. "Okay. You'll need a medical and physical fitness assessment done. My clinic is available for you, if you want."

I nodded, swallowing the anxious bit in my mouth. "Yes, please. Thank you."

The video played yet again in my mind. Then the comments followed like I was reading them all over again. That pushed my decision further.

"Tomorrow."

Mrs. Cantwell lifted her face. "Tomorrow then."

We resumed eating, each knowing the weight of this moment for me.

I'd cried more in the bathroom after the video. I saw a caption scrolling at the top, "Wit, sang about dodging relationship potholes, but literally fell into one herself, having being dumped by her fiancé." More tears came tumbling.

I'd cried and blown my nose, then applied some makeup. Hopefully, my eyes weren't visibly puffy. If they were, the Cantwells didn't react.

"Mrs. Cantwell?" She looked up again. "I'd like to help you with the garden."

Her lips curved in a smile. "Great. Take two."

I felt my eyes narrow. "Nah, I'm not going to fall on my behind."

We both laughed, lifting the tension.

"Sure, Candace. The seedlings arrive in a couple of days, and I sure do need the help."

So much love here. So much acceptance...

The comments, they were like swords through my heart, all at once. Venomous hate was poured at me. One commenter said I didn't fit the stage because I drowned myself in burgers and fries.

To be honest, they weren't far from the truth. I just wouldn't say it that way. The last one I read really got me. "She'll never lose the weight! Forget her. Her career? Press delete." It repeated in my mind. The pain of such dismissal...was unimaginable.

After lunch, I walked to the sunroom and sat there—for two hours straight. Did I want my critics to be right? Or would I challenge them with action?

Can I prove them wrong?

Their comments were hateful, but if I didn't do something, they'd be proved right.

My career could end. The excess weight could kill me.

As I sat there, head in my hands, staring at the lush greenery beyond the glass barriers indicating new life with spring, I chose.

I will *fight. I* will *prove them wrong. I* will *show I can do this.*

I can *lose this weight.*

Stretching out my feet and arms, I imagined them smaller, slimmer, more toned, looking gorgeous. "I'm beautiful. Now I just have to get healthy."

I rose with determination.

Striding to the living area, I picked up my phone and flipped it upward. I'd watch the time go by.

But I won't simply watch. I'd make it work for me.

After reentering the bedroom, I changed into a tank top and tights, then I made my way to the elliptical and pressed On.

I wasn't waiting for a medical test to tell me what I already knew. I needed to lose weight, short and simple.

I climbed on, shoeless, and began to work the machine back and forth slowly to acclimatize.

I've never done this before. It was hard at first.

The pressure burned through my arms and reached my lower back. I grunted but kept on it. I pushed the handle, swung it back and forth, over and over until it read, One Minute.

I was panting. My eyes threatened to flee their sockets, but I closed my lids briefly and continued pushing. Five Minutes. I breathed hard. Minute by minute, I was getting there. I slowed when my arms felt like they were on fire, literally unable to push further.

I climbed off and sat on the couch. Ten minutes later, I climbed on again, surprised that it became easier. I pushed and continued until the machine read Fifteen Minutes. I climbed down, dragged my feet off it, and sat on the ground, breathless. Sweat damped my top, and a chill radiated from the ground.

I pressed off the ground, and climbed on the third time. I kept going until it read, Thirty Minutes. This time, I was done. I couldn't do one more. I limped to the bathroom and climbed into the shower. I'd showered before, but now, soaked with sweat, I needed round-two shower. And I smiled, for a good reason. I just crushed fifty minutes on the elliptical!

I made my way to the bedroom after my shower, still worried. I had no song. Every attempt ended up in blank pages. Frankly, I'd grown tired of carrying a blank notepad around.

Time was passing. Every day brought the need for a song closer.

I sat and curled my feet up halfway. Leaning against the headboard, I uttered a desperate prayer.

Lord, please give me a new song according to Your Word in Psalm 90:3.

Opening my eyes, I immediately caught view of the pillow. I'd stuck a notepad beside it in case something occurred to me late at night. Armed with a pen, I tapped the ballpoint along the booklet.

Nothing came. I drew a line along the borders. I just sat there waiting like God and I had an appointment and He would drop a song from heaven. Couple of minutes later, I laughed, a little in frustration. If there was a perfect place and time to get a song, it was now. It was here. No distractions, no people, and with nothing else on my schedule.

My phone rang. It sounded alien. No one had called for a while...

except insistent telemarketers. I leaned over the bed and yanked it from its charger. Bad idea. It knocked the bedside lamp side to side until it rested still.

I held up the phone and sat straight, feet swung low.

Ugh. In that time, I'd already missed the call and gotten a voice-mail. I played it. It was Matt. He asked me to call him back right away. He sounded urgent. I felt scared but chose not to make any assumptions.

Lord, please take control. I pressed Redial.

"Hey, sis, what's up?"

"I missed your call. The voicemail said to call you back right away. What's going on? Everything okay?"

Concern I'd heard in his voice outweighed the brief silence. Uh-oh.

"I don't know, Candace. I got a call from one of the team members, saying John called members of our team to his office for a quick meeting."

Well, that was sufficient to get me worried.

"Only our team or everyone?"

He sneezed.

"Bless you."

He cleared his throat. "Allergies. Thanks. Ben said he got there a minute or two ago. From the looks of things, it's just our team, no one else."

Worry rose in my heart and made me swallow hard. I tried not to express it. "Did he say what he wanted to talk about?"

"Has John *ever* given anyone a meeting agenda, Candy?" He laughed hoarsely. "He calls people. They show up. That's the way he works. You know him."

I shrugged. I did know a little of him. He'd made passes at me when I'd first started with the label. I'd crushed it, fast. I had only one agenda, to sing, and nothing came in front of that—nothing. Since then, he became a mean bean. I never bothered. He was the deputy talent director then so we had very little dealings.

"Okay. Keep me posted on what you hear all right. But for the record, I don't like this. At all."

He cleared his throat again. "Neither do I."

Before I forgot, I added, "Take care of those allergies, Matt."

He groaned. "I knew you'd say that. Sure, I will. Meanwhile, you go write those songs, and I'll get back to you as soon as I hear something."

CHAPTER 12

I passed the time doing laundry, ironing, making my bed, setting my light blanket in place, and folding up dried clothes. I had an assistant in New York who did these sort of things for me regularly. Out here, I was on my own. But I didn't mind. After all, I did these chores for myself growing up. I liked the scent of clothes fresh out of the dryer. Their aroma said, "Clean."

All done, I sank into the lounge chair in the sunroom, with my phone in hand. I checked it. Nothing. I exhaled. No text message, no missed call, no voicemail. I had been checking every half hour since my brother's call. Waiting for news.

If it was the quick meeting John implied, it should be over by now —unless he had something up his sleeve. That scared me.

I paced the length of the sunroom. I should pray. But I was too scared, and too tense to utter one word, even in my heart.

My nerves stuck on edge. I rushed a hand over my hair, long black strands sweeping into my fingers. I sat on a chair, facing the bright windows. Maybe they'd cheer me up. The sun had risen around eight and grown hotter.

"Candace, I was searching all over for you."

I jumped at the voice.

Mrs. Cantwell hovered in the entryway, gloves in hand, with sand on them.

My hands rose to still my heart.

"Sorry, I didn't mean to scare you."

I half-nodded, and half-waved. "I didn't hear you enter." I was far from the door anyway, but my mind was much farther. My feet touched the ground, and I stood. "I was just...here. Did you need anything?"

She smiled, nodding toward the hallway. "Come. I want to show you something. You'll like it, I promise."

I trotted behind her as we made our way to the back garden, past its small white gate. We turned a corner and emerged to a wide space. Certain crops of different varieties had started budding, shooting up off the ground.

A tall palm, already planted before I came, about six feet high, waved at the side. I'd never come close enough to see its height before now.

She stooped. "Watch the peppers. They could be quite sneaky. Their leaves crawl everywhere." She was right. A trail of pepper stalks, still green and tender, lay across the path.

Cutting carefully beside it, I planted my feet a few meters beyond. "Look."

I bent over and examined. One tomato crop hid beneath a crop of green leaves.

She pointed at it. "I tended this for weeks. It wouldn't, couldn't grow. I thought, hmmm, maybe it's the weeds. I weeded the area surrounding it, and then applied more fertilizer. Then I watered it every morning. Still after two weeks, there was nothing. I complained to my husband last week and you know what he said? 'Leave it alone. Just let it be.' I didn't get him. Usually for this sort of thing he'd say, 'add more water or prune the leaves or get other crops out of its way, then it will grow.' But this time, no. I was offended because I'd done all those. But then I left it alone, like he'd said."

She straightened, and I did so too, the laugh lines around her eyes coming alive as she grinned. "Then this morning, I came out, lo and behold, it was growing, and reaching up—stunning! Here I was, toiling and working and pushing it, but at God's time, effortlessly, it sprouted and grew unassisted. Not because of anything I'd done, but purely by the hand of the Maker of all things."

Taking off her gloves, she lowered them into a farm basket she usually carried with her to the garden. Her eyes pinned me. "Candace, whenever you push and toil and dig for something but it does not yield, hand it over to God and let it go. He will perform it in His due time. That is what I learned."

I wasn't sure whether I wanted to thank her for sharing or be scared. I was banging at heaven's gates for a song—for weeks. I'd received no answer yet, not even a line to start with. Should I just let go and let God? What did that even mean for me?

I chose to nod. "Thank you for sharing, Mrs. Cantwell."

Instead of going back to sit and brood about my problems, I might as well stick around. "Do you need some company? I could weed some, or whatever you like."

She grinned again. "I need you to dig. I can't bend this waist any longer. My knees are gone too."

"I can do that."

She pulled a pouch closer. "I'll hand you the seed, and you put it in the ground. C'mon, I'll dig one to show you."

She crouched low. "Of course, we'd need to redo the flagstone path from here to the side of the building, but I got to get special stones first. Jim can take care of that tomorrow."

She dug into the ground, dropped some seed in, and covered it up. "Just that deep, and you pop three seedlings in it each time. The width should be about an inch or two apart. Here." She handed me the gardening tool.

I accepted it, bent over, and began digging. This was so much better than my worry session!

The sun burned hot when we both packed up from the garden. She returned to the main house, and I to the residence, feeling spent.

Gardening was hard work! Weeding a small section of the garden seemed simple but took me half an hour. Then I'd fed Mrs. Cantwell tomato seeds in between, which she sprayed on the cleared ground and watered. She threw some dried grass over the seeds so birds couldn't pick it off the ground.

She worked with vigor, focus, and dedication. You'd think she was performing surgery not planting a garden. The organized appearance of the garden spoke volumes of her attitude. Everything—save the wandering peppers we'd almost stepped on—was in its place.

She showed me how to get a garden started, how to make a plant bed, and plant the seed that stayed atop the ground and those that went beneath. She also showed me how to gauge which direction to guide the crops as they start to grow, to ensure they face the sun without struggling. We harvested kale and green peppers for dinner.

"I'd like to do this again," I'd told her. She said, of course. It was fun, and I enjoyed it.

Lunch followed a quick shower. But waiting to hear from Matt drained me. I tried to focus on other things, but every passing moment spelled something wrong.

Now the sun was turning a reddish hue over the horizon, darkening the sunroom. I picked up my notepad and went to sit outside, savoring the lush dusky greenery.

I could never have predicted where I was right now.

This time last year, I was singing at a school fundraiser for cancer awareness in Mexico City. Thanks to my Hispanic roots, there was a huge turnout. People supported me. Some even brought free tacos after the performance, saying they'd thought we would be hungry.

Such kindness! I was moved. I'd told them I'd try to come again this year. Little did I know my life would be so different. I could still go if they invited me. The songs would be Christian this time—if I wrote them, that is.

I sighed and returned to the bedroom. Spying my phone's light come on, I rushed to it and picked it up.

One message. Breath held, I clicked.

"You have been enrolled in a participant survey…" I tightened my grip and bunched my arm as if to toss the phone out, but restrained.

"Ughhhh." Sighing, I stretched out on the bed then burst out laughing. Why was I so tense? I could just praise God, and thank Him, just because...

* * *

THE BUZZING of my phone against the desk woke me sharply.

Time? 5:15 a.m.

Groggy, I picked the call.

"Hello?" I cleared my throat then coughed a bit.

"Candace? Hello?"

My lashes flew open. "Yeah, Matt?"

His voice sounded hushed, like he was trying not to be overheard. "Yes, it's me. Sorry to wake you but... listen. I need to tell you this. Today, I learned they are going to end things and charge you for all the lost revenue for the last concert you were supposed to perform. We'd forgotten it. They're meeting to cancel it at noon."

That shook me awake. There was one more concert. A cancelled concert. I thought it had been taken care of.

I jerked up from the bed and sprang to my feet. "You sure, Matt? They couldn't do that. I never said I'd stop singing, I just said I wouldn't sing the songs I sang before becoming a Christian."

He tapped on the phone, his impatience radiating through the distance. "To them, that means you're out. They've got others willing and ready to jump in and sing those songs. Face it. They want the money. They want to keep the audience. If you're going to do something, you have until twelve o'clock." He snuffed. "I knew John was going to turn on us! He's so unpredictable."

Wrong time to sulk.

"Matt, I'll be in New York before twelve. Don't tell anyone—especially John. Everything is going to be fine, by God's grace."

Deep inside, faith sprung. I was sure. I trusted God, and I hung up.

I raced to the closet. Flipping through clothing, I selected two, top and bottom, and laid them out on the bed.

Quickening my steps into the bathroom, I slid my pajamas off me, tossed them onto the railing, and entered the tub for a quick shower.

Minutes later, I returned to the bedroom, toweling with one hand, and tossing a few items into my purse with the other. I dressed up, then rushed through some light makeup. I wasn't going down there looking run-down.

Brushing my hair back, I pulled the long, dark tresses into a bun, leaving some loose onto my back.

Whipping my hair while I performed my songs used to make me feel powerful. Now, I struggled to keep hair off my face while sweating it out on the elliptical.

I exhaled, calling for a taxi. I wasn't going to bother the Cantwells for a ride this early. Dispatch said it would take eight minutes to arrive.

My mind wandered to John Akum. Director for talent management. Not the nicest guy. He hated me from day one. Thankfully, he didn't choose me to sing with Global Sound Records. With his trademark goatee, I'd recognize him from afar though his meanness made it even easier across the country.

We endured one another for years. I wouldn't be surprised if he was "punishing" me for my recent choice. But things were different. I couldn't waltz in there and behave like I was one of them. I'd dropped the ball at the play for the anthem. That effectively altered the terms of a long-standing agreement. Nevertheless, I'd stand up for myself against being tasked with losses not yet incurred just because I elected not to sing their chosen songs.

Buttoning up my shirt, I searched for creases and found none.

I straightened up and cast a glance at the mirror. Nothing appeared amiss.

I belted at the waist, and slipped my feet into solid black heels.

Picking up my luggage, I exited the residence, cautious for wet ground. Thanks to spring weather, it now rained often.

I rummaged through my handbag for my phone. I found it stuck inside my notepad where I'd slipped it in last night. I was going to try to write songs this morning. Hah, not today.

I headed to the main building to inform the Cantwells. I knocked on the door, with Burpees For Breakfast, smiling while recalling how

I felt the first time I laid my eyes on it…my reaction was so different now.

Mrs. Cantwell stood, clad in a black wide coat. Striped pajama bottoms ran down her legs to meet her socks.

"Sorry for the early rap. I got a call from my brother about my contract. There's a meeting so I'm going to New York. I've called a taxi. I should be back later today or tomorrow, God willing."

Her hair was rough, and she rubbed her eyes. Good thing I apologized for waking them.

She nodded and widened the door. "The Lord go with you and keep you safe. Let us know how it goes. We'll see you soon, dear."

We hugged.

The taxi hummed as it pulled up the driveway, red lights brightening when he hit the brakes. I headed toward it, and the door thudded shut as Mrs. Cantwell returned inside. The driver exited the cab and walked over to open the door.

"Good morning. Headed to the airport, correct?" He held the door wide as I slid in, then closed it, walked around, and entered the driver's seat.

I adjusted my coat, which had slipped in behind me. Summer was only a few months away, I encouraged myself. 'Bout time for some warmth.

"Reagan Airport, please."

He switched the ignition on. "Yes, ma'am."

CHAPTER 13

*A*rriving at the JFK airport, an hour ago was the easy part. I'd done enough to disguise myself not to be recognized, thanks to an oversized winter hat, cheek-wide sunglasses, and a thick scarf. I'd called my brother to let him know I was around.

Hopping into a taxi, I headed toward the Global Sound Records headquarters in downtown Manhattan, a few blocks from my apartment.

Everywhere seemed different. The noise level was higher than I'd gotten used to. Sirens blaring, sound systems booming, car horns tooting …it soon felt a little too much. I'd lived with it for so long, I was numb to the mix. Now, I wondered how I could write anything, let alone award-winning songs, with so much activity. The vibrancy… something about the excitement of this city must have blurred the noise to me.

The driver pulled to the curb, and I stepped out of the taxi, careful not to get knocked aside by the forceful throng of people. Everyone appeared to be in a hurry.

I cut a slice through to the building's entrance, avoiding getting my foot stamped. A chill struck my skin with unwelcome familiarity, spreading goose bumps all over me. I craved the warmth of heated indoors. My anxious mind, on the reverse, needed some cooling.

Lord, please help me at this meeting.

A boisterous security guard, armed with a charming grin, swung wide the large doors. I smiled in gratitude. The musical note on the wall brought back memories of my first visit.

Freshly recruited, and ready to sing my heart out. So many dreams...of writing and singing whatever songs suited my heart and selling one million records flooded my mind. Dreams... They'd come true, mostly.

Dreams have a way of pushing you in the right direction. Facts can snap you back to reality fast enough too. I chuckled. But God always wins in the end.

My career had taken off all right. Singing my own songs?

No! Not in the contract, I was told.

My songs were rewritten several times, until they became something totally different. The label's management chose places I went, where I performed, and which organizations I supported according to the label's needs.

In fact, I served at the pleasure of Global Sound Records. Simple. My songs weren't mine.

I did get famous, I landed great endorsements, and represented some good causes. But I lost myself in the process. I ate junk food while in the recording studio. Bringing food inside was against the rules, but I sneaked in snack bars, or candy bars—anything in a wrap and small enough to fit in my pocket. When you're in there for endless hours, you forget about time. You focused solely on getting your voice, the rhyme, the tone, and the lines right. And being passionate about what you sang. Going out to get food was out of the question. Most times, I had deadlines to meet.

Even my covers were out of my control. A cover used for one of my albums was too...steamy. I requested something simpler and was told, "It won't sell". My brother told me to let it go. My songs were more than their cover. I wish I'd stood my ground. My next album, if it happens, will represent me better.

Stepping into the elevator, I pressed Eight, hoping to catch John before the meeting. Ascending the elevator to the top floor, I pondered what I'd say.

I tapped my feet repeatedly, my high-strung nerves every bit impatient with the elevator's stoppage at every floor. So many thoughts flooded me. I'd hoped that a few days of solitude would guide me, but I felt more confused now than on my first day at Day Spring Farms. The only thing I was sure of: God took me there for a reason.

The elevator chimed, and I emerged on the eighth floor. John's office was to the right of it. I walked toward his reception desk. The staff there appeared new.

She was slim, formally dressed in a black suit and black pants, with her hair poured on one shoulder.

"Hi. How can I help you?" She flashed a clean white set of teeth and didn't seem older than seventeen.

"Hi. Is John's office still here? I'm one of the artists."

She nodded. "Yes, it is. However, he's currently busy now. Can I take a message?"

Of course, he's working hard to nail my future.

I shook my head. "No thank you. I'll wait."

Her smile faded.

I didn't bother.

I came prepared.

Even if they tossed me out, it wouldn't be because I didn't put up a fight.

"All right, have a seat, and I'll see when he's available."

More like it.

I approached the set of chairs resting off the wall and sat as my stomach knotted.

I was faced with a couple of issues…First, I wasn't invited to this meeting. Second, John never liked me. Third, I wasn't sure, having come all this way, that I would be let into the meeting—especially if the goal of the meeting was not in my favor.

I exhaled.

Lord, I made this trip by faith in You…

"Hey, Candace! How nice for you to stop by. Today." John, looking crisp in a navy blue suit and red tie, stood above me.

I smiled, broad as I could, not missing his stress on the "today" part. "Thank you, John. Pleased to see you too. I learned that there would be a meeting in one hour. I'm here for it. I hope you don't mind."

Arching up a shoulder, he hesitated. "Sure. I mean you came all this way. Don't want to waste gas money, right?"

More like flight money, but he didn't know that. "Thank you."

He pointed toward the cafeteria. "We got some time before the start. Just enough for you to grab something to eat and join us then?" He dropped his chin to the side. "You might need some energy. This is not like the first time."

He did remember the first meeting. Everything went breezy.

I was chosen and signed on the same day, thanks to a voice that impressed their scout team.

Today, I'm one leg out the door.

Easy, Candace.

"Well, don't we all need energy?" I chose to ignore the insult, but stayed focused on my goal.

There was no need to pick a battle before it actively began.

As he walked into his office, I knew he was right. Though I had taken a snack on the plane, it wasn't enough to hold me for long. I needed food. My stomach's growl confirmed it.

I entered the cafeteria, hoping that eating something would ease the knot in my stomach. But my mind worked away.

If only I'd learned another skill in all this time...like, I don't know, how to organize concerts or represent an artist—something to hold onto, in case music failed.

Sure, I had a degree, but with no work experience, who would hire me?

"Some coffee, please. Add scrambled eggs and toasted whole-grain bread with low-fat cheese, veggies, pepper and salt. As a sandwich, thank you."

The bright-eyed cashier tapped on the machine, expertly taking my order. *See there. Someone who knows their stuff does it as second nature.* Just like music was to me.

Why was I finding it so hard to write a new song? Might it be the fear of doing this alone? I sighed.

Maybe eating breakfast at noon would ease my tense stomach. Or not. Either way, I couldn't eat something heavy right now. My stomach churned as though in response to my internal monologue.

Stepping off to the side, I waited.

A lady at the other end and her little girl also milled around waiting for their order number to be called. A man leaning on the counter seemed anxious, tapping his fingers on it. Others who stared at the order display screen appeared too hungry to care.

I couldn't help but wonder how so much uncertainty lay at the heart of most human endeavors. Yet we rise every morning, leave our homes, and expect something good to happen. Every human being has faith; most simply don't use it. Only the degree of faithful expectation varied.

My phone buzzed, and I raised it.

The Bible App—Daily Scripture.

"See, I have set before you an open door and no one can shut[it]." Revelations 3:8.

I laughed. How timely. This door was more than halfway shutting in my face. Worse still, I don't see another one opening anytime soon.

"Here you go, ma'am." I raised my head to the cashier. My order was ready. "Thank you very much." I accepted the complimentary lunch soup bowl and my sandwich. Seats were off to the side. I slid into one with more width between the chair and table.

Soon after I sat, I opened it and began to eat, starting with the hot soup. The heat was welcome. Done with the soup, I crossed to the sandwich.

They included lettuce at the center. Ordinarily, I'd have pulled it out and tossed it in the trash because I loathed greens. But I had goals now.

I bit into the food as someone tapped my shoulder.

Covering my mouth with one hand, I turned, sucking up a string of onions dangling from the corner of my mouth.

A young man, teenaged, stood in front of me with a sheet in hand.

I waved instead of speaking, thanks to my full mouth.

He smiled. "Sorry to bother you. I wanted to say I recognized you. You're Wit. You have a beautiful voice. I was there where you sang the national anthem." He bowed a little. "I'm sorry you fell. Hope you're okay." Slight color rose to his cheeks.

I swallowed the last chew bit, overwhelmed and moved by the heart of this young fellow, who didn't look a day over seventeen or eighteen.

"Thank you. That means a lot to me." Laying down the bread, I wiped my hands with a napkin, and then shook his hand firmly.

He smiled again. "And don't listen to what they're saying online. You can lose weight. In fact, you should, just to wow 'em."

I felt my brows rise in unison. "To wow 'em, huh?"

Something about the faith this young man had in me, worked up faith in me as well. His words entered my thirsty soul like chilled water.

"You want my autograph?"

He handed me the sheet and smiled big. "Of course. That's what I brought this for."

I took the sheet. "What's your name?"

"Eric."

After signing the paper, "Eric, go wow 'em!", followed by my name, I handed it to him.

He peered at it. "Why did you date it?"

I'd hoped he'd ask. "Because I want to remember today is the first day someone else believed in my ability to lose weight."

He nodded with apparent satisfaction, and then walked away.

It should be almost time for the meeting since I'd spent the first half hour waiting for my food order. I rolled up my half-eaten sandwich and put it in my purse, before striding back to John's office—11:55 a.m. Five minutes to go.

* * *

I ENCOUNTERED THE RECEPTIONIST AGAIN. This time, I took a seat beside a group of gentlemen and one lady, all seated, and all busy on their phones. None bothered looking up.

I slid out my phone. I had a missed call from Matt. He must've called when I was eating. I was about to call back when a shadow crossed my view.

"Candace."

It was him. I didn't see him walk up to me. I rose, and we hugged.

"Were you inside John's office?" I cupped my hands, unsure.

"Yeah, we were hammering out some stuff. I'll gist you later." He craned his neck and peered at the tail of a sandwich wrap sticking out my purse. "May I?"

I let the bag slide, then I opened it wide. "Sure. Help yourself."

He pulled it out, unwrapped it, and took a bite. "Hmmm. I had no idea how hungry I am. Thanks, sis." He slammed his teeth like his life depended on each chew.

"I got here as soon as I could after we talked. A few of us were in John's office trying to crank out a deal that doesn't involve paying lost revenue."

I hurried him to the end. "And?"

He swallowed, with his Adam's apple bobbing.

I wasn't sure if the deal meant good or bad. I waited, handing him water. He drank some.

"It's off the table."

I exhaled. *Thank God.*

He readied for another bite. "There's one snag though. They want one more concert to recoup the funds. They're not gonna let you off on that."

I gripped my purse harder. "Do I still have job, Matt? A contract?"

He stared at me like I'd spoken an alien language. "Candace, they were going to throw you under and forget you. You would've been in debt for millions if we didn't hammer out this deal. There's no contract. That ship sailed the moment you told them you weren't singing their songs anymore. This is cleanup we're doing right now."

I sank back into my seat while he ate, oblivious to the cloud that'd settled on me.

No!

This wasn't the end of my music career. I made a personal choice of faith. There was no reason to punish me by taking away my source of livelihood, my passion.

CHAPTER 14

"All right everyone, you can enter now." The receptionist ushered us into John's office.

The lady and the men beside me entered first, followed by my brother and I. He tossed the emptied food wrap into the trash bin, wiping his mouth and hands with a napkin I had handed him.

I had no idea those others waiting were here about me.

I swallowed, feeling a little nervous, but I summoned courage. Eric's words minutes ago gave me hope for my future. I might not have a contract, but I had God.

We filed in, fitting around the oblong desk. The office had been occupied by the former talent manager, Jack, the one who hired me.

He liked me and gave me more opportunities than John did. When he left and John took over, the only new functions I attended were those with little visibility. Others were split among other artists within the label. I didn't complain because I was doing well. My fans loved me. I sang and performed live on various shows across the country. Considering my background, I felt lucky to have a record label's support for my gift. My goal was still to write and sing songs I'd written without someone overwriting them and make a living out of it. That would spell success to me.

For now, survival it was.

John strode in, sheet in hand. "Thank you all for coming in. As you know, we're here to discuss terms for settling our agreement with Ms. Candace Rodriguez. We're all aware she no longer sings for the label."

Nope, I was not letting that slide. "Excuse me, that is incorrect. I no longer sing the songs I used to. I'm open to options where I sing what is more closely aligned with my Christian faith."

One of the men jumped in, "Don't you mean like a choir?" He gave a slight eye roll. "If you want to join the choir, by all means do so. *This* is a record label. We are in business. Businesses make money. You are not making money for us right now so I don't see any reason to keep you."

Ouch. He came loaded.

Another man—more senior, hair grayed-out—leaned across the table, placed a hand on the younger man's shoulder. "Easy here, Francis. Let's hear John out. But let's not rule the girl out completely just yet. John?"

I sat back into my seat. Fair enough. I was still in the fight.

"Right. As I was saying, there are expenses for events and for logistics already paid for future performances. Not to speak of staff for her with contracts to serve till the end of her contract simply because we ran things overlapping."

A third man, clad in gray suit and seemingly the oldest among them, leaned forward. "How much are we talking here?"

My heart beat wildly.

Matt's earlier words came to mind. He sat at the opposite side of the table looking more nervous than I was, chewing his pen, eyes pinned on John.

"Two million dollars. We're eating the rest of the cost as determined earlier." John cast a short glance toward my brother who nodded.

Two million? I swallowed. This was tough to say the least.

The men and the lady exchanged glances.

They were coming to a decision.

If I was going to say anything in my defense, it was now. But I didn't know what to say.

Desperate, I raised a hand.

Oh Jesus... I whispered in my heart.

"Excuse me. There's one thing we're forgetting here." All eyes turned, and laser-focused on me.

My eyes fell low in uncertainty.

Candace?

I cleared my throat, lacking words.

Something dropped in my heart just then and my lashes flew up.

I smiled and sat up tall, chest out, and my gaze roamed the room, one person to another. "I am a talented singer. I have made this label money, in millions."

John twiddled his fingers.

I regarded him then shifted focus to one of the gentlemen who began to smile. I nodded to him as my gaze swept across the room again.

I rose to my feet, towering above everyone. "I can still make you the money owed."

John tapped his finger on the desk and sprang from his chair. My guess was, this wasn't going as he planned. He scowled in response to my claim.

"Tell me how? I mean, you're not singing now, are you? Let's make this quick and let's—"

"No!" I thumped my fist on the desk, sending some sheets of paper sliding to the edge.

He jumped back and stopped still.

I leaned forward, glared at him. "You will let me finish."

Well, I had everyone's attention with that.

Candace? I silenced the voice of skepticism, and stamped it shut.

"Like I said, I can make you the money you need. I just require a few things. First, time. Twelve months from now, from today, I can host a concert. But I will need recording equipment. I need a logistics team ready and a digital team."

I cast a glance to John, who'd disintegrated my team, then the gentlemen and lady, who hadn't uttered a word.

Silence fell around the table. The man who'd smiled, the same one who'd said I shouldn't be written off yet, looked up. "One year you say, Candace?"

I met his gaze. "One year, sir. That's all I need."

For some reason, God made this stranger support me when I needed it most.

Matt's mouth dropped wide. He'd never seen me like this. I'd never been like this, like a lioness protecting her cub, my only babies, being my songs.

"What about venue and don't forget songs?" John pressed. "They're important too."

I smiled broadly.

Oh thank You, Jesus!

I glanced at him. *You never give up, do you, John?* But there was no need to share more details with him now.

"I got it, John."

He shook his head. "You're bidding for time. If you got the location, who's paying for it? Us? 'Cuz I'm not—"

I held up a steady hand. "Location's already fully paid."

I wasn't sure if I was still talking about land...or about the sacrifice of Jesus for my sins, dreams, and life. That He bought back all I'd lost. Gave me a new life, new beginning, and a fresh start. A life I could only dream of having. I saw it now, there was no denying it.

John postured himself, and crossed his arms with a stubborn glare. "Where is the venue then?"

The challenge in his eyes were unmistakable. He knew I'd likely stretched a few things.

I backed off my seat, and walked up to a white board behind him. I picked up a sharpie and wrote, "Day Spring Farms Circuit, 265 Hope Lane, Beltsville, Maryland."

I dropped the sharpie, and turned to the people. "What's today's date, please?"

They scrambled through pockets, browsed through their phones, and seemed shaken from their intense focus on me. My charm bracelets jingled as I tucked stray hair behind my ear.

The eldest man's eyes shot up. "April 10."

I wrote again. "April 10, next year."

"That's the date for the concert," Matt emphasized, having somehow found his voice.

The man who'd challenged me first looked up from his phone. "It's a Sunday."

Jesus…Emboldened, I continued.

"Yes, with your support, I can do this. I will perform the concert on April 10, and it will be streamed live. There will be cost of entry online and in person. We can work out the details for fees later. If by the next day you do not have two million dollars, then we can talk."

John perched on the desk. "Songs?"

Right.

"Working on that." It was more like hoping on that. A two-million-dollar song…

The man who'd first given me a chance nodded, as though he admired my doggedness.

"Gentlemen and ladies, if Candace could net us two million in twenty-four hours, I say we start an inspired music arm of the company!"

Laughter broke out across the table. And then applause.

John laughed longest, in scorn. He didn't think I could do it. He'd made that abundantly clear.

The eldest gentleman in gray suit stood and extended me a hand. I shook it firmly.

"You got yourself a deal. We'll see you back here on April 11, a day after the concert. Good luck, Candace. You'll need nothing short of a miracle to pull this one off."

I acknowledged his truth in my heart but didn't say it. "I'm counting on it, sir."

Everyone else rose.

I looked toward Matt who was rounding the table coming to me.

John pointed at him.

"We need to do paperwork for this agreement. I'm assuming you're still representing her?"

By her, John meant me. He knew my brother did not share my faith values and he was pushing that fact to the fore.

"Of course. Let's do this." Matt turned to me. "Candace, I'll talk to you later."

My flight wasn't until four p.m. "I'll be downstairs at the lobby waiting."

John stood. "How on earth did you secure a farm? Of all places to hold a concert?"

He turned up a nose, then shook his head. "What a flop it will be! I get it. You're buying time. I see this happen all the time."

I had to stop him. He was gaining the attention of two of the men we'd just met with. They drew closer. One of them observed me with a raised eyebrow.

I stepped up to John, standing face to face. "This is neither a joke, nor a fraud. I'm a music professional and I take my career very seriously. This is a real concert. You better give me everything I need for it, because it will be a success contrary to your expectation. If you can't afford a ticket, you best let me know. Excuse me!"

I stormed out the room. Not giving him the dignity of another glance. Time to get to work. I muttered to myself, "God can handle this!"

I'm going back to Maryland.

I'm losing this weight, and I'm writing songs for this concert.

If nothing else, I'll wow John!

* * *

JB

I depressed the accelerator, exited the garage, drove down the driveway, and merged into the street. The sky loomed dark, like it was preparing to rain.

Again. I sighed.

But this was April. What else if not rain?

Except it snowed for two days prior, leaving five inches of white snow yet on the ground.

Then rain fell atop it. Ice might not be too far away. I had better double-checked on the de-icer for the walkway to the animal pen later.

My mind then strayed to Candace as I rode up the driveway at the Cantwell farm. I hadn't seen her since they came for milk pickup.

Recently, Mrs. Cantwell came on her own, then her husband.

I parked, turned off the engine, and stepped out of the truck, slammed it shut, and opened the back door. Pulling the cart of milk and meat, I lifted it up.

I'd asked Mrs. Cantwell not to bother coming for them, then I promised to deliver the products to her doorstep. She was elated. No one wanted to contend with icy ground. I walked up to the door and rapped the door knock.

Mrs. Cantwell emerged and swung the door open. "JB! Thank you so much. I wondered how I was going to get some milk with Jim at the clinic and Candace out of town."

Really? "She's out of town?"

Mrs. Cantwell led me toward the kitchen.

"Yes. Something about her music."

I thought you didn't care....

"Is she coming back?"

Mrs. Cantwell shrugged. "Yes, but I always leave room for what God leads each child of His to do. You know, that's something none can control."

She'd obviously noticed my heightened interest.

My eyelids fell a little. "True. Where would you like these?"

She pointed to the kitchen table. "Up there should be fine. Until I find time to cut the meat and refreeze them."

I did as she asked, noting how tidy the kitchen was. The stove did appear well used.

"Thank you so much, JB."

Bowing out of the kitchen, I strode toward the door.

There, she held it open while I made my way outside and turned.

"Have a nice day, Mrs. Cantwell."

She flashed a broad grin. "You too, JB. And say hi to Ms. Patty for me."

I walked to the truck, and pulled the door open.

Some snow clung to my boots. I shook them off and climbed in.

When I started the truck, the engine roared. I made a U-turn, and headed back to the farm. But I couldn't stop thinking about what she'd revealed.

Candice went back to New York—for her music?

I thought she was working on new, Christian songs?

Unless she caved… I swallowed.

I pray not.

* * *

CANDACE

Arriving back to Maryland was a double-edged return. I didn't ask the Cantwells whether they would yield their space for a concert before I announced it as a fact miles away. I wasn't sure whether they had plans.

I had acted upon faith—in desperation.

As soon as I alighted from the taxi, I paid the driver and walked around the house to the residence, planning to put down my purse before alerting the Cantwells to my return.

The sun shone high, and its brilliance belied the chill still in the air.

I unlocked the doors and entered. I couldn't help but ponder what my brother and I had discussed after the meeting. He'd said he was shocked how I rose up and took control. He'd also never seen such informal negotiation turn the tide with a finalized management decision. There was neither precedence to what I'd done, nor the kind of choice for a concert location I'd made, except perhaps Woodstock. But that was long ago.

I'd told him I needed his help.

Everything I offered at the meeting I based purely on faith in God.

No actual plans were on ground, since I had no idea this would happen.

No song had yet been written, and I had no chance to explain things beforehand because I didn't know what I was going to say before I said it. I laid out the facts to him, vulnerably.

I told him I'd simply prayed and asked God to take over.

His reaction was mellow. He grew less impatient when I spoke of God and faith. Clearly, the encounter had impacted him in a good way.

Then he told me some news about himself. He was moving, him and his wife. He wanted something new, and separate from music, possibly a different venture. My concert in April will be his final one. His news surprised me, but I was glad for him.

I smiled, and assured him that was fine with me. He was free to move on. After all, beyond the concert, there was no saying where my life headed. I could only pray and hope, trusting God to lead me forward.

Now back to Maryland, I had no fiancé, no song, and no manager —and excess weight to lose.

I'd told myself I could lose this weight, over and over during the flight. I wrote it down. Then repeated it up to a hundred times. "I can lose this weight." The more I said it, the more I believed it, and the more plans I formulated.

It would be hard. But in one year, I'd stand before the whole world. I vowed to look new, better, and healthier. I could not believe how much my thought process had changed from even the singular act of repetition.

I searched out Scripture for possibilities and added it to the mix, now I recited, "With God all things are possible."

I leaned over and set my purse to the side, sitting down on the bed. I had less than one year to change my life, my body, and write at least one new song. Which by the way, I'd perform live, and it would be streamed online for people to pay and watch—all on April 10.

I laughed, ecstatic at the victory I won in New York, wondering where things could have been had I not gone to the meeting.

I was grateful for my brother's help too.

I set my hair free, letting it fly loose on the sheets. Lifting my leg up the bed, I closed my eyes.

Success was my only option.

I would perform the concert, and I'd look good doing it. The earlier I started the better.

First step was heading to Dr. Cantwell's clinic for the medical assessment test. I checked the time. It wasn't too late yet. I could still do it today.

I'd not gone for anything medical for years, afraid of what I'd hear. Who wants to be told they were fat? That was always the first thing they said. I had to prepare snap answers to retort. I got tired of doing that, so I stopped going.

But now I had to know.

I leaned forward on my arm to find Mrs. Cantwell standing in the doorway, smiling.

"Sorry, I didn't hear you enter."

She nodded and copped a spot on the side of the bed.

"I know. You were lost in thought. And smiling, really smiling. You left the door ajar, and I was coming from the garden. I guess things went well in New York?"

How do I break the news?

"Um, sort of."

Rising to a seated position, I faced her. I wasn't sure where to begin.

"I'm no longer under contract. That's the bad news. I can do one more concert to offset the record debt. That's the good news."

She glanced at me questioningly. "All right. And?"

She saw I still had something coming.

"The concert will be hosted by me, and it needs to make two million dollars in one day. On April 10, next year. I volunteered your farm as the location for it. I'm sorry. I didn't know what else to say or how else to raise the two-million-dollar balance from my contract."

She shrugged. "They're a corporate entity. They need to make money so I wouldn't blame them too much if I were you. Now, let's figure out how to get this place ready for a concert shall we? I'll tell my husband."

I halted her hand as she rose, about to leave.

"Thank you so much! I also want to lose this excess weight before the concert. I want to look good."

She patted mine. "Wonderful! Let's help you get stage ready then. As a matter of fact, I did some weight loss thing years ago. Remind me, and I'll give you what I have. You can do this, Candace. "

I shrugged my arms back into my light sweater and stood.

"Meanwhile, let's get you to the medical check-in my husband suggested. It's a good place to start."

I felt as though something had shifted in the foundation of my life. Nothing had physically changed. But a lot had changed in my heart. I was glad I went to the city. The trip changed my perspective.

I followed Mrs. Cantwell out.

My job wasn't done until I completed the medical check.

And I wasn't waiting. I was getting it done—today.

CHAPTER 15

The sun had crested over the horizon as Dr. Mrs. Cantwell and I headed to the clinic. Her husband was already there and would be notified once we arrived. We drove into the parking lot, found a spot cleared of snow, and slid into the parking space.

Shoveled spaces were gold on days like this.

"JB came over earlier today. He asked after you."

I grabbed my custom-made, milk-white leather purse, ready. "Really?"

She snapped her seatbelt off, and we exited the vehicle.

"Yep. I told him you were in New York."

We neared the entrance.

"He asked if you were coming back."

I opened the door and held it for her to enter first before following.

"I said it depended on the Lord's leading."

There were patients—mostly adult women, plus few children—quietly seated, waiting to be seen. The waiting area had a cozy feel. An aquarium sat atop a table by a single sign-in station to the right.

After spotting two empty seats next to each other, we sat there.

JB had asked about me? He'd never seemed interested enough to be curious.

On second thought, I strode to the reception desk area, signed in, and returned to my seat. While we waited, I employed the time to search out a couple more Scriptures to assist me.

Phil. 4 verse 13: "I can do all things through Christ who strengthens me."

Another good one I found for my music was, Psalm 40:3: "He put a new song in my mouth, a hymn of praise to our God. Many will see what He has done and be amazed."

I worked on memorizing them.

Fifteen minutes later a nurse in a white coat appeared.

"Dr. Mrs. Cantwell? This way please." The nurse offered Mrs. Cantwell a friendly smile.

Mrs. Cantwell smiled back, giving her a loose hug. "Hello, Beatrice. How are you? How's your family?"

"They're all doing all right. What brings you here today?"

Mrs. Cantwell waited until we'd walked out of earshot to respond. "Our friend here wants to have a medical assessment test done. Mainly checking her vitals, weight, BMI, blood tests, and the like. You think you can do that today?"

The nurse drew her lower lip through her teeth, glancing down the hallway. "Sure. Give me one moment to check on something first." She led us into an empty room by our right. "Please wait here. I'll be right back."

I sat on the lone chair while Mrs. Cantwell leaned on the examination bed. "Candace, you're taking a huge step here today. I want you to know I'm proud of you. It may be a tough road ahead, but you can do this."

"Thank you." I folded my hands in my lap and smoothed my Outfitters red cape-length, hoodless shirt, worn over jeans. My large, twin silver fancy-stone engraved bracelets jingled. They were my favorite pair. "Your support means a lot to me. My mind's made up. I know it will be hard, but it's worth it. I'm going to give it all I got."

The nurse reentered, with a booklet in her hand. "Come with me this way, please."

She turned to Mrs. Cantwell. "Would you like to wait in here or at your husband's office? He's examining patients right now. Another doctor will see your friend and you get to see him once he's free."

Her suggestion made sense. I'd prefer to see someone other than her husband, for decency's sake.

"Sure, I'll wait in his office."

She gave me a hug. "I'll see you when you're finished. Let me go find out what my good fella has been up to since I last came here a couple of weeks ago."

I smiled and followed the nurse up the hall. Then we made a left turn to a wider hallway.

"I'm sorry we had you wait. I had to make sure the bed we need to weigh you on was available."

I frowned. "A bed? I thought you use scales?"

"Yes, but from observation, your weight appeared more than the scale could measure. So, I didn't want you to become embarrassed out there. We have the bed in a private room. The results are accurate up to decimal places."

I weighed more than the scale capacity?

Great!

The sarcasm bit.

How could I, Candace, weigh more than a scale measured?

My heart broke for myself.

I maintained calm and followed her into the large room. The bed dominated the center.

She picked up some kind of control mechanism and pushed a button.

"You can undress if you like or simply lay down and we'll begin."

I marched toward the bed. "I'm climbing on right now."

She pointed to a measure screen by the side of the bed.

"That screen will display the number. The weight of the bed and everything on it has already been subtracted. Only your weight will be recorded."

I nodded.

"Okay. Let's begin. Leave your shoes on the ground, please."

I did and sat on the bed, then I swept one leg up after the other. I braced my hand on the side, adjusting to sit properly. Then I laid down.

She pressed a button, and the bed began to lift higher. "Remain as still as you can until the reading is completed."

The bed creaked at a certain point, but kept rolling up. A beep sounded, and it stopped.

"Its reading now."

We both waited—I, with bated breath. My entire future hung on the number, my future and how much work I needed to put in to conquer it. She on the other hand, simply did her job professionally.

"Anytime now." She smiled to ease my tense glare at the screen.

I smiled a little, then heard a beep and jolted to the screen—350.1 pounds.

What?! I swallowed a sharp intake of breath. That couldn't be. Could. Not. Be. But the number stared me in the face.

She clicked her pen and wrote it down with no expression on her face. "All right. We're going to go get your blood work and other tests done in the first room whenever you feel ready."

But instead I dropped my head in anguish.

Every word she'd said I heard, but they went out the other ear.

I burst into tears, crying into my hand.

How could I weigh this much? I thought it might be 280 or something in that neighborhood. But 350s?

I did this to myself. So I had to undo it.

She came to my side and held me briefly. "Please don't feel that way. This is not the end for you. It is something you can change. The number on the scale does not define you. You are worth more than this, and you can prove it if you want."

I'd never heard anyone in a hospital tell me that. Their responses were always something either cold and impersonal, or downright demeaning.

I wiped my eyes, not trusting my voice. Then I rose from the bed after she'd lowered it to a point where I could sit and put my legs down.

"How tall are you?" She began scribbling things on a notepad.

"Five feet ten."

She wrote it down. "When was the last time you got a medical exam?"

I shrugged. "Don't recall. It was years ago."

She leaned on the wall. "Your age?"

I glanced up. "Thirty-one."

She wrote it. "Okay, Candace. Let me explain. Medically, you're categorized as super obese. Which means your Body Mass Index is quite greater than 30, which is where it should be. Based on your weight and height, it's actually 50.2."

She waited.

"What would a healthy BMI be for me based on my information?"

She ran the tail of her pen across a sheet then looked up.

"Healthy BMI would be 24.8 as indicated by the National Institute of Health, and you will need to weigh 173 pounds to be at that BMI."

I tried to do the math. "Then I need to lose about 180 pounds."

"To be exact, 177 pounds. If that's what you want," she added, as though trying not to offend me.

"Yes, it's what I want. Plus I've got twelve months to lose it."

Saying it out loud was my way of telling it to myself. Maybe the more I said it, the less daunting it would sound.

But my mind was made up.

I will not climb onto a national stage to sing weighing as I do now.

"Thank you for your assistance."

She smiled. "Just doing my job. Let's move to the other tests if you please."

I stood, more determined than when I laid down and reassured myself.

I will lose this weight.

It is possible.

CHAPTER 16

*A*fter arriving at the residence, I'd gone to the bedroom and simply stared at myself in the mirror.

I told myself some hard truths. Like that I could no longer put my weight secondary. I was too fat for my own good. I could not hide under loose clothing and fancy jewelry any longer. It was time to face reality and to change it into what I wanted.

I left the residence and walked over to the main home.

The scent of freshly diced onions reached me from the kitchen entrance. Mrs. Cantwell had told me to stop knocking and retrieve the key from under the flowerpot, unlock the door, and enter.

I'd said okay, but since I arrived, this was the first time I did so.

"Coming in!" I shouted from the door to alert her.

As I opened, she peered out from the kitchen, a long cooking spoon in one hand. "Come." She ushered me to enter. "You'll like what I'm cooking. I got these fresh from the garden this morning."

Fresh kale and green onions stuffed a basket on the table. "I may have gotten too much, but I'd rather we ate them than that the rodents did."

I guessed I needed to begin to eat these kinds of food if I was going to meet my goal in twelve months.

"What are you making?" I peered at what she diced on the cutting board, curious. Onions.

She placed a wide pot on the stove. Her multitasking skills fascinated me, being unfamiliar with the kitchen since I ate out a lot.

With one hand, she positioned the pot on the stove. With the other, she snatched the lid and set it on the side. She sprayed olive oil onto the pan. Smoke rose instantly.

Next, she poured in the diced onions and lowered the heat with the other hand in one fell swoop.

I stepped to the side to not get in her way.

"Remember, when you stir fry, use low heat."

My keen observation did not escape her notice. I stifled a grin.

"Sometimes, I mix in the veggies first, other times, the spices go in first." She tossed in garlic, fresh basil, and mint. The aroma was to die for. And she was not done yet.

"When we were growing up, most of our meals were beans, rice, or tacos and the like. They were basically carbs rich. Our parents didn't have much, so we ate what was affordable. I'm glad I can do better now, thanks to having more resources."

She poured in the veggies, lowered the heat further, sprinkled salt and pepper from her shakers, and then stirred the mix. "Even people with more resources find healthy food too expensive in cities. I think we're simply blessed to live on a farm."

She placed the spoon down and covered the pot. One step over to the sink, and she washed her hands. "Let me show you something."

She marched from the kitchen.

I cast one glance back at the stove as I followed.

"No worries. A timer will go off as soon as its due."

She read my mind again. Her wisdom floored me.

We climbed the steps to the bedrooms and entered a room opposite the stairs. Clothes stacked three rows of racks from the door. More spilled from a wide, polished, supported wooden sill, occupying an area where a bed should be. It was like an active walk-in closet.

I gaped. These were more than mere clothes, they were quite classy—party-like and functional as well.

"Wow." I moved through the racks.

A low whistle slipped through my teeth as one dress caught my eye.

Set aside from the rest, it dangled in a transparent hanger, the covering displaying the dress clearly. A knee length, royal blue satin overlaid with gold lace trimmings at the top cascaded from the hanger. Brilliant white pearls adorned the neckline in a twirly pattern. A gold broach pinned the top, on the left side. A delicate white scarf swung stylishly tied across its middle.

"Beautiful!" I said, more to myself than her.

But it was a small-sized dress—one I could hardly ever dream of wearing.

She crossed to where I stood admiring. "Yes, it is. It's a custom-made gown for when I delivered a speech at the University of Maryland. A friend of mine, who now dresses famous actresses, created it."

I ran a gentle finger across a discrete side zipper opening, admiring the ends of the hand-sewn scarf. "This took a lot of work."

"I know." She nodded. "And she's never made another like it. She said no one will pay her enough to do so. Making a dress so special was something she only reserves for dear friends like me. I was humbled."

She folded her arms and took a deep breath. "What you don't know is that it took six months of very hard work for me to fit into this dress. Our youngest son was seven when I got invited. I had very few months, maybe eight, to fit into medium from an extra-large.

"So I told my friend my predicament, and she went and made this dress. Then she brought it to me one month later and asked me to hang it where I could see it every morning until I fit into it."

My eyes traveled from the dress to her. "What did you do?"

She cracked up. "Of course, I did it. Every. Single. Day. I would walk from our apartment in town to the gym, leave our son at the daycare for an hour, and exercise."

Her brows rose. "Finding time wasn't easy, let me tell ya. I struggled, and cried many times. But I knew I did not want to stand on stage and have rolls of fat sticking out anywhere because this dress was unforgiving."

We both laughed.

"For sure it is." I spread it out, waving a hand lengthwise. "I mean look at the waistline. You can't hide anything here even with waist trainers. At all."

"That's what my friend had said." She pulled the hanger off the rack, and held it out to me. "And the dress is now yours, Candace. You take it. Put it in front of you every day, until the day you wear it to perform your song."

My mouth dropped open as I received it from her, but stood frozen. I pointed to the dress, to her, and then the alarm went off downstairs.

She sprang out of the room, waving a hand. "Close the door behind you, will ya?"

I took one step after her and stepped back, carefully unhooked the dress off its hanger. I laid it across my arm still covered and went after her, shutting the door as she'd asked. I made my way down the stairs and into the kitchen as she placed the pot on a glass cooling platter.

She waved the spoon. "Not in the kitchen. You and that dress do not belong here. It should be hung up in your bedroom."

I'd forgotten how rare the piece was, as I got solely concerned with coming to tell her how much I didn't deserve the dress and couldn't take it so I don't ruin it for her. "Thank you for this." Was all I could say in response.

On her urge, I left the kitchen and hurried, making my way to the residence. When I entered, my phone was ringing. I contemplated keeping the dress or answering my phone first. I chose to hang up the dress. I could call back whoever called me. After hanging the dress up on the closet and leaving the closet door partly open so I could see it, I made my way to the bedside where my phone sat. I picked up the phone but I'd already missed the call so I checked the ID. It had been Matt.

I dialed him back. "Matt, sorry I had something in my hand that I needed to put down first. What's up?"

"Guess what? I have a new gig!"

Whoa. I didn't know he'd find something so quick. "Oh? What?"

I winced. He must have heard the caution in my voice.

"I'm starting my own business, distributing musical equipment. Like a middleman for record studios, concert performances, and road shows."

I wasn't sure how to react. "Congratulations, bro." I was happy for him, but I had one concern. "When do you start?"

There was the crux.

"Next year. I told the suppliers I needed until May, and they were cool with it."

What relief! "You scared me there for a minute."

"I wouldn't do that to you. You know better."

I exhaled in relief, glad to know I still had a manager for the concert. I would hate to face such daunting challenge without his support, given his experience with music and with my career.

"We'll find you a new manager after the concert. But you can never start too early to look."

I smiled. "Like how you got your new gig, right? No, I'd rather wait until the concert is over. I'm juggling a lot right now."

I wasn't going to tell him about the weight loss plans. I was very serious about it, but I'd hate to raise his hopes and then dash them. It was better to let him see me losing weight when it happened. "I'm happy for you."

"I know. By the way, what do you do on a farm all day? Harvest corn?"

I realized that he'd never been to a farm before. So he'd naturally be curious.

"I don't know. Maybe you should come down here to see for your-self," I teased.

"Hey, I might take you up on that." He laughed with delight, as his tone rose a few notches.

That wrapped up our conversation.

"Good talking to you, Matt. See ya."

We hung up, and I shoved the phone in the pocket of my jeans this time.

I'd formed a habit of not taking my phone along with me since coming here, and that wasn't a good habit.

I returned to the main residence. "I'm back!"

Mrs. Cantwell was already setting food on the table. She was fast.

"I had a call from my brother."

She glanced up briefly then continued setting up the salad bowl. "I wondered what took you so long. But then I thought maybe you needed a moment alone."

She laid the napkins next to the clean dishes, and someone knocked.

"Oh," she whispered. "I'd invited JB for dinner. He was so kind this morning, so I called him up and asked if he could join us and he said yes."

"What?!" I scanned my jeans and crinkled t-shirt.

She waved me away from the thought. "Don't worry. I'm sure he's worse dressed than you. He doesn't seem like the fancy type."

I gave a hurried look toward the stairs leading up to the bedrooms. "And Dr. Cantwell?"

She shrugged. She knew where I was going. I wanted another person here, a rescue squad sandwiched between him and me.

"He's stuck at the hospital working late. He said there were too many patients today so he stayed for an extra couple of hours." She bustled toward the door.

I busied my hands laying out the remaining two napkins, wrapped them, and placed them on the table. Their voices filtered in, and I leaned on the wall separating the kitchen from the dining area. I smoothed out my shirt and brushed stray hair aside then stood tall.

Shortly, they emerged into the dining room. JB walked behind Mrs. Cantwell. When he sighted me, he flashed a brilliant smile. I smiled back, noting his blue jeans—like mine—under a formal shirt.

Well, he was a bit more dressed up than me.

He had one hand in his pocket. That appeared to be his casual stance.

"JB, I thought I'd steal you away from those animals that love you too much to let you leave your farm. They can be so possessive."

"Especially the goats," he chimed.

Mrs. Cantwell took a seat next to me. "Please. You both, sit. Enjoy."

JB sat opposite, directly across from me.

Mrs. Cantwell said a quick blessing then handed me a bowl.

Our eyes met briefly as I passed the bowl of mashed potatoes to JB. "Want some?"

"Thanks." He took it, scooped some, and handed it back. "I heard you were down in New York?"

His cautious gaze studied me a little too closely. I shifted my attention to my plate. "Yeah, just for a day. I had a meeting."

I could still feel his eyes fixed on me. "How did it go?"

Mrs. Cantwell and I exchanged glances. "Good. All things considered."

He took a bite of the grilled veggies.

"She's going to host a concert here in April, next year. That's the bottom line. Right, Candace?" She was already publicizing it.

I haven't written a song.

I chuckled. "I gotta write the songs first. But yes, a concert here on the farm is in the works. A Christian concert. On April 10."

He drank some water and put the glass down. His hands were hairy, but appeared supple. Farmer hands? Definitely not.

"Congratulations, Candace. That's good news." A smile lit his face, as though now relieved.

What did he think I went to New York for? "Thanks."

Mrs. Cantwell inclined her head, pointed her fork to his plate. "Now you eat up. Candace can bear witness of how hard I worked over on that stove to cook this and keep the food hot."

"If anyone knows her way around the kitchen, it's Mrs. Cantwell," I agreed, sipping water.

I cleared my throat.

"You don't cook?" Mischief twinkled in his measured glance.

Mrs. Cantwell caught the question. "Of course, she does. We were in the kitchen together for some time."

Did that suffice?

"I'm from New York. We eat out a lot, so kitchen time is minimal. Since coming here, it has increased exponentially though."

He also reached for his water glass then dug into his meal. "Living on a farm can do that to you." He turned to Mrs. Cantwell. "How are the crops doing?"

Mrs. Cantwell pointed to the table. "That's what we're eating. They're doing great. Last year was bad. It was our first time farming the land here. This year, we went ahead and replaced it with imported soil, far from land humans have trod much to preserve the natural integrity of the soil."

JB's brows arched. "Must've cost you lots."

"It did, but it was well worth it. I'd rather know what is growing my food than be ignorant."

I dug my fork into the broccoli. Why did it have to taste like paper?

"Did they do better? The crops?" JB asked, eating his meal with zeal.

"Yes!" Mrs. Cantwell gave a vigorous nod. "Way better. Fruits taste better, veggies appear greener, and the tomatoes are more fleshed and varied in their appearance. My husband thought we should start a business selling whole soil. Go figure."

He nodded toward the door. "How far did they transport the soil?"

Mrs. Cantwell cleared her throat noisily. "Alaska."

"Whew, quite a long way to fetch sand."

"Yeah, it's one of the few places with affordable soil humans haven't trodden much, to optimize plant growth. We've been able to re-soil half the land. The other half is yet to be done. We decided to wait until next year after we've planted this year and seen how the crops fared."

I glanced up from my food. "That's why the portion farther from the road isn't planted?"

I'd seen it the day we fetched milk from JB's farm. 'Twas huge.

"Yeah, and God willing, that's where your concert will happen. We'll need to lower the grasses, of course, and fence off the crops on the planted portion, but those are minor fixes."

I turned to JB, resting my fork and reaching for the water jug. "How about the animals? Are things working out?"

He raised his chin slightly. "Yes, they're good. I can't complain. It's a learning experience when you have to figure out how to milk a goat. And protect chicken eggs. Let's just say that it's a whole new way of living. But I have good staff, and I'm learning, and improving the way things are done."

He drank some water again. "Your music?"

Nothing had changed since the day we met so I wasn't ready with an update. "I'm working on it."

I repeated the same thing I'd told Matt.

When will my response change, Lord?

He smiled. "It will come together at God's time."

"Amen."

Mrs. Cantwell rose. "I'll grab us some dessert." She strode into the kitchen as we ate in silence.

He laid his fork down, and copped a serious expression. "Months ago, I'd prayed for you. God laid it on my heart."

I stopped eating, then put my own fork down.

He raised a hand. "Not to meet you in person, no. I watched the video where you fell, by accident, while searching for something else. The Spirit led me to pray for you and I did. I was still in Kentucky, minding my business. I didn't know you. Didn't think I ever would."

He chuckled as he recalled, then he shook his head. "I resisted, but God wouldn't let me. The burden to pray stayed so I continued praying for an entire week. Until the day I came here, that was when it lifted. That was the day we met."

That must be the reason for the weird look on his face when I introduced myself!

He prayed—*for me?*

I swallowed.

The revelation was a little much to take in.

His eyes were pinned on mine, and I was unable to run from them. An insistence, or a sort of dare, lingered in them.

I tore mine away, feeling overwhelmed.

"I prayed every kind of prayer for you—for strength to stay in the faith, for your music, and for courage to follow divine leading, and stability to stand in the faith after your fiancé moved on." He shrugged. "You name it. I was never going to meet you, so I wondered why I had to pray for you. I almost told God that I was sure there were others praying and He didn't need me to. But the burden wouldn't leave, so I prayed until it lifted. I didn't know when the right time to tell you would be. Until now."

He reached a hand across. "You're a woman of courage, Candace. God loves you. I want you to know you have a friend here any day, any time."

I took his hand. Brimming with gratitude, I shook it firmly, almost hesitant to let go. "Thank you, JB. I mean, thank you for praying for me. I'm very grateful. God bless you."

I let go as Mrs. Cantwell arrived with dessert.

But by then, I had almost lost my appetite. The fullness of my heart sealed my stomach shut.

Here I was, seated across from someone who labored for my soul —without knowing me. And I'd never even cared to find out anything about him.

Mrs. Cantwell noticed the silence. "Everything okay?"

I was close to tears so I chuckled instead. "Yes."

She pointed. "Dig in then. You both stop staring like I just served brussels sprouts for dessert. It's carrot cake."

Good thing, I like carrot cake.

"Trust God," Mrs. Cantwell had said a long time ago.

I did now.

CHAPTER 17

*S*itting at the sunroom, bright and early—the sun not even up yet—I sobered as I remembered how I first started in music. I'd heard songs on the radio when my dad drove me to school. I'd sing along with the rising and falling crescendo, matching those on the airwaves.

I was seven the first time he took me to a local concert. I stood in line, and waited with other excited kids for an autograph. I was able to get one after two hours' wait. Dad said we had to go home. He had to work the next day, and it was almost midnight.

Mom had it framed, and placed it in my room. It was the first thing I saw when I woke up and the last thing I'd see before lights out. The seed of music grew inside me with every view.

I sighed. Those were the good days.

Leaving my notepad and pen on the lounge chair, I walked to the sunlight slicing through the distance, too faint yet.

When I turned sixteen, I had my first formal audition. My brother, Matt, twenty-one then, was my greatest supporter. He believed in me. He told me that I could do it. That I had a good voice but so did the others at the audition. It wasn't easy and I was scared. But I gave it my all. I was chosen as a backup singer for a fundraising event performance then.

It wasn't big, but it was a starting point. My parents grew concerned. They wanted me to focus on school. The problem was, music was more important to me. I went to classes, did my homework, and graduated, then moved on to college.

But every waking hour when I wasn't in school, I spent practicing, listening to the famous artists' albums, and honing my voice. I sowed countless hours and I spared nothing. Be it in the shower, watching TV, riding the school bus, or sometimes walking home from school. And the nickname, Wit, began. I'd answer questions in song. They thought I was being smart. Little did they know that I was simply maximizing my practice time.

Midway through college, I impressed a talent scout, and he signed me on to a two-year contract. I performed at small events first. Then larger ones.

I sang lively songs, carried people along. I especially loved hearing their voices fly along with mine.

After graduation from Fine Arts, I went full time into music. Granted, I wasn't in the big wigs, but I held my own.

My audiences weren't huge, but they were sizeable. When my contract came up for renewal, the executives said the label was doing poorly.

They needed to reinvent the artists and the music. Most artists left seeking greener pastures. I figured I'd stay with what I knew…Moreover, my talent director was kind. So I renewed my contract, and chose to wait and see.

Then without warning they sold us to a separate organization, Global Sound Records. That coincided with when Matt and I lost our parents. It was caused by a hit and run accident. It totaled their vehicle. The driver responsible was never found. His tags were unregistered, and he'd fled on foot.

I was so grieved that I wasn't thinking clearly. When I returned from the funeral, everything changed. The song choices became heavily edited.

I didn't like it so I complained, and asked Matt as my manager to intervene. But he couldn't do much, having limited power.

Every time I objected, they referred me to the contract. I was there to do their bidding. My voice was simply a tool. But I still sang.

My first single, titled "Wit" for my nickname, was a hit.

People loved it so much they said my voice was incredible.

The executives said that I had saved the label.

They wrote more provocative songs. I sang them. They sold and made even more money.

I was getting miserable, and was losing myself. Some of the lines stuck with me for days, ringing though my mind, into my subconscious.

As hard as I tried, I couldn't get them out, I couldn't think straight.

I felt stifled. I longed to go back to the little girl who sang simple songs along with the radio…but listeners wanted more and more.

The entire period became a daze.

I lived through it.

But I didn't feel it.

I was like a walking robot, singing so I could eat.

Matt, on the other hand, was so engrossed in the fame, that he didn't grasp how I was sinking fast.

I smiled though I was miserable until one day when it all changed.

I strolled to the lounge chair and sat, threw my head back, and closed my eyes.

It was one sunny Sunday afternoon last summer, that I strolled past a nearby church because I was bored in my apartment. It wasn't a large church, maybe a hundred people were in there.

It was loud and boisterous from what I heard outside…I could feel the excitement filtering out.

I wondered what they were so happy about when I was nothing but miserable.

I entered, sat in the last row as worship ended and the pastor began preaching.

I listened to the sermon behind huge, dark sunglasses lest anyone recognized me.

I still remembered the message titled, "Who Are You?".

By the time the preacher finished, he had completely described my present life. The lack of fulfillment, living to please, while searching for meaning.

Everything he said was a package deal.

I hurried out as soon as the ministration was over. But the message haunted me all week. I returned to the studio, unable to sing those words again.

They tasted like poison on my tongue.

Next Sunday, I surprised myself and returned, aching for more.

Five Sundays later, I'd had it. I was so burdened.

When the altar call came, I removed my sunglasses lined with tears, went in front of the church, knelt down, and received Jesus.

That afternoon, the pastor baptized me and encouraged me to continue walking in Christ.

My life became lighter.

I had new strength, and a new life.

I told Matt and he was aghast.

First thing he asked was—"What are you going to be singing about now that you're church folk?"

I froze. I had not thought about that at all.

I'd been simply overjoyed.

I shrugged it off, and told him I could sing at official events.

But then, there was Ray. Ray returned from his summer trip and I told him too.

It was different with him because we were in a relationship and were already engaged. Though I knew we should cut ties, I held on. I loved him, and didn't want to lose him. But I knew that we couldn't sleep together any longer. That's when he moved into the separate room and our relationship grew strained.

As for Global Sound Records?

They didn't like the news either. I was their top talent, and I was loved nationwide.

They'd complained that there was no time to groom new talent to replace me.

I wondered why no one actually stopped to think of my wellbeing. I was happy now, and living a meaningful life.

I asked for, and they booked me to do some official events. But the revenue was too small and couldn't sustain the contract's terms.

Confused, I spoke with the pastor. He prayed with me, for God to lead me. He said he couldn't tell me what to do because God led us all individually.

The storm began when I cancelled all my tours.

Word got out that I was now a Christian and would not sing my old songs.

What an uproar it led to. An unimaginable, hateful venom was poured toward me. As though people could not wait to rip into me.

I got vilified, and called terrible names.

Out on the street one day, someone threw rotten bananas at me.

So I was forced to stay indoors. I asked Ray to please move out. He didn't mind since we weren't intimate anymore, but I still wasn't going to let him go. Though our worldviews were no longer compatible, we'd been together for many years. So I clung to him.

The day he packed and moved, I cried my eyes out, and locked myself in my bedroom. What I did was right but that didn't make it any less hard.

Then I waited on God. I fasted and I prayed.

The day I fell on stage was my breaking point. It literally drove me off the cliff.

I suspected that the label stood by me probably because they expected me to change my mind.

Now they know. Without a job, fiancé, or song, I'll stick with Jesus.

My soul was worth more than those things.

I understood now why God would have JB—a man I didn't know who lived miles away—pray for me.

After all, whoever left the known and entered into the unknown—with no guarantees? I chuckled with an answer.

Only one who's got Jesus by their side—and was prayed up.

* * *

THE SUN HAD SET when I walked to the main house to ask Dr. Cantwell some questions.

I'd received my medical test results in the mail earlier and I studied it. I'd already eaten lunch at the residence.

The report was mostly numbers. I could hardly figure out what they meant, but I compared the standard/expected lines with the patient's lines. To say there was a huge gap was an understatement.

My cholesterol numbers had a flag symbol next to them. The line for vitamin D read "low". The line for my body weight read, "increased risk for heart disease, diabetes, stroke, and heart failure".

My weight, which I already saw at the hospital, read 350 pounds. The sheet began to drop from my hand. But not before I'd read the recommendation, "advised to commence a weight loss program. Monitor cholesterol and fat intake to improve health."

That was the bottom line.

Because of the late hour, I knocked. But the door rested slightly ajar, so I entered, wrapping my coat more tightly.

"Have you even bothered calling in the past six months? I don't know what's going on with you, Jim." Mrs. Cantwell sat sobbing in the living room, phone tucked in her ear.

I met Dr. Cantwell's troubled look with an apologetic one. "I'm very sorry. I didn't mean to intrude. I can come back." I turned and headed out.

Dr. Cantwell marched up, followed me out, and shut the door. "No need to apologize, Candace. What can I help you with?"

Was this the right time? I glanced at the door.

His jaw was set hard. Whatever the problem, it wasn't easy. He stood on a higher step, and I on a lower one.

"I'm truly sorry. If I knew I would not have barged in."

He waved a hand. "Candace, you did nothing wrong to apologize for. Every family has such moments. Now, could this have anything to do with your medical report?"

"Yes, I wanted to see if you wouldn't mind taking a look at it."

He accepted the sheet, and bent to read under the porch lighting from below the rim of his glasses, nodding a couple of times. "For someone at your current weight, I expected most of this. I'm being honest with you. But there are two things I'd like to flag here."

He gave me a fixed look. "Your cholesterol is too high. I would advise you stop consuming processed fat. Fat from milk and olive oil is wholesome and should meet your needs."

I swallowed hard.

"Secondly, like you mentioned days ago, you should begin to exercise. Start with three days a week, then up it to maybe five, depending on what you think you could handle. Then supplement that with eating a healthy, filling diet, and you should begin to see results. However, when you start, you will be prone to lose weight quickly. As time goes on, it gets harder to lose even a few pounds. These are good steps you can take now."

He went up the steps toward the door. "Wait here, let me go get you some literature I've found useful. You might find them beneficial too."

He entered the house then emerged with two books soon afterwards. *The Daniel Plan* and *The Maker's Diet*. You'll find a lot more resources online, but I'm old school so I like to go with something bound with a hard cover."

I smiled. So did he. "Thank you, Dr. Cantwell. I will read these. Have a good night. Please extend my regrets to Mrs. Cantwell."

He nodded. "You're welcome, Candace. You have a rested night as well."

I returned to the residence, steps light with hope. I had all the resources at my disposal *and* medical guidance. I could make getting healthy and my weight loss a reality.

I tried not to focus on the scene I'd walked into. I was sure that whatever it was, they'd sort things out. People always do. Meanwhile, it wouldn't hurt to pray for them instead of trying to know what the problem was.

My phone rang.

Matt was calling. "Hey?"

He sounded like he'd been sleeping and just woke up. "I wanted to see how the songs are coming. The label is pressuring me to give them something. Have you written anything yet?"

His tone came out sounding testy.

I swallowed. "I'm working on it, Matt. It's not easy you know."

I wished he knew my frustration!

"It's not so hard either. You have to give them something, Candace. You can't keep everyone waiting like this."

I didn't appreciate the pressure but still, I struggled and controlled my voice. "I said I'm working on it. Good night, Matt."

He hung up.

CHAPTER 18

I went to sleep with a heavy heart. The stress had finally gotten to me. I slept fitfully, tossing.

The following day, I woke up and was so worried that I skipped my morning meditation on the Word.

I simply wasn't in the mood.

I had to get out, and go to somewhere to release all this tension. I strode into the bathroom and ran a quick shower.

I dressed, called a taxi, and informed the Cantwells that I was going to town to pick up a few items. When I arrived in downtown Silver Spring, I alighted from the taxi and entered the shopping mall.

As I roamed from store to store, my thoughts joined in my wander.

No one performed a concert without a song—no one. I knew that for a fact. And here I was without one.

The frustration mounted and a strong desire for something to soothe my ache grew as well.

I perused hats in a boutique store then I saw a workout hat and bought it.

What else?

I entered a sport store and got myself some workout gear,

complete with a short sleeve top, brown leggings, a white sports bra, and one black sweatband.

Taking the escalator to the lower level, I entered another store, and bought two pairs of sneakers, topped with sunglasses for working out outdoors during summer.

Even though I was on a farm where no one knew me—well, except the Cantwells and JB—I couldn't be too careful.

Speaking of JB, recently, I hadn't been able to get him out of my mind. The ease with which we chatted, having just met surprised me…I was comfortable talking to him, more than I'd been with Ray. I was never so comfortable with anyone that quickly. Since the night he told me he'd prayed for me, something just clicked.

I pushed him off my mind now and focused.

There was no telling where my music career was headed. I had to find out before I got too far ahead of myself because the direction could be downhill.

I helplessly pondered whether to buy the sport watch I was currently inspecting.

My thoughts strayed to the concert.

What if John came up with something else to stop me with? What then?

My stomach knotted as I grabbed the watch and walked to the counter to pay for it.

The lady cashier, about half my size, accepted the watch and rang it out. "Your total is 129.99 dollars and cents."

But I wasn't focused on her. A wet, dripping, colorful vanilla-chocolate ice-cream cup melted beside her and beckoned.

My mouth watered, as my eyes glued to it—until I realized she waited for payment. "Oh, sorry."

I swallowed, pulled out my bankcard, and swiped it, pressing in my pin number.

My resolve melted with the ice-cream cup.

"Where did you get the ice cream?"

She pointed toward the left end of the mall. "Down by the last stall, next to the west entrance."

Oh, that's why I didn't see it when I entered. I'd come in through the east doors.

She flashed a broad smile, like she'd made a new friend, and whispered, "They've got a sale going on. Buy one, get one free of the same size."

I could already imagine what size would satisfy my gnawing hunger.

Two cups wouldn't be enough—but it was a start. I accepted the bag with the purchased items. "Thank you."

She waved as another customer walked up to be rung out.

I made my way to the other side of the mall, my pace quicker this time than when I'd entered. I perceived my target before I arrived. Vanilla flavor wafted into my nostrils, and my mouth watered.

I reached the store and queued up behind the last guest.

The line moved quickly, and I was soon standing in front of the cashier, waiting to take my order.

Everything inside me screamed, "Stop!"

But I wasn't listening. My body had taken over.

"Can I have one cup of vanilla and chocolate ice cream, large, a second cup with strawberry and peach flavor, mixed?"

A petite redhead filled the cups as I watched eagerly.

Someone passed me with theirs—chocolate and vanilla, mixed.

That was such a tantalizing sight, I couldn't wait for mine.

I stilled the voice in me, fighting for me to walk away.

I'd come this far already so why leave…

She handed me both cups then I paid.

At a round table to my left, a couple rose with their children, ready to leave.

I stepped aside, allowing them passage.

Setting the bags with my purchases down, and my purse on the next seat, I placed both cups of ice cream, two spoons inserted, and some napkins on the table.

Pulling the spoon from my large-sized vanilla chocolate serve, I delved in, satisfying my guilty pleasure.

Thoughts about my weight loss goals faded.

I dug deep for my second scoop. The creamy satisfaction on my tongue felt elating.

Glancing up, I spotted a burger and fries shop next door.

This is going to be a good day!

I'd feed off my frustration.

I stretched my legs underneath and got down to business.

* * *

MORNING CAME, and with it, the sluggish consequence of everything I'd done the day before. I roiled in bed, tummy bloated and hurting.

"Candace? Good morning!" Mrs. Cantwell's voice sounded chirpy.

Ugh, so not suitable to my mood this morning.

I scooped the blanket closer while listening to her on the call.

Something about me coming over for breakfast.

With everything I ate yesterday? Guilt flooded my mind.

Ha! Not a chance.

"Oh no, thank you. I'll pass on breakfast. Thank you."

Silence trailed on the other end.

I'd never passed on a meal since I arrived.

My refusal, however subtle, didn't escape her notice.

"All right, see you at lunch then," she calmly replied, still tried to sound cheerful, but an edge had set in. She'd guessed there was a problem that I wasn't eager to share.

Afternoon came and my phone rang again. I was still rolling around in bed, wishing I could forget what time it was.

"Candace, I've set up the table for lunch. See you soon."

Silence followed.

I don't want to eat anything! I wanted to shout into my pillow.

I didn't know how to turn her down, not to be rude. "Sorry, Mrs. Cantwell. I'm not having lunch today."

The silence was on her end this time.

"Are you all right? Is something wrong?" She sounded like she would like to shake me into some reality if we stood face to face.

I wanted to shout, "Everything is wrong!"

"Nothing big. Just skipping…"

She hung up.

Well, that went…err… okay.

I finally dragged myself off the bed and headed to the bathroom to clean up. The best I could do while sulking was to shower.

When I stepped out of the shower, my stomach grumbled more than a few times but I ignored it. Serious hunger pangs set in around three. I felt like I was going to pass out.

I bent low, with my breath down to whimpering. I staggered to the sunroom and sunk into the chaise lounge feeling faint.

Waiting for the feeling to pass, I drank some water.

My eyes brimmed with hot tears.

How could I?! Why did I eat so much bad food yesterday? What was I thinking!

I'd decided to get healthy. Was the solution moving backward?

I staggered to my feet, wiped the teardrops, and returned inside just in time to hear a rap on the door.

Without opening, I knew who it must be.

Mrs. Cantwell.

"What's going on, Candace?" Her hands flew in the air.

I left the door open and went back in, her steps following. We sat down and her eyes pinned on me.

I lowered my gaze. "Ever had two tubs of ice cream, when you set out to have one scoop?" I shot her a quick glance.

Her arms dropped to her sides. She sighed. "You binged."

I nodded, feeling a cry close.

"And now you're starving to make up for it. I tell you that never works. Why did you do it?" Her question could have torn at my very soul.

"Frustration. I have no song for the concert."

She was quiet for a minute then rose, and beckoned me. "Come. I want to show you something."

Despite my little energy, I followed her into the main home.

As we entered, fresh baked confectionaries assaulted my nostrils.

My mouth watered, and my stomach followed with an audible rumble. I pressed a hand against it.

In the kitchen, she set an empty bowl down. She rounded the kitchen table to the fridge while I waited, lifting onto my toes. She removed two bananas, placed them on the counter, and then reached for the blender. Pulling it outward, closer to the edge of the kitchen counter, she turned.

"I have a cure for my ice-cream binge sessions I'd made years ago. I had one such session a couple months ago. Things weren't going so well with our son, Jim. I laid awake all night worried."

She grabbed a container from the cabinet and screwed it open, then she scooped a spoonful of its contents into the blender. She returned to the fridge and came out with a jug of milk.

Pouring some into the blender, she peeled the banana and added it as well, and topped it with some ice. She pushed the lid of the blender closed.

With one press on the Blend button, the mixture went pasty. She pressed again, but held it for longer this time. She poured the thick mixture into the clean bowl and plunked a spoon. "Now, this looks good if you ask me, and I'm loving it."

She fed some into her mouth. Then she went back to the fridge, brought out two bananas, the ice cube tray, the milk jug, and set them on the table next to the powder container and blender. "Your turn. If you're hungry."

After one look at her, I peeled the bananas with hurried hands. Tossing them into the blender, I poured two scoops of the protein powder—one scoop was too small—and then in went some milk. Then I topped it with ice cubes and covered the blender. One hand on the blender's cover, the other on the button, I blended to my heart's content.

Mrs. Cantwell already brought a second bowl out, laid it on the table, and went back to eating hers.

My mouth was watering as hunger pangs tore at my stomach.

I stopped the blender when it turned creamy, opened it, then poured its contents into the bowl, using a spoon in the bowl to scrape out what stuck to the side. I wasn't wasting any of this when it looked so appetizing.

Putting down the blender, I pulled out the second kitchen stool and sat to enjoy.

As soon as the first scoop made it into my mouth, it melted in sweet savor on my tongue. Its taste was creamy, naturally flavored, and thick. "Just like ice cream, but much healthier."

Mrs. Cantwell was already halfway through her bowl.

I frowned a little. "Isn't this too much for one sitting?" I'd heard portion sizes were it.

She chuckled. "Well, not if you're having a bad day—and if you haven't eaten at all. So go ahead, no judging."

I scooped another one into my mouth, savoring its sweet, and creamy taste.

She pointed at my bowl. "Approximately 250 calories in comparison with 800 calories for the same serving of ice cream, with the protein powder being optional. That's a good alternative if you ask me."

I loved it.

"What is its name?"

She smiled. "Most people call it 'banana ice cream' or 'n-ice cream'. More than enough fun names for it if you ask me. The important part is this, people are substituting unhealthy meals with healthy ones. You know no one can succeed in weight loss without proper nutrition, both for content and in portion control. If you'd like, I can teach you what I know."

Having started with banana ice cream, I wanted to learn more, much more. "Yes, please. Everything."

We continued to enjoying the meal, my stomach grateful.

"God Himself will provide you a song, Candace. You just have to trust Him and His timing—which is hard. I know it's always tough for me. Maybe for you too. Focus on your part. He'll do His when the right time comes. We like to know everything now. But He wants us to trust Him instead, so trust and obey as the song says."

I smiled. "Lose my crutches, and trust God. You said that the first time we talked. I guess it still applies."

She nodded. "Exactly. I'm glad that you still remember."

But it was so hard to do!

"I sure will. Thank you."

CHAPTER 19

* * *

*W*e stayed in the kitchen as Mrs. Cantwell showed me various recipes, kitchen equipment, and a kitchen measuring scale. I learned as much as I could.

"You could come in here to cook anything you want, anytime," she'd said.

She shared healthier alternatives, like using olive oil instead of butter. Eating lots of veggies to fill up rather than much carbs. Drinking a lot of water by sipping as long as I was awake. Brushing my teeth at night to prevent me from eating a late night snack. And if I had to eat something that late, to have a healthy snack bar on hand.

She gave me a cookbook she'd developed for herself years ago when her children were young and she'd tried to lose weight in a healthy manner.

It was a treasure trove.

She shared her workout schedule and told me to only do what I could now, then do more when it got easy, keeping it hard. She shared so many tips, and there was so much to learn, but I was determined.

As I thanked her and left, armed with all the information, books, recipes, tips—and of course, my leftover banana ice cream—I made up my mind.

Yesterday would never happen again, if I could help it.

* * *

"GOAL—TO lose 177 pounds in twelve months." I wrote it down, then tore out the sheet, rubbed some glue-stick I'd found on the desk then blew on it to dry. I folded the blank portion backward then taped it to the elliptical machine.

There. It would be in my face every day.

This goal was front and center. Focus, JB had said.

That was exactly what I'd do. I hadn't seen him again, which was good. I had time to focus on my goals.

I climbed onto the elliptical and began working out.

My phone rang so I stopped to get it.

"We're having zucchinis for dinner tonight. I got way too much zucchini in the garden. You in or not?"

I swiped sweat off my brow with a towel. "Oh yeah, count me in, Mrs. Cantwell."

A notepad and pen sat on the edge of the machine's display screen. I placed them there in case a song came while I was working out.

When she hung up, I refocused. My arms felt like they were on fire since I got on the elliptical. Pushing it back and forth, I alternated with applying pressure using my feet for cycles when either limb got tired.

I glanced at the timer. It said fifty-nine minutes. One more minute. Every part of me wanted to stop.

Everywhere screamed but I didn't. I planned to go an hour. So an hour it would be.

If I fainted, I was pretty sure Dr. Cantwell and his wife could perform CPR.

So there was no stopping for me!

My ears tuned to that timer like nothing else. I'd never paid such close attention to a clock. One minute—is long!

I clung to the handle of the elliptical like for dear life. Rolling my feet forward, I moaned with every last bit of strength I could muster, fully geared to stop, but waiting.

C'mon!

Five seconds later came the sweet chime.

Finally!

Climbing down was work. I staggered and my knees shook.

Applause rang from the doorway. I glanced up sharply with hands rested on my trembling knees.

"Excellent job!" Mrs. Cantwell walked in closer and peered at the elliptical. "Sixty minutes, 700 calories burned at low resistance level. Amazing, Candace. Look at you soaked and sweating it out."

I glanced at my shirt. Sweat had truly soaked me. Wow! I was too engrossed on the machine to notice.

I rose, still feeling like my knees would buckle. I changed my mind and sat on the ground instead, laying flat, my chest rising and falling fast.

Mrs. Cantwell walked to the elliptical, wiped it down with a towel, and replaced it with a fresh one that I'd hung on the other handle. She tossed it in a laundry basket by the far wall. "Candace, you moved a mountain today. Do this every day, and I tell ya, no one will recognize you six months from now."

"That's the plan."

She returned to the doorway and stopped. "You know, this may be a farm, but you gotta start locking your door. People can be funny sometimes."

"Sorry, I forgot. I'll lock it behind you."

She nodded. "Oh, I'd suggest you soak your feet in Epsom salted water, to relieve the pain from the grinder you just put yourself through. You'll find some in the cupboard under the bathroom sink. Couple of minutes' soak should be enough."

I straightened a little, then groaned.

Yup. She was right. My leg muscles screamed, protesting every movement.

"Thank you, Mrs. Cantwell. Good night," I shouted toward the doorway.

She had asked me to call her by her first name. I'd insisted on adding her marital title. I figured if I couldn't call her doctor every time, the least I could respectfully do was call her Mrs. She didn't seem to mind then. Plus, she was twice my age.

I walked to the bathroom, limping a little, and peered in the cupboard, in search of Epsom salt. There it was, deep inside.

Bending over, I reached behind a can of mentholated dusting powder from India, said to be for heat rashes. I made a mental note that I'd need it for my neck when summer arrived. A hot balm application for sore limbs, and a first aid kit also stood in the way. I skipped them.

Wow, this place was well stocked for my recovery. I'd simply remain focused on my goals. Pulling out the salt, I turned on the tap and got ready for a soak, rolling up the hem of my pants. The salt went in first. Then I turned off the tap and sat, with my legs in the water. This was just the beginning. By God's grace, tomorrow, I'd do this all over again.

* * *

I COULD HARDLY BELIEVE that it was now eight weeks since my first day working out for an hour on the elliptical, and ten weeks since I arrived on the farm. Exercise became part of my daily routine. I was always moving.

"Did you talk to your brother yet?" Mrs. Cantwell asked as we plucked the last patch of weeds off the garden.

We had begun tackling them last week. But they'd added more garden land behind the house for pumpkin seeds, so we cleared it too.

My hands no longer blistered like the first two weeks here. We worked away as some music from the radio on my phone supplied us much-needed encouragement.

I sang along, usually louder when I was alone, or if she went into the house to fetch some water or snack for us.

Her husband had joined us for half an hour then left to keep an urgent appointment with one of his patients. Today, I was quiet, listening to the songs, ruminating on the words, applying them to my life, and to my situation.

"We spoke a couple of weeks ago." I wasn't ready to tell her that I was afraid to hear more bad news so I hadn't called Matt.

I dug my fingers beneath stubborn weeds growing around a rock leftover from the special stones we'd used for the flagstone path. Leaning over, someone blocked my sun. I put up a hand to my face to shield my eyes.

I jumped to my feet before thinking, landed in his arms—sand and all—and wrapped my arms tight. "Matt! How—I mean, when—you're here! Wow!"

He pulled us apart and spread out his hands. "I thought I'd come in and surprise you. Look at you! How much weight have you lost? You're looking good, Candace."

I swung around for a full view.

"How much?"

I wasn't dwelling on the number, but I'd been curious so I'd rode with Dr. Cantwell to the clinic two days ago to get weighed.

"Seventy pounds to be exact! I'm so excited, bro. I'm down to the 200s—283 pounds right now. Ninety-five to go in nine more months." I could've told him that the new habit of drinking almost a gallon of water per day had significantly cut down my hunger pangs. Plus, Mrs. Cantwell cooked veggies in such a way they muscled out my carbs considerably—and that sped up my weight loss, not just exercise. But that would be too many details for him.

I swirled, showing off my progress.

He laughed, spreading out his arms further in admiration. "Whopping seventy pounds! You're doing this full time, all day long. Okay, time to take a break, sis. We need to celebrate. Let's party tonight."

I felt my face fall. "Sorry, I can't. My schedule is to write a new song tonight, or—um—pray about it at least."

Mrs. Cantwell smiled. She'd been careful not to get squished in between us. "I suggest you both join us for dinner then instead of going into town. Matt, it's nice to finally meet you. We have ample room in the house. That gives you two more time to catch up. I'm sure you have a lot to talk about. You don't need a hotel. Plus it could be late by the time we finish dinner."

Matt dipped slightly. "I was going to book a hotel, but this sounds like a better idea. Thank you for the offer. I'm only here for a day. I wanted to check on Candace, see how she's doing. Also would love to assess the land, the venue for the concert, so I'll know what we need to order, if you don't mind."

"Certainly," Mrs. Cantwell agreed. "I'll have one of the men escort you to the grounds and show you the land tomorrow. It might need a little bit of trimming, but it can hold up to the wear of human feet."

We packed up and headed out, Mrs. Cantwell to the main house, Matt and I to the residence.

"I'll see you both around seven thirty for dinner."

Matt veered off to his Jeep for his luggage. I entered the residence to shower and change. My routine for the day was up on the wall, and I'd been consistent.

Wake up at six to pray. Workout at seven until nine a.m. Help at the garden from ten till lunch at noon. Laundry and cleaning in the afternoon. Walk around the farm in the evening at five. Attempt to write a song when I return. Eat dinner and then go to bed at nine or ten depending on whether I had something I needed to do to prepare for my exercise the following day. Pretty straightforward—except the part about writing new songs.

I plunked down the couch, dressed in a clean shirt and jeans. I gathered my hair into a bun. I'd washed it so it still felt damp even though I had blow-dried it.

Matt strolled in about a half hour later. We sat and talked then went to town so I could show him a few good places I'd discovered.

* * *

THE BLAST of sharp onion flavor hit my taste buds with gusto. I smacked my lips, relishing my grilled chicken salad. Matt, seated next to me, busily sliced through meatballs, while our hosts sat on the other side of the dining table. Mrs. Cantwell dug into her roasted beef sirloin with her fork and knife, pushing veggies on her plate to the edge.

"Matt, how's the commercial side of music faring these days?"

Matt sucked in his dangling string of spaghetti into his mouth faster to respond. "Up in the air as usual. Which is why I'm switching to the equipment side of things."

Matt engaged with Dr. Cantwell about the history of commercial music production. They traded updates while Mrs. Cantwell and I chatted about the latest trends in workout wear I'd seen out in town.

In the course of eating, we learned that Dr. Cantwell was part of a campus music group in college. He said his parents warned that if he didn't focus on his education, he would be eating off goodwill on the streets. As he put it, that ended the band dreams.

His band mates got tied up with their studies, but he said the few times they performed were memorable. He'd advised me to not put my dreams on hold, while waiting for tomorrow, because tomorrow may be late. Life shelled out new responsibilities each day, and it got harder finding time to do the things you love.

"We're happy to donate the land for the concert. I'll cancel my engagements to be there front row," he'd added.

"Thank you, Dr. Cantwell."

All that time meanwhile, I smiled but my heart pounded. *Candace, you have not written any songs—not one.*

It kept on until I sat, almost physically shaking. Everyone was getting excited for a concert whose songs have not been written.

This was real pressure!

CHAPTER 20

*A*fter dinner, I bid Matt and the Cantwells good night. I went to my bedroom to lay my workout clothes out for tomorrow, like I'd done every day for the past eight weeks.

But the first six weeks were tough.

I read Mrs. Cantwell's workout plan where she documented when she exercised to lose weight.

She'd written detailed information about what she'd eaten, done for exercise, how much she weighed, including off-the-record cheat days, written in red ink—and in block letters. Probably to keep her from repeating the mistakes.

I tried to follow her pattern, but tweaked it a little, since I was much heavier. I incorporated the daily evening walks for one hour to my routine. Sometimes, I'd be so worn out and beaten by my elliptical workout or the gardening, but I did not skip my walk.

When storm predictions loomed, I walked inside the residence, from the sunroom to the bedroom, back and forth until I completed the one-hour walk.

The elliptical workout never got easier, as I'd mistakenly assumed. It got harder—every single time. I struggled, but I now complete one hour and forty-five minutes on the elliptical, building an extra minute into my routine each day.

I wrote down my workout plan for the next day in a notepad.

Satisfied, I was off to sleep.

Hours later, I roused to the sound of Matt's voice on the phone in the living space of the residence, giving instructions to someone about equipment.

I was still in bed, groggy and sleepy-eyed. Yawning, I rose and made my way to the closet. I must've forgotten to lock the door last night—again. I needed to post a reminder or something.

Catching my glance on a mirror, I covered my disheveled hair with a hair wrap, rolling the length into a bun.

Yanking a big jacket over my nightwear, I wiggled my feet into house slippers. When I walked into the living area, he was still on the phone.

He motioned me over, wrote something, and handed it to me. "The bathroom?"

I pointed and whispered, "Left turn."

He dropped his phone on the table, slipped on his Bluetooth, and headed to the bathroom.

I checked the time on my phone. Eight. I'd overslept. I went over to the sunroom to pray.

Noise filtered in from outside. I tried to block it out and focus.

I jealously guarded my prayer and worship time. I'd grown to enjoy fellowship with God. I learned a lot from listening to the Christian radio station and to the pastor's exultations at the Cantwells' church, Miracle Assembly, every Sunday.

Beginning my day with the Word of God and offering praise to His Holy Name refreshed me, every time. I bowed my head as I knelt on the plush small rug I'd bought a few weeks ago. Leaning over the chaise lounge, I poured out my heart to the Lord. Of course, letting Him know of my need for songs, never stayed far behind.

Five minutes later, Matt emerged at the sunroom to find me praying. I didn't look up, but I heard him walk back to the living area.

When I was done with my quiet time, I joined him there. He lifted his head a little when I entered, then refocused on what he typed.

"Tell me about these people you're staying with. What do you know about them?"

I shrugged. "They're nice and truly Christians. They opened their doors to me just like that. You know, folks are rarely so nice, especially for someone you don't know how they live, and for someone in the public eye. But I guess God led me here." I sat on the couch, at the sole space his laptop and notes didn't occupy.

"They've taken good care of me since I got here. Fed me, even clothed me, inspired me to lose weight and change my lifestyle. I'm grateful to them."

He peered, observing me with a fixed look. One hand slid under his jaw.

"Are you happy? I mean, I know you and Ray broke up, but I don't know how you'll find someone out in the middle of nowhere. You can't be single forever, Candace. You have to settle down. Time is ticking."

Tell me about it.

"I know. You might not understand this, I'm praying and I know God will lead me to the right person at His time. I need to focus on improving myself. I got a lot of work ahead, Matt. Sometimes it feels so daunting, this weight loss journey. I know I'm losing weight, but it's hard work, very hard work."

I brushed off a hair strand. "It requires my complete focus, if I am to succeed. I will get married by God's grace, and have a family too, but Candace needs to fix Candace, before getting attached. I want to be whole before I marry, so I'm sure I'm not leading the person to do the work God could have done in me, had I given Him the chance."

He listened as I spoke, his face expressionless. "Okay." He put his laptop away and sat up. "What about the songs? It's almost nine months to go. You think you might have something soon?"

He must've noticed my drawn silence at dinner. A tinge of impatience colored his tone. I used to have the first draft of a song ready for him and the team within a month. Four had passed, and not a word.

I rose, rubbing my neck. "You know, when you're threatened by your label, it's not exactly a creative spur to write songs. It hinders creativity, all that pressure."

He sighed. "I know. What they did was unfair. We can still find a way to win this."

I looked up, taking my spot on the edge.

"They want two million. Let's target making three." He tapped a pen on the couch.

"In one day?" I nearly screeched. "That would take…a major miracle, Matt. How do you propose it?"

He placed the laptop on the floor, off to the side, and grabbed a sheet.

"Explore every option. I was thinking, for starters, if we have enough songs, we could set up preorders for them as singles on online sales channels, and then gather them as an album separately. Different price ranges for each selection." He demonstrated with his hands, like he was envisioning it. "We could also produce at least one thousand copies of the album for sale at the concert. While you perform, people can buy the albums from volunteers in stands. The proceeds from the stands go to us, because it's not really part of the show. The label owns the concert and all revenue from the entry fees, up to two million. That's the deal."

He drew a line then an upward arrow. "Those who listen to you online, their revenue also goes to the label up to two million. But everything else belongs to you, because they did not sign a renewal of the contract and you are not under any obligation to hand any excess revenue to them."

I stared at him, speechless.

He shrugged. "I read the fine print. For a month—carefully."

That sounded like a great plan… *If* I had songs already written.

"I don't know what to say. It sounds good—I like it. I mean, if we can do it, sure. As long as we don't break any rules, let's go ahead."

That is, if you ever happen to write the songs, Candace. Time to silence my voice of doubt. Permanently. "God will help us. We can do this."

He smiled. "Exactly what I was hoping to hear. Put on your singing shoes girl; we're about to turn the tables!"

We chatted about family stuff for another hour before he went to discuss the venue with the Cantwells. Later, we bid goodbye as he left to catch his flight to New York City.

* * *

EVERY WEEK I made the milk runs to JB's farm. Every time I saw him, he was active. At the animal pens, hauling feed, taping fences, chasing chickens, the man was never idle. For six weeks in a row. He wore a formal shirt most times. Certainly not a farmer by trade, but dedicated to it nevertheless.

During my evening walks, I spotted him at the boundary of his farm near the road, note and pen in hand, jotting things down. I usually turned and walked back before he saw me. We chatted more each time I went for milk. I began to like him. I noticed little by little, his farm's outlook changing.

First, the chickens were freed from their cages, and left to roam in the land with barricades so they didn't stray. A massive delivery of grass was dumped on a part of the land, bundles up to six feet tall.

The following day, the goats and some cows fed on them. A covered stand went up beside the road, where a few patrons stopped to buy eggs, fresh meat, and gallons of milk. Then a sign went up JB Organic Family Farms. Bright red letters on a barn background with a phone number printed underneath. The bold signpost was dug into the ground, rose about twelve feet tall and hugged the road's edge, impossible to miss. Floodlights attached to both sides shone bright on the words, even in broad day light.

I thought that was a smart move he made.

The next week, I set up my rolling cart where I typically did—at the front of the farm shed where they sold gallons of milk. A large truck idled beside me, loaded with the same-sized gallons. Farmhands stacked frozen, labeled slices of variety of meat on the opposite sides of the open truck. Three men taped something to the side of the truck. I didn't wait to see what.

I picked up my supply of one milk gallon, a stack of frozen chicken, some goat meat, and goat milk and loaded them onto my rollable cart. Satisfied, I paid the service staff in cash and placed the change in my jeans pocket.

"You know, you can now pay with a bankcard or credit card. We have Square now," a baritone voice rumbled beside me.

JB stood elegant and tall, hands in his jeans pockets, wearing a smile and a crisp, clean brown shirt.

This was only the second time I'd seen him wearing jeans.

I also noticed that he rarely smiled before today— he always had the look of a perfectionist focused on making sure nothing fell out of place.

But not today. He appeared relaxed, even a little nonchalant—as if he had no care in the world.

I smiled back. It was hard to ignore his charm.

His brown hair, brushed back, revealed a scar along his hairline. His firm jaw made his lips appear thinner.

I tore my eyes away, and focused on securing the cart's cover.

Without another glance in his direction, I replied, "Thanks, good to know."

Considering his diligence, there was no doubt he'd be great at anything he ever chose to pursue.

On second thought, my curiosity got the better of me. "What's up with the trucks? I saw them being loaded up. Are you moving?"

He laughed, his stance relaxing. His shoulders had inched high when he'd walked up. "Like I could move an entire farm! No, not at all. I'm expanding our supply channels to make room for more customership. Growing the business but also reforming it into a full organic farm. The previous management did what was necessary to keep the farm going, but I want the farm to be truly a whole source of good health."

I nodded in admiration.

His voice was firm but soothing. Somehow, it made my worries melt away.

"That's why you're grass-feeding the cows."

His long lashes flew up, a glint in his eye. His full lips widened to a broad grin. Then he pointed toward the closest pen where green grass feed still stood. "Glad you noticed. Yes, I've changed the feed here for the goats and cows, and let the chicken roam free within their areas."

He scratched his head with a wary hand, brown curls tumbling over. "I've had to chase quite a few chickens... but it's worth the exercise."

I laughed, then sobered up.

He laughed a little too.

He seemed to have a habit of leaning on his left foot when relaxed. One thing was clear from his stance—he was enjoying our conversation.

"Sorry, I wasn't laughing at you. It was just funny to imagine you chasing chickens." I halted my cart from rolling away as I'd taken my foot off its stopper.

He glanced narrowly at the full cart. "You know, I could walk you back with these. It looks heavy." He reached for the pull. Something about speaking with him took the edge off so I didn't mind.

But recalling the last time he'd made us an offer to help, I turned to see. Only one customer stood at the shade buying eggs. The lady attended to him. Good. I didn't want to make the same mistake twice.

"Sure, thanks." I handed over the pull of the rolling cart.

CHAPTER 21

We strode out of the farm onto the tarred road, toward the Cantwells'. He pulled the cart in between us while I swung my arms, grateful to be cart-free. "You're looking good, and so much slimmer."

I felt a little self-conscious as his eyes skimmed me.

I shrugged, making light of it. "Thank you. Nice of you to notice."

He laughed loud. "Only someone who can't see wouldn't notice! You've lost a lot of weight in a short amount of time. Congratulations."

I smiled, forcing my eyes to stay on the road.

"This is my fourth month on a weight loss and fitness journey. I was blessed to have factors working for me many people didn't have—time, opportunity, health, and resources. When you lack one of these, it takes longer. But I'm also doing it the healthy way, not starving myself."

He glanced at the cart he was dragging. "Yeah, I can see that."

We both laughed. But I halted him briefly with a finger tap.

"Now you know I'm not the only person eating and drinking all that, or I might add more fat than I lost!"

He roared with laughter. His voice, powerful and strong, set off a turmoil of emotions inside me.

"I know, just kidding. But seriously, you've done well for yourself. I saw you a few times when driving to town, walking in the evening from the Cantwells'. Such dedication deserves applause and recognition."

I nodded, acknowledging my gratitude. "Thank you, JB."

The more we talked, the more I found myself relaxing. We walked at a leisurely pace for a couple more minutes.

I had to ask. "So what brought you here—to a farm?"

He was quiet, matching my stride without pressure to go faster.

I glanced up. Our eyes met, and he smiled. I felt safe in them.

"God. God brought me here. I would never have chosen to be here." Sure, of course. He wore crisp shirts and formal pants 99 percent of the time. No one wears crisp shirts on a farm.

I probed further. "How?"

He rubbed his jaw. "It's a really long story. I can simply tell you that it wasn't a smooth ride. I came here not knowing what to expect. I knew nothing about farming."

My mind strayed to our last serious conversation. "Why did God lead you to pray for me, even when we didn't know each other?"

He bent over, picked up a broken piece of bottle, and tossed it off the road. "God alone knows the answer. I can tell you, the night he led me to pray, I was online learning about farm management. My grandma was moving, and the former manager resigned, because he was retiring to Mexico. She needed someone so she asked me."

I imagined how inconvenient that must've been. "I'm guessing bad timing was when she asked you to come?"

He flashed a smile. "You have no idea. But I prayed, and God led me here. And so far, so good."

"What about you? What brought you here—to a farm—like you so rightly mentioned earlier?"

Curiosity breeds its kind.

I shrugged. "Same as you. God. God brought me here. More accurately, tumbled me here. I fell off stage while performing the national anthem, as you already saw online. I fled and came here to seek refuge and a new beginning. You know, new songs, and a new body image. I grew tired of the life I was living. My new life as a Christian did not fit with who I used to be. I came here for solitude, and to learn."

He swapped the cart as we reached level ground, no longer sloping. He walked next to me, cart now on the other side. "This has also been a learning experience for me. When I can't see the whole road, I focus on the very next step, praying that God guides my way. I don't know where the road leads, but I'm being faithful with what God has called me to do right now, while waiting for the next stage."

Wise, discerning, humble, and patient!

Unlike me, impatient for songs... I was not groomed to wait. Everything was quick, ready, and ordered. For the first time in my adult life, I had to wait for something, a thing I was desperate about and only God could give.

"So how are the songs coming?"

Exactly my thoughts, JB.

He'd caught me unawares. "Um—" I could say, "Coming." But I was tired of it. I chose otherwise. No need to appear strong while I was sinking.

"There's nothing yet. I'm waiting—not so patiently—for God to give me a song. Just one."

The hint of frustration in my voice must have seeped through. He got quiet, and looked up at the sky. Lightning flashed, though no rain showed.

He pointed at it. "See that lightning?"

An approaching car zoomed past.

"It makes everyone uncomfortable, it even feels dangerous. But lightning carries nitrogen which is essential for plant growth. You can't wish for the nitrogen without the lightning, Candace. You'll get the songs when your lightning strikes. Question is: are you seeking the nitrogen content while avoiding the lightning source?"

I swallowed and didn't look up. His words sunk deep. Why did I want a new song? What kind of song? Was I ready to completely allow the Lord's leading in choice and wording?

Right questions indeed.

We were almost at the Cantwells', our pace slowing down when our conversation really started. His face lightened with a curved smile.

"Many days I wake up and ask God why I'm not back at Wall Street, selling stock, making money, and trading high. It's what I know how to do without thinking."

Your crutches…

"Days I wake up and want to lie back down because I'm in a farm of all places." He slowed even more. "Times when the sun burned hot and I'm chasing a chicken around, when I'd rather be in an air-conditioned office or training junior stockbrokers."

He faced me fully. I also stopped, and our gaze locked for the first time since leaving his farm. "But this week, I realized something. Wall Street experience was sufficient grace for that time of my life. God gave the chance and the skill. It doesn't mean it's the only thing He planned for my life."

I glanced away as we began trotting.

"Throughout history—except when Israel arrived at the Promised Land—once Christ came and resurrected, God rarely left His children rooted in one place perpetually. The church is a body in transition. We are the church. That means God moves us to where He needs us, not necessarily where we would like to be. So, part of being a true Christian, is being flexible in allowing God to lead you to where He needs you—whether you like it or not. And to realize that, through you, a divine purpose is getting accomplished."

He chuckled. "When I realized that, I stopped waking up waiting for the day when I'd leave this place. In fact, I'm prepared to stay permanently if that's His plan."

He handed me the cart as we arrived. "You stay in Him, and He will give you a song when you least expect it."

I nodded.

He'd given me a lot to think, and pray about. He'd opened up to me too. Something told me he rarely did. "Thanks for walking me home, and thank you for sharing your experiences with me. I appreciate it."

175

He smiled, then leaned in closer and dusted something off my shoulder.

"You are quite welcome. See you later."

He avoided addressing me by name. I'd noticed it since the first day I'd gone for milk. I chuckled remembering he'd actually called me "ma'am" to which I frowned and he caught it. He never did that again.

* * *

I DETOURED to the main house to drop off the items first. Upon entry, I met Mrs. Cantwell at the living room.

"All smiles now, huh? No more grunting on the elliptical?"

I laughed. I'd entered, not realizing I wore a smile. "Those work-outs are grueling. Have you tried this elliptical?"

She sighed and shook her head. "Not a chance. My son, Jim, bought it last Christmas. I never climbed on it. I'm fine just walking. That stuff looks daunting. You're doing great even getting on it at all."

My thighs, ankles, and arms paid the price for it.

I placed the haul one by one on top of the kitchen counter.

Mrs. Cantwell stepped over, opened the fridge, and began to load in the items.

"I happened to peek through the window and saw you and a certain someone having a conversation. Seemed intense…was everything okay?"

Our eyes crossed as I placed the last milk gallon on the table, and I nodded, my lips twitching.

"Yeah, we chatted but there was no qualms. He helped me wheel the cart home." I wasn't willing to divulge details of someone else's life without their consent.

Her twinkling eyes narrowed. "When a man starts walking you one and half miles home, honey…" She coughed playfully.

I laughed. "It was just conversation. He is nice. And he was a gentleman."

We went on to prep meals for the rest of the day. But JB stayed on my mind.

I knew there and then, I wanted another conversation with this man of deep understanding.

* * *

THE SUN ROSE and found me, arms wrapped, feet curled, sitting on the chaise lounge, and waiting—for a song. I tapped my pen absent-mindedly.

My mind roamed.

What if all of this is a mistake?

Coming here, waiting, praying for a song? Huh?

I remembered the blue dress from Mrs. Cantwell hanging off my closet.

What if I don't lose all this weight in six months' time? Sure, I'd made progress, but what if everything I've done wasn't enough to get me across the finish line? How would I face the world knowing I'd failed myself? I crouched my head in my hands and moaned.

This is too much! I can't do this.

Lord, please free me! I'm only one person, one human being. I can't do all this...

I rose. It was dark when I came in here. The time had said 5:50 a.m. My sport watch read about eight now. I dropped the pen and notepad, grabbed a bottle of water, left the residence, and walked outside.

It was hot. Summer was here, yet I had no song...

I'd hoped. I'd prayed. I'd waited. Still nothing...

I began walking, with my heart sinking heavy, and tears close.

Not a stanza, or tune I could hum and fill out the words.

I felt...empty, and without purpose. It was one thing to call your-self a singer; and something else to actually sing. I walked past a lamp-post, then a fire hydrant next, and continued.

I traveled in the direction of JB's farm. When I got there a half hour later, I tromped past it and didn't stop, and I didn't glance either. I kept going. Something had to give. I wouldn't continue like this.

Wandering aimlessly in life, with no purpose, and no fulfillment. Precious time was ticking…

Sweat soaked my face, neck, and arms.

The shirt glued to my skin.

After another half hour, the sun burned hot by the time I made it up the hill. I'd never made it this far.

No cars passed me anymore, just farmland stretched far as I could see on both sides.

My ankles hurt.

But I kept going.

Lord, I only asked for one song. One. Something to wipe the shame off my face. I left New York, and came here. I knew no one. But I simply trusted.

I stumbled on a piece of rock. I kicked it to the side, dusted off myself, and kept walking.

The sun beat my head fiercely.

I felt my brain thumping inside, with my heart pumping hard trying hard to keep up.

Tears flooded my vision, and a sob broke out.

Lord, why am I here if You won't give me a song? Why?

The road path came to an end ahead. The farmland faded behind me and light brushes took its place.

The road now had sand, with rough grasses growing from cracks in it.

A small felled log laid across at the end, marked as a roadblock for anyone sure enough to get so far.

My body trembled.

I'd run out of water long ago.

I'd walked, prayed, worried, and thought. Everything weighed heavily on me.

When I reached the felled log, my eyes spun. My legs burned. My ankles hurt sore. My thighs felt bruised.

I still kept going. I was carelessly crying aloud, my stinging throat baring my frustration, and pouring them forth in tears.

There was no one here to hear me.

I felt shoved to the ground by the sheer weight of responsibility surrounding me.

My faith in my ability to write a song waned.

Sharp heat tore hard into my back, burning hot, but I couldn't care less.

I had no idea how far I'd traveled. Staring at the felled log, I collapsed to my knees, weak, tired, frustrated, and fed up. I pressed a knee against it for support.

I bowed my face into my hands between my knees and let out a cry from deep within my soul.

A cry of one name. "Jesussssss!"

Twenty-two weeks and not a single song. I'm out of patience, out of time, and out of hope. Answer me, O Lord!

Tears tumbled as I shed more in my heart than out loud.

My breath grew raspy.

The air felt thin, and my body grew heavy.

I got lightheaded and dizzy, eyelids drooping.

Running feet thudded close behind me, but I was too tired and had no strength to turn.

I swung side to side, my head twirled, and the back of my head was set to hit the ground.

Firm hands slid behind my neck.

A face came between me and the sun.

"Candace! Breathe." The face seemed familiar.

JB.

I grabbed his arm. "I've got a song!"

Joyful gratitude welled from within, as I felt a smile tug the corners of my parched lips briefly.

I inhaled a deep breath, and my arms fell asleep beside me, as everywhere turned brightly white.

CHAPTER 22

 B

CANDACE RODRIGUEZ. I'd seen it on her face. The flicker of interest that had flashed in her eyes while I walked her home yesterday. But as fast as it came, it was gone. And sadly, I knew the reason.

The problem was that I wasn't in the league of her past relationships. I was a farmer. She didn't want a farmer. The glimmer of hope that what was laid on my heart had a chance of becoming real, died there. Saying good night to her then was saying bye to any chance of a relationship.

I'd made up my mind so I spoke to God in prayer last night.

God, what you placed in my heart to ask her, she doesn't want it. I can't force her.

Moreover, she was famous, and had lived a high life. I wasn't sure that I could keep up with it, nor with the publicity and temptations accompanying it.

In addition, I didn't know how serious she was in her faith.

Was this just a passing phase? Or was it permanent? I swallowed hard.

Jesus was my everything. Any woman I approached now, I intended to marry, and Candace Rodriguez left a lot of doubt in my heart.

Until now.

After laying her head gently against the ground, I rushed to my truck.

Pushing the gear in reverse, I backed up until she was adjacent to the side doors. I left my door ajar, ran over, and lifted her.

"Argh!" I grunted. No one else was around to assist me.

Somehow, I lifted her upper body to knee height. Three paces and her head touched the seat. I pushed and slid her in headfirst into the chair and then shut the door.

I ran back and entered the driver's seat.

Pressing into drive, I raced toward my farm.

Within two minutes, I parked across the lawn and jumped down. One hand on my keys and the other on my phone, I shouted to one of my men who casually loaded produce onto a truck, "Get me some water! Fast!"

He raced into the house while I called emergency services.

"Hello, I need an ambulance at 265 Hope Lane, Day Spring Farms Circuit...."

The man returned, and I sent him off again. "Get the Cantwells!" He knew them. I'd sent him to deliver Grandma Patty's letter to Mrs. Cantwell when I was out negotiating for new freezers.

He ran off.

I opened the back passenger door and ran to open the opposite door to allow cross ventilation.

Lifting her head, I splashed some chilled water onto her forehead, as it felt hot to the touch.

Kneeling on the base of the truck, I cradled her head in my arms. She appeared so vulnerable and tender.

My heart filled with love for this creature, worn from the troubles of life. I wished good for her, and wanted her to know that she was stronger than her tests if she stood rooted in Christ.

Her hair, pure black and peach-scented, fell onto the seat, and subtly blended in with its dark leather covers. I held her, hoping and praying.

God, please, give me another chance, and I'll ask her. If she says no, I won't like it...but I'd have obeyed You.

* * *

CANDACE

"Where am I?" The bed creaked. The lighting was dim, and curtains fluttered to the breeze of an air conditioner.

"Hospital." Someone stepped close and peered in my face.

The shoulder length red curls and petite shape ID her. Mrs. Cantwell. To her right stood JB, then Dr. Cantwell—as they all lined the left side of the bed, observing me.

I pressed back against the pillow beneath my head.

"Why? I mean, what happened?" A smile then stretched my face when I recalled it as I urgently scanned side to side for something to write with. I saw none.

"The song! Pen. Paper! Now, please!"

All three scrambled, and searched.

I spotted my phone next to me on the bed. I grabbed it and began typing fast.

"Got it!" They stopped the frantic search and stood, waiting for my fingers to stop.

My thumbs fired away at the phone's keyboard. Then...full stop.

I grinned, threw my head back, and laughed.

Mrs. Cantwell folded her arms, a hand on her chest. Her huge relief—for me—spread across her face.

Placing my phone on the bedside, I cleared my throat and glanced at each of them, face to face. "Wait, what was wrong with me again?"

They looked at each other and burst out laughing.

Dr. Cantwell waved a dismissive hand and turned to his wife. "She's all right now. We might as well help them discharge her."

Dr. Cantwell and his wife slipped out of the room. His wife leaned back and waved a small hand before their backs disappeared, leaving us both alone.

JB stood silent by my bedside. Then he bent over, took my hand in his, and squeezed it. I remembered his words, his face, and that moment of my surrender.

He was looking into my eyes softly, a softness I hadn't observed before. "You fainted. Medically, that's what happened. They're suspecting dehydration. You were in the sun and exposed to it for too long in very high temperature."

I ignored the mild chiding in his tone. After all, he saved my life and earned the right to say that. Had he not been there... I squeezed the hand he still held over mine and smiled. "Thanks for saving me. I don't know what I would have done."

He nodded slightly, lips drawing thin.

Something weighed on him. I'd seen that look when he told me about his Wall Street fall. He withdrew his hand slowly.

Now I remember. He'd called me Candace just before I passed out. That was the first time. But I'd seen the look in his eyes at that moment....

Oh, Lord!

He pulled a chair over and sat. "You're welcome. Now you owe me a whole concert."

I chuckled. "We can make that happen. Now that I got my song."

JB leaned close, his arms rested on the raised side bar. He gazed into my eyes, fresh concern lining his. "You scared me. You were lucky I was driving in as you walked past my farm. I'd wondered where you were headed so I made a turn and came up to see you falling."

He rubbed his forehead. "It was tough finding help. I got you into my truck and sped to the farm."

He carried me? I swallowed, fearing my earlier thoughts were true but not totally embracing them. He couldn't love me. He was being a nice neighbor. That was all.

"I called an ambulance. Then the Cantwells came. You were still breathing. Luckily the medics didn't need to do much."

He placed his phone into his shirt pocket. "I told them you were probably out in the sun too long. And it was still very hot. So they pumped you with IV fluid."

Wincing, I stirred my head away. I'd caused so many people trouble due to my desperation. "I'm sorry for all the trouble. I should've turned back once I ran out of water."

He leaned in and touched my hand as his eyes scanned my face. "The song, was it worth it?"

I smiled, tilting my chin. "JB, I've prayed and waited for almost six months for it. Yes, it was worth every minute."

I turned to the side. "All this while, I wanted a song everyone could accept, including non-Christians."

I shrugged, feeling suddenly vulnerable. "A moral song, not necessarily a Christian song. I could sing, 'you, we,' instead of 'Lord, Jesus, I'. Stuff like that."

I chuckled again. "Who was I kidding?"

He pinned a hand to his jaw, fully attentive.

I looked him in the eyes. "That was what I prayed for until that day on the hill. I let go and embraced all of Christ. I surrendered all of me to Him."

My voice cracked. "I'd given up so much. I was scared of going all-in. As I walked along that road, my frustration peaked."

I bowed and shook my head. "I had a choice. To go back to my former life and hope for the best, or give all-in to Jesus and allow Him to control my music."

I placed a hand to my mouth as the memory of that victory flooded back.

"My music is my life. Whoever controls it, controls me. Jesus has it all now and I've got peace." I wiped a stray tear. "The song came in my moment of surrender. It flooded me like an awareness, it flowed stanza by stanza. It wasn't a song as much as it was an experience. I was seeing it in my mind's eye. It felt incredible!

"If I'd given in sooner, maybe I could've had my song earlier…" I swiped another tear. "I'm just glad He answered my prayers. Truly." Joy tore through my tears.

JB took my hand again, and leaned closer to the rail. "Jesus said in Scripture, 'You can't put new wine into old wineskin, you need a new wineskin for new wine. Your waiting was not wasted. You've grown. He's changed you on the inside. The new you can pour out His praise unhindered. Congratulations, Candace. You've broken through."

We joined both our hands, and I squealed in delight, the IV line dangling along and all.

"I can't wait to get back to the farm and sing it!"

He eyed me quizzically, withdrew his hand, and pulled out his phone. "My phone has a voice recorder. Wanna do a rough draft now so you don't forget it?"

My phone's memory has been full a while leaving no space on it. If I used his, I could always tweak it later.

"Sure," I said. "Let's do it."

He entered the password on his phone, and it unlocked. Then he glanced up. "Oh, password is 1225, you know Christmas Day. I'm telling you in case you need to retrieve the song later, and I'm not there."

Whoa! Wait, did he just trust me with the password for his phone?

Ray never did that. I recall our fight over it. Safe to say, it wasn't pretty.

"Um, okay thanks."

He held out the phone to me. "Whenever you're ready, Candace."

At his prompt, I drew in a deep breath, sat up a bit, and then braced a pillow on my back for support. I leaned into his phone facing me. It was already recording.

I closed my eyes, and focused on the Lord, with my heart full of gratitude. My mouth opened, and I let the song flow out as I'd seen it play in my heart:

FEARLESS LOVE

CHORUS: I hold onto Love, Fearless Love,

I cling onto hope, endless hope,

I dig in the fight, the fight of faith,

The fight of freedom,
The fight of love,
Fearless Love.
VERSE 1: I've had enough,
Fear making me run,
Scared out of my wits,
What does tomorrow hold?
Where will I end?
Will my past or future rule?
No more will fear run my course.
CHORUS
VERSE 2:
I press delete on all my fear,
Doubt, tears, and pain take flight,
I let go of anxiety for tomorrow, pursue today,
Minute by minute, hour by hour,
Held by Christ, helped by faith,
Believing in Fearless Love.
CHORUS
LAST VERSE: Today the sun rose, I did too,
A fresh slate on which to dream,
On which to hope,
On which to work,
Powered by Fearless Love.
CHORUS

I repeated the chorus twice for good measure, in case I lost the tune later, and then sang the verses.

Done, I opened my eyes. JB was staring at me, his eyes wide, and smiling ear to ear. He pressed the phone to stop recording. "Sorry. I just couldn't—that was amazing! I could literally feel it. "

He looked up, put down his phone, and rose, applauding.

Tears of appreciation filled my eyes. "Thank you. I will tweak the verses later, but the chorus is good as is. Thank you so much."

Dr. Cantwell and Dr. Mrs. Cantwell strode into the room. A

doctor followed closely, and a stethoscope hung from his shoulders. "You okay?"

"Yes, I'm okay. Can I go home now?"

JB pointed to me. "She's got a great song. You got to listen to it!"

Mrs. Cantwell rushed forward and grabbed my hands. "Praise God!"

She drew closer. "All those days at the garden, with you muttering in prayer. I knew what you must be praying for. I didn't want to increase the burden by asking. I'd prayed for you instead. I'm so happy."

She turned to her husband, and he nodded.

The other doctor looked at me and smiled. "We'll get your discharge paperwork started. Your vitals appear okay. You should be fine to go."

Dr. Cantwell exclaimed. "You all heard, let's help get this princess home. She's got a song to work on!" They clapped in celebration.

The moment stamped deep in my memory. Three strangers had become family to me, and they were now key to my divine destiny.

Thank You, Jesus!

CHAPTER 23

*M*rs. Cantwell ushered me up, gingerly guiding my steps.

"I can walk, you know."

But she wouldn't have it. She cooked up a storm for dinner and brought me food to feed an army.

"I can't eat all this. If you gave me three days, I still couldn't eat it all."

She shrugged. "Then I suggest you better get started."

She stopped at the door. "You'd better eat enough, or I'm calling the doctor."

I laughed. "Are you threatening me to eat?"

She pretended to be serious. "Yes, I am."

With those words, she shut the residence door and left me alone with my thoughts, surrounded by trays of food.

I bowed my head. "Father God, thank You—for everything. The food, the song, and the peace. I have rest in You, in Jesus' name, amen."

I picked up my spoon, but felt like I wasn't done praying. I bowed again. "Thank You, Lord, for what it took to get me here. It took all of You working on all that I am, changing me, transforming my mind. All the way…"

I felt a song coming. I dropped my spoon and raced.

Notepad!

I'd lost it on the road earlier. "Argh!" I frantically searched my purse.

Found one. I ran to the couch, tore off a piece of paper, and wrote, hand scribbling fast.

ALL FOR YOU – LYRICS

VERSE 1:

Part of me cried, part of me sang,

All of me waited, for You, my God.

Anything broken, everything You changed,

Better than new, better than the old.

CHORUS: This is me, but this is You,

The new me is all of You,

Is all for You.

This is me, made new by You,

All of me, shows all of You, Jesus

And only You.

VERSE 2: Now I'm complete in You,

Now I cling to You alone,

Because I'd fallen but now I'm risen,

To meet You again,

To be all You made me to be.

Now I'm free,

To be me, to believe,

That all of You is more than enough,

For me.

VERSE 3: All of my days I will sing of Your praise,

Sing of Your glory,

The power that made me free,
All of me, is all for You, Savior,
And all of me, is all for You, Lord,
All of me, forever for You, Jesus!
THANK YOU, JESUS!

I put my pen down and laughed, then wiped sweat off my brow. Whew!

I struck gold twice in one day!

I continued working on the stanzas, fine-tuning them. I pushed the tray of food aside. On second thought, I remembered Mrs. Cantwell's warning. So I grabbed an apple and took a bite. I began to sing out aloud, alter tones, sing in soft tunes, then louder ones.

A rap at the door interrupted me.

I turned. "Come on in!"

I hoped I'd yelled loud enough.

"It's me. I brought a visitor. JB. I know it's late, but he insisted on coming to check on you before heading home. May we come in?"

What? Mrs. Cantwell—and JB?

I peered down. I hadn't changed from the clothes I was taken to the hospital in.

Too late to change now. "One minute!" I smoothed out my blouse, slipped under a light blanket in bed, and stretched out my feet.

That should do it. "Come on in."

They entered and met me chewing an apple.

Mrs. Cantwell observed me narrowly, then looked over at the table.

"I—"

She raised a hand so I fell silent.

Uh-oh.

"Two bananas and an apple." She turned.

I waited then responded. "Yes."

She smiled. "Good job. Now you can chat with him while I stack these up."

JB walked in tentatively, steps a little unsure. "Just wanted to see if you were settled in okay. If you need anything, call me."

I was grinning ear to ear. Then I raised two fingers.

He stared at them appearing a bit confused. Then he got it. He bridged the gap in two strides. "Another song!"

"Yes!"

He embraced me then let me go.

Mrs. Cantwell stopped, a plate midair. "That is fantastic."

JB yanked his phone out. "Have you recorded it yet?"

I shook my head, and pointed to the piece of paper. "I literally just wrote it."

He halted, phone still held out. "You got a tune?"

I chuckled. "Sure yeah."

He pressed the Record button.

They listened as I sang, chorus and verses till the end.

They looked at each other, then at me, with their mouths agape.

"Wait. Was it the banana or the apple that induced the song? 'Cuz I can get you more."

We laughed. Mrs. Cantwell and her food jokes always made me crack a smile.

"Neither. Blessing the food did it."

I was feeling a little weak. Delivering two songs in one day, after passing out wasn't exactly how I'd figured this day would go. JB, who still had his phone in hand, stood close.

"Can I have your number, please?"

I wrote my number on the paper and gave it to him. I figured we'd need to communicate regarding the songs. He took it.

"I'm so grateful for your help with the recordings. Thank you."

He nodded. "I got you, Candace."

Our eyes locked. I broke the gaze first and turned to Mrs. Cantwell. "Thank you for the food, Mrs. Cantwell. Mighty kind of you."

"You're welcome. Now you rest that pretty head o' yours."

She lifted the dishes and moved toward the door. JB trailed behind closely.

* * *

I REACHED for the ringing phone. "Hello?"

Brittle laughter cut through.

"Wit!"

I knew the voice but I was still trying to place it…

"Just checking to see how things are going?"

Oh. John. Ugh.

I pressed the phone close to my ear and sat, disillusioned. I was supposed to start my workout at seven.

It was 7:02.

"Hi, John. Is there a problem?" I knew he was never good news.

He cleared his throat. "Not that I know of."

Silence.

God, what has this man got up his sleeve this time?

"I've approved all you asked for. Team, backup equipment, stage construction…everything. I'm just not sure if we have any…songs yet." His brittle laughter followed again, and this time it sounded more like an ancient broken record.

He mocked me.

Well, surprise, John. "Yes."

He coughed as though my answer choked him. "Oh."

Silence again.

"Okay. Do you need anything else to make this happen, Candace?"

I'm totally done with this man's antics.

I ground my teeth close to the phone. "Just one more thing, John. Do me a favor, stay out of my way!"

I shut the call down and tossed the phone to the couch, breathing hard.

That was rarely the type of cardio I'd prepped for.

John was set to mock me?

I'd blow his mind. I climbed on the elliptical, with renewed zeal burning in my soul.

Workout time? I set it to two hours.

Difficulty level? High.

I pressed Start and began to row hard, giving my all with each pull.

I'm working for my After—and nothing will stop me.

* * *

"Scrambled eggs, quinoa, grilled salmon fillet, chopped spinach, and sprouted Ezekiel bread, with a cup of tea." She placed the meal in front of me.

I smiled. My kind of ideal breakfast.

This woman has done so much for me. I couldn't thank her enough.

She poured more ice tea into our individual cups.

"Mrs. Cantwell, thank you. For everything. For taking me under your roof at my toughest time, and for supporting me. I'm grateful to you and your husband. I don't know what I would have done without you both." My voice cracked a bit with emotion.

She came close and whispered, "Thank God instead, Candace. 'The earth is the Lord's and the fullness thereof.' Wherever God leads you, you stay there, you occupy, because you know He owns it all. We are glad to help you. Now you finish your meal or I'll help you out." She winked. Dr. Cantwell joined us right before I was done, and his wife had waited for him to arrive before she began to eat. That was something they typically did.

We both laughed as I set about my meal, relishing every bite.

Back at the residence later, I showered, soaked my feet in Epsom salt, ironed a few clothes, and slipped into a long summer dress. I turned and checked it in the mirror. Size XL, no longer XXXL. I felt accomplished.

I looked quite different from six months ago!

I saw the changes more now. I twisted for a fuller view.

Not bad.

I raised my arms. Hmmm. I still got some work to do there.

I chuckled.

I hated push-ups. But they were working these arms nicely. I walked to the bed and grabbed my purse.

It was time to go. I exited the residence, and passed the flagstone path, as I made my way to the home. Turning the corner to the steps, I ran straight into JB. "Oh, I'm so sorry!"

We both staggered then steadied ourselves.

His lips curved into a smile.

"I guess we could never meet in a non-clumsy manner."

I grinned, feeling a tad nervous.

He scanned me head to toe, eyes filled with admiration. "You, for one, look much better than yesterday. Looking good, Candace."

He called me by my name, for the third time.

Candace…

I rushed a glance through my attire. "You mean while I was fainting, or wearing the hospital gown?"

"Both." He offered a steadying hand and I took it.

"Thanks. So do you. You look good, and you're not in a shirt today."

He was wearing arm length tees and jeans for the third time, not trouser pants like I typically saw him wearing. Scent of his aftershave tickled my nostrils but I focused on the Cantwell's main home.

"Ah, well, I'm not on duty right now." He glanced at my hand, where my purse hung low, before letting go. "Where are you off to?"

I pointed toward the road. "Oh, I'm heading into town for a few items. I was just going over to tell Mrs. Cantwell."

"Can I drive you to town?"

I did want to avoid having to wait for a taxi to and back. I hadn't even called them yet. Plus, he could insist.

I nodded and smiled. "Okay. I accept."

We walked up to the stairs and at the top step, right before I knocked at the Cantwells, JB took my hand in his.

I twisted, curious.

His face contoured with a serious expression, brows drawn together. A worry line creased his forehead. "Candace. I need to ask you something."

I shifted to face him fully. "All right."

His lips thinned, as though struggling with putting the words out. Behind me, inside the Cantwells home, voices approached the door. I guessed that it could be Mrs. Cantwell. She probably saw me walking over but didn't see me enter yet and was coming to get the door.

I fixed my eyes on JB, giving him my full attention. I didn't make to pull my hand away. The softness of his palm and firmness of his hold felt quite comforting.

We'd gotten closer over the past two days, more than the friendliness we shared during my weekly dairy run.

He stared into my eyes, searching. Our gazes held.

I'd never really looked this closely at him before. I'd been busy either buying dairy, eggs, meat, or falling down. So much hope etched those sandy brown eyes. His straight nose dauntingly sat above full lips.

"All things are possible to them that believe." His long lashes fluttered.

No sooner were the words out of his lips than the door creaked open behind me.

I spun.

Was I seeing things now?

Familiar brilliant blue eyes slammed into mine, with the force of the past sweeping into my present.

My grip on JB tightened. Then I let his hand go and turned, eyes and spine steeled.

"Ray," I said casually, making him know we had nothing special any longer.

Mrs. Cantwell scanned me. "Candace, I was coming to let you know someone's here to see you." Her sharp expression mirrored my resolve.

The pain of his let down soared to the fore of my mind.

I smiled at her. "Thank you, Mrs. Cantwell." She reversed and went back into the house, leaving the door slightly open.

I should've spotted the rental cruiser parked in front of JB's truck at the driveway before now but I wasn't paying attention. Even if I saw it, there was no way to tell that it was Ray.

First things first.

I looked at JB. "Please give us a minute. Thank you."

JB firmed his jaw and looked from Ray to me. "I'm meters away if you need—anything."

I simply nodded as he walked away.

Emotions fought inside me. *Do I yell at him, tell him off, or just walk away like he isn't there...?* I struggled to keep my emotions in check.

I'll show maturity instead...

"Hi," I said flatly.

He chuckled, and then frowned. "Really, Candace? That all you can say to your fiancé?"

I stepped up sharply, and stood toe to toe. "Ex-fiancé! I trust you got your ring and stuff back several months ago?" My emotions got the better of me on this one. I drew a calming breath, walked to the corner, and stood under the large tree with the dangling red toy car.

Why—?

He came up behind me.

I swung around. "What are you doing here, Ray? Who told you where I am?"

He laughed. "Candace! Living on a farm? Had to come see for myself. I got it from your brother."

Matt....

"What do you want?" My phone buzzed, and I looked down.

It was a text message. "When the past comes calling, don't answer. It has nothing new to say. JB"

I smiled then faced Ray.

"I wanted to see if we're, you know..." He talked but wasn't really saying anything at all.

So typical of him. He was here to see if I missed him so much, or was so lonely on a farm that I'd throw myself into his arms.

His rules, for my obedience? Not a chance.

I looked him right in the eyes. "We were over the day you called and told me so, the day I fell. Remember? You walked away, not me. I wasn't strong enough to leave you then. Now? I'm a completely different person. Thank God. I don't need you, Ray."

He grew soft. He leaned in a little, seeking to hold my gaze. "Candace. Remember the day I asked you to marry me? How happy you were. We were supposed to build our lives together. Until you..."

changed. You asked me to move out. I did, didn't I? We can work things out."

I wasn't going to fall for this, though the nostalgic memory twisted my heart a bit. I *was* happy the day he proposed. It was in fact, one of my happiest days. At the top of the Empire State Building. He and my team composed a song ending in, "will you marry me?"

I was overjoyed. *No, I can't afford reminiscing right now.*

Too much was at stake…

I fought back tears—tears I'd held in since the day I reached this farm determined not to shed them over a man ever again.

"I don't ever want someone who makes me feel needy or power-less. Moreover," I chuckled, "someone once told me that you and I don't mix, like oil and water. Remember? Goodbye, Ray."

I turned, but he grabbed my arm and swung me to face him.

JB jumped out his truck and Ray gave him a rough look. I beck-oned on him not to intervene.

I returned my attention to Ray, and then glanced down at his grip on me.

He stepped closer with hurried breath.

I'd never stood up to him before. Until now.

He wasn't used to hearing no.

"I got something you might want to hear."

My mouth curved downward. "Speak."

He positioned himself like he was about to score a major point. "All right. I talked to Global Sound Records. They're willing to have you back if you'd only agree to sing what they've arranged for you."

I should have known. Bait and hook. "Hmmm. What would that be?"

He shrugged. "The final songs you composed with them. I don't know the details, I didn't ask."

I stood up close to him, eyeball to eyeball, and laughed. "You know, Ray. If you had shown up seven days ago, I might have been tempted, desperate even and caved."

I pointed downward, my lips as firm as my made up mind. "That

197

was then. This is now. Tell them Candace said no thank you." I bristled. "Enjoy your trip back, Ray."

I shrugged off his arm and walked way.

When I got to JB's truck, he held the door open as I climbed in. Its alloy rim sparkled in the sunlight.

Waving to Mrs. Cantwell, through the window, he shouted, "I'll return your princess in one piece."

Mrs. Cantwell laughed, shutting her door. "Sure! See you, Candace!"

That, in Mrs. Cantwell-speak, meant "we haven't talked about what's going on yet".

I waved to her too. The truck roared into the street, and I glanced and saw Ray returning to his car as my past disappeared in the rearview mirror.

CHAPTER 24

"*W*here do you want to shop first?"

I shrugged, glancing from side to side at the stores we drove past in downtown Silver Spring.

"I need a scale, a weight scale. The store should be about three blocks over on the right, after a stop sign." I'd found the shop on the internet.

I pressed Refresh on my navigator app.

Shortly, we reached the store, and he parked. He followed me into the store.

A sales associate greeted us at the entrance. "Welcome. Can I help you find something?"

I stepped up to her. JB followed close behind protectively.

"I need some weight scales. I found the—" I pulled the slip of paper from my pocket and read it out loud, "Taylor Model 7506 Glass Electronic Scale, said to be quite accurate and to measure up to 400 pounds. Do you have it in stock?"

She pointed in a direction, opposite the entrance. "If we do, it will be in the fitness section, along the far side wall. You should locate it easily, under scales."

I walked down to the fitness aisle; JB stayed close, but not too close. He stepped aside to take a phone call while I continued.

There! I recognized its transparent glass and iron base features from the online picture. Lifting it, I read the tag.

"Hmmm...39.99. Not bad, for something you buy once," JB offered.

"And never again, except batteries." I chuckled, flipping the back to check for them.

He pointed at it as I found a pair, taped to it. "Right. Batteries you do have to replace. This looks good, and it should work."

With my choice finalized, we walked to the register. "I didn't want to always wait until we go to the clinic to check my weight. It is good to know what it is any day, anytime."

He nodded. "Good decision. Never sacrifice convenience if you can. It's always better to have your own stuff." Was he still speaking of the scale?

We paid, and exited the store. We made two more stops for sneakers, socks, and food. After grabbing a meal, we headed back to the farm.

* * *

JB

The best way to capture the image of a rare beauty, is to squat low to its eye level, or even lower. That's the secret of photography.

The secret of love? The same, except you crouch even lower. Candace Rodriguez did not happen into my life by accident but by divine design.

The master architect lowered the barricade, felled her false foundations, and led her to my path.

As I finished the phone call with Mrs. Cantwell on the delivered package, eyes fully admiring Candace while she joyfully shopped, I could only wonder what her reaction would be to the discovery of what my heart held safe for her.

"I'm glad you went with me." Her dark intuitive eyes flew to mine as we drove back.

"And I'm quite glad that I came along." There were so many words yet to be spoken between us, but I was willing to wait.

* * *

CANDACE

As JB roared the engine and slid into traffic, a wind-blown loose strand of dark-brown hair fell to the side of his face in a spiral curl. I resisted the urge to help him tuck it behind his ear. In a moment, he instinctively tucked it, and I tore my eyes away. He tilted his head slightly, clicked the blinker, spied the left side mirror to change his lane, and slid past a crawling garbage truck.

Looking him over, there was nothing strikingly dashing about him or superficial to chase after. But he was treasure whose worth lay within. It took time to draw it out. His quiet spirit was homey and welcoming, restful.

That drew me. He used a hand to push his hair back, revealing the scar that disappeared into his hairline. "How did you get the scar?"

He didn't look. "An accident when I was a kid."

"Oh, I'm sorry."

I could tell he was fighting battles, just like I was fighting mine.

"How long have you been off Wall Street? A year, two?"

His jaw tightened. I'd sure struck a raw nerve with that one.

"Seven years." He gripped the wheel tighter.

"The higher you were, the quicker your exit when things crashed." He threw his gaze sideways. "But I should've seen it coming. I mistook quicksand for solid ground until I sank waist deep."

He sighed. "If not for the Lord…"

He grimaced a grin, a nerve twisting in his neck.

Again, he depressed the blinker, signaled a right turn. We exited heavy traffic off the I-95 Highway then entered lighter but slower traffic, headed toward the farms.

He glanced quickly before making a right turn. "I forgot I didn't get there on my own. That it was God who made my hard work turn successful."

I exhaled deeply. "I'm sorry."

"No need." He shook his head. "The only thing I'm sorry about— was that spending all my savings wasn't enough to save my mom from cancer. She died not too long ago."

This man was rugged outside, but gentle inside.

He fell, but didn't allow life to keep him down. I admired his determination and respected him even more now.

I wasn't sure if I would've liked the rich, Wall Street stock trader JB. But the one sitting across from me now? Was a remarkable man.

"Don't hate me okay, just one more question."

His razor-sharp instinct and discerning eyes stared into mine and stirred something deep I'd rather keep down. His gaze flew back to the road.

Did he feel that? I did. A connection beyond words.

Finish up your cup of curiosity, Candace.

"Is JB your real name or short for something?"

His eyes jerked from the road to me in a split second, then back on it.

I'd crossed a line. He ground his teeth and pressed his lips.

Too late, curious cat.

He blinked severely, his arm muscle rippling as he gripped the wheel tighter then softened. "Its not something I typically share. Jabez, that's my full name."

Got more questions, Candace?

Not for a long while.

Everything must have to do with his name. Jabez. How... I coughed and stopped myself. Enough for one day.

I glanced at my hands, unable to bear the pain evident in his expression.

Clearly, I'd drummed up something he'd rather keep buried. He must've thought highly of me to share it.

"Thank you for telling me. I'm sorry if I crossed a line."

JB straightened, navigating a final turn. "I knew you meant well."

We'd arrived to the Cantwells' farm.

He parked, then hurried over and opened my door.

"Thank you." I gladly stepped onto the familiar turf.

He reached beside me for the shopping bags. He carried them up to the door of the residence and leaned them against it.

I slowly followed.

He took one look at me, and he burst out laughing.

What was funny? "What, JB?" I crinkled my eyes for emphasis.

He pointed at my feet. "Your feet are sore. I see it in your walk."

I smiled, exhaling.

Can we add observant to the list of his attributes? I'd hoped though, that he wouldn't notice.

Hand pinned on my waist, I tilted my chin. "Laughing at my soreness, are you?"

He laughed even harder, his arms crossed.

I wagged a threatening finger. "Don't you laugh too hard, because I promise I'm coming over to get my belly of laughs too, when those chickens send you running after them in hot pursuit!"

He still laughed a little but took steps away from me.

"How did you know?"

His eyes narrowed. "I do move this body once in a while and I get sore too. Ever heard, 'so sore it felt good'? I don't believe that—at all. Sore hurts."

He wasn't into sugarcoating.

I picked up the bags, searching for my keys. "I'm still coming."

He shrugged playfully. "Suit yourself. The chickens aren't going anywhere. Hey, you never know, they might even like you."

So he's got tough skin, huh? I smiled.

I had a friend like that in college but we lost contact. Now it was good to have someone to trade laughs with.

"It's a deal, JB," I said as he began walking to the road, and his slight bowleg curved with his steps.

I unlocked the residence door and piled my stuff inside. When I entered, it appeared a little dark, so I switched on the light.

A wrapped package sat on the desk. I strode toward it. The only person with a second key was Mrs. Cantwell. A solid white cardboard tag dangled from on it. Red ink scrawled, "Open. It's a surprise."

No sender, and no return address. This had to be local.

The tag folded closed like a card.

I flipped it.

The same pen and penmanship scrawled, "For a fearless lady" on the other side.

I glanced at the door. I could go ask Mrs. Cantwell who the sender was.

She might tell...or not. I sighed. *Open it already.*

How hard could this be? I ripped open the packaging carefully, starting from the side.

The content felt flat at the center and felt hard to the touch. A firm, solid item.

"Hmmm." I carried it to the couch, sat down, and lifted it to see the base.

A convenience seal was lightly glued to the bottom.

I peeled it and released the rest of the wrapper.

A Fragile: Handle With Care sticker affixed it there.

After taking it off, I opened the package completely, and set it on my lap. It was a piece of art, engraved in cultured glass.

"Beautiful!" I gasped.

Engraved flower images decorated the corners. Imprinted letters chiseled into the glass core. A deep blue color painted over them.

I touched the bold words at the top. "Fearless Love". The chorus, in smaller, but equally breathtaking print followed them.

Only one person had heard "Fearless Love". Same person to whom I sang it at the hospital and recorded the lyrics on his cell phone. JB. I ran my fingers across the rough indent of the words, feeling the love of every carving.

There were no stanzas. He must've remembered that I'd said the verses weren't finalized. He made this for me. Overnight. While I was recovering, he was working. What kind of man was this?

"Wow."

I laid it gingerly on the couch and raced to the main house.

Mrs. Cantwell didn't answer when I sang out a greeting.

"Hello?" Maybe she was upstairs. I walked deeper into a dark house but it was very quiet.

I headed into the kitchen.

A handwritten note sat atop the counter and I flipped it over.

Candace, if you're reading this, the hubby and I are out visiting a young friend of the family who just delivered a baby boy. We'll be headed back around seven p.m. Hope you enjoyed your trip to town with JB? Cheers.

P.S. A little gift came in for ya. It's at the residence. Enjoy!

Yup, I'd seen it already.

I placed the card down flat so she'd know I'd read it. Then I went to the fridge.

Pulling its handle, I bent over.

Out came the salad, baked chicken, and basmati rice I'd made two days earlier. Heating up the mix, without the salad, in the microwave, I grabbed a fork, and spoon and filled up a glass of water.

I didn't take sufficient water while downtown because I didn't want to need a bathroom break on the road.

Which wouldn't make sense unless you're someone who drank a gallon of water per day, and as a consequence, would pee like twenty times!

I grinned as the microwave beeped, and I picked up my food, set everything on a tray, and made my way back to the residence, ready to sit and eat up.

I needed the block of time from now until tonight to focus and finish writing the two songs I already had—"Fearless Love" and "All for You"—and pray over them.

I should call JB to thank him. On second thought, it was better, I'd conveniently go over during my regular evening stroll. I rose, found a hook nailed to the wall near the PC station, then hung up the art, with gratitude welling in my heart.

Hours later, I went to see JB like I'd promised myself I'd do.

True to type, he was out on his farm working hard. I found him at the chicken pen, wearing rubber boots, pouring in some feed. As he opened the gate, a hen followed him out. He tried to chase it back in, and it flew toward the opposite direction.

I laughed so hard my sides hurt.

He grunted. "It's not funny."

I laughed louder, pointing at the chicken wobbling over his head. But it didn't perch on him. It flew over him, aiming toward me. I turned and fled but stumbled over something and crashed to the ground.

I flipped around, and leaned on my elbows, with my back on the green grass in time for the chicken to land on my tummy. It flapped its wings and cuckooed.

I screamed.

JB held out a hand. "Stay calm, Candace. It won't hurt you."

It kept cuckooing loudly.

I shook in panic.

"Calm? There's a live chicken on my tummy!"

He approached, but the chicken turned its beak toward him, forcing him to stop.

"Help me, JB," I muttered.

He took his shirt off and rolled it into a ball. "Hang on, Candace." Eyes pinned on the chicken, he took a step sideways, handing me the balled shirt.

"What am I supposed to do with this? Smother it?" If he thought I was staying calm, he had another thing coming.

"You'll see…" His eyes remained trained on the chicken.

The chicken bent low, and something warm plopped on my belly.

Excreta? "Oh no!"

The chicken ruffled its feathers then slowly trotted off my tummy but stayed close, and appeared guarded.

I raised my head.

A raw egg, not excreta. It laid an egg on me!

I laughed. "Use the shirt to gently pick up the egg."

JB shuffled. But the hen rushed forward, and he froze in his steps again.

"It's protecting both you and its egg. As you move it, keep the egg visible at all times, lay the shirt with the egg on the ground, as low as possible, where it can see it."

I did as he said, gently picking up the egg, and placing it inside the shirt, then laying both on the ground with the egg on top. The bird got close, then saw its egg, and stopped.

It sat over the egg and stopped its cuckoo as JB assisted me to my feet. I dusted off sand and grass.

JB was smiling. "I told you they'd like you."

I punched his arm. "For egg-laying purposes!"

* * *

JB

I jolted from sleep only to realize that I was dreaming. My chest rose and fell quickly as did my recollection. As I ran a hand over my hair, my fingers stumbled over the reason for the nightmare. How I got the scar on my head. I shuddered at the memory and took a deep steady breath, exhaling from my mouth. Sweat damped my shirt.

I hated nights like this when that altercation between Mom and Dad when I was a child morphed into something worse. Everything changed then.

There, I'd sworn to be a better man than my father. To treat women with respect and courtesy. Of course, I couldn't tell Candace everything that led to this scar—at least not yet. Sharing that it was an accident was sufficient. After all, it was. Preventable, but an accident nevertheless.

I sprang to my feet and hurried to the bathroom, a few feet away. Reaching there, I splashed some cold water on my face. The nightmares had stopped when I came to Day Springs, until tonight.

I strode back to the bedroom, after turning off the tap.

What time was it? I peered at my phone. Two a.m. I've got a couple more hours of sleep to go. I slid back behind the covers, praying I could sleep again—and this time, uninterrupted.

CHAPTER 25

 ANDACE

SIX WEEKS FLEW by in a jiffy. I focused on my workouts and developed my songs further.

They were time consuming. I couldn't help as much in the garden like I used to, except on the weekends.

I tried waking up early, earlier than six.

But it didn't work because I groggily dragged my feet all day. On the days when I tried that, I could hardly get through one workout. So I chose to stick to the six a.m. wake-up alarm. When I tired from working on my songs, I searched the internet for new workout ideas. I found quite enough to make creative adjustments.

This week, I even began something new. A thirty-minute, body-weight-only workout. Day one, I nearly passed out. It was brutal! I couldn't complete the reps, I had to stop most of them halfway. And at the end, I was soaked.

Thanks to my consistent weight loss, loose skin wiggled under my belly, arms, and thighs. I'd already chosen to do everything naturally to tighten my skin. That got me into strength training—hard, sore, strength training.

A few times the soreness kept me indoors recovering for three straight days.

Then I'd start again, but slowly. My body began to adjust and accept it. It did my loose skin a world of good, but a long journey still awaited me.

Today alone, I did five sets, with ten minutes each of push-ups, squats, mountain climbers, as well as different variations of planks, sit-ups, and side crunches.

Right after, I laid back on the ground, exhausted. I chose to do these, in addition to my daily cardio routine, every other day because they left me feeling terribly sore.

With five months to go, and forty-five pounds to lose, I gave it everything. I bought a pair of ten-pound weights for my power walks outside too.

JB got more involved in supporting me. He drove me to buy jump ropes and exercise DVDs. He'd encouraged me when I got into routines like plank jacks, jump squats, knee raises, and burpees.

I still hated burpees.

But the more I did them, the more comfortable my body became doing it. I was literally exercising the greater portion of the daytime. I always kept things interesting so I don't get bored.

I added weighted lunges, weighted step-ups, and jump rope skipping—even though they were tough on my tummy because of loose skin, so I wore trainers.

I'd worked out using full water bottles for weighed squats. The impact burned underneath my arms by the fifth squat.

The ten-pound weights?

Ha. Different story.

It literally pulled me toward the ground as I tried lifting it in the other direction. I got through three squats the first day, dropped them, and danced the rest of the time away.

Put simply—they were too heavy.

My daily calories consumed averaged 1800 for my body weight. I learned to make sure I covered all my food groups every day, and at each meal, when possible.

Fats in the form of olive oil, protein in form of meat and eggs, nuts, fruits, alkaline fruits like watermelon, and veggies comprised my staple.

I was grateful for my support network, especially JB.

JB and I now texted back and forth every day. He'd usually encouraged me at the start of every week, asked about my goal for the week, and then he'd text me encouragement, or one verse of Scripture or a motivational quote.

And I saw results. I changed wardrobes twice—at the three-month mark and recently at the six-and-a-half-month mark. I now wore size L.

I only wished that I could better tighten this skin.

But I learned so much online from social media. From observing other people living a fit lifestyle. I applied what they did, tips they shared, especially caution against using excess salt and oil and how these impact weight loss.

They drank lots of water, like I had been doing from the beginning, unaware that it significantly aided my weight loss.

They moved every two hours. I struggled, but I tried to move every three. I already exercised at least two hours per day plus walking in the evenings.

Recently, I added a rest day for Sunday, to help with my muscular healing and recovery. This allowed me to rise early to pray. Then prepare for church with the Cantwells.

My stomach area still frustrated me. I wore skin tights to keep the skin in when leaving the farm or when someone was joining us for dinner. I wore jeans to maintain top form when I knew JB or anyone close to the Cantwells was visiting so as not to seem unkempt.

Today, JB texted me, and said that he was coming over this evening to see me about something important. I grew nervous, but I prayed and chose to stop worrying. I hadn't offended him as far as I knew, except the day I'd asked him personal questions.

Yet I was nervous. JB didn't ask for time carelessly. He wanted my full attention for something, and I could only wonder what.

* * *

TOUGH DAYS HAPPENED OFTEN for me in my fitness journey. Whenever I said "I can't go on" or "I can't do this" while performing burpees, an image of Eric in NY who believed in me would flash through my mind so I'd press on.

When I was tempted to cheat on my meals with something unhealthy, I'd recall the video comment that said I must be somewhere stuffing my face with cake and ice cream and I'd stop.

When I got tired working on my music, I'd remind myself of the last comment: "She's wasted talent." So I'd get back up.

JB taught me to find motivation in the negative things people had said, and make them spur me toward my goal.

These drove me, and pushed me more than the workouts did.

The workouts were hard, but I stuck to it.

A lot of days, I'd cry in the midst of a tough workout session, but I dried my tears and pressed on.

Others struggled online too. Knowing I was not alone in this fight helped.

I'd also toughened up after I realized—*I* had to do this. No one will or can do it for me. I was fighting for me, and for my future. I had no other way out but through. However hard it was, I'd do it.

I set my weight loss goal by one-pound goal each time, until I conquered it. Most times, I lost two at a go. Then I set the next one pound less goal. Big goals daunted me. But one pound each time? I could handle it.

* * *

"CANDACE? JB IS HERE FOR YOU."

Words I'd partly expected, and partly dreaded.

"Thank you. I'll join him soon." I packed the workout gear I'd taken from the dryer into the closet. I pushed the weights to the corner and out of a clear path, and went outside.

Fall air, a little breezy for November, kissed my cheeks. It felt a little dry but the golden leaves swirled by—and they were quite colorful, alternating between green and brown colors.

I faced chilly mornings again after the warm summer weather we'd enjoyed.

I walked up to the front and found JB under the toy-car tree, seated on a low branch, dangling keys in his hand.

He grinned broadly as I approached. "Hey, Candace."

I leaned on the husk of the tree, close to him. "Hi."

His new haircut suited him, his hair now stopped at the nape of his neck, was curled to the side, and he was clean-shaven too. I held back a chuckle. He was way too cute for a farmer.

Staring up at the sky, he reached out his hand without looking and I took it.

"Clouds are gathering. It might rain tonight."

I couldn't believe how much he'd become a part of my daily life, how much adventure I'd had with him, how much progress I've made with his help. He gave and asked for nothing in return.

"Better than windy." Spring in New York City could be quite breezy.

"Any weight changes this week? And it won't bother me if you said no, because I know you're working hard."

I raised a forefinger and huffed. "One pound, JB. Just one after three days of work! And today's Friday."

He took the raised finger and lowered it gently. Then he leaned in and whispered. "That's one pound more than last week, Candace. Celebrate it."

I looked away, feeling unsatisfied. "I know. But I've worked so hard. Every day, except Sunday." I exhaled long. "I just want more results than I'm getting."

He smiled. "Then what I'm about to ask, might be timely."

I eyed him, noting how much calmer, and peaceful, he appeared compared to when we were both new to these farms months ago. "Okay. Spill it."

He drew in a deep breath and released my hand. "I'm inviting you to go hiking with me, just us, next weekend at the Great Falls. I heard it's a nice area to hike. I think you'll like it. Plus, it will be a different kind of workout for you."

Well…Warmth filled me. This was what he wanted to talk about?

"May I add, it's also a date. First date for us—officially, if you say yes."

Oh, now, *that's* what he invited me to talk about.

A date!

My gaze fell on the lush green spinach spilling off its bed to the other side of the far garden.

Those vegetables! I'd fixed that last week. I'd even torn my garden overalls in the process.

My attention returned to JB… I should've known this was coming. He was right though. We'd had a couple of prior run-ins and "drive dates", if I could call them that. The day I fell and he rushed me to the hospital was our first run-in. Then count in the egg-laying "chicken date".

I turned sharply. "Wait, how is my chicken doing?"

He startled, and was probably expecting a serious answer. But I was quite curious. He chuckled. "Its doing all right. The egg is now a chick."

I glanced at him, surprised.

He shrugged, his voice lightening up. "The egg was special. I didn't sell it. Instead I allowed it to hatch."

I smiled. "I'd like to come see it sometime."

He nodded. "Anytime you want."

I met his gaze, with seriousness this time. "May I think—and pray —about it first? I mean, I'd sure like to hike with you, but I need clarity on the date part, if you don't mind. I'm sorry if that's not the answer you were—"

"No, no," he cut in. "That's perfect. I'm glad you said so. Let me know okay? We could go in about a week's time if you're in."

"Okay. I'll be in touch."

I'd doubled my walking distance for a couple of weeks. It helped with pushing my fat loss percentage. So I knew that I was going to walk past his farm during my evening walk.

"Candace, have you tried running?"

I laughed, waved my hand in rebuttal. "Oh no! Don't even get me started. The elliptical, walking, and strength training, I do—in that order. But I don't run."

My answer was definite and defensive enough to drive my point home.

He stood up. "Just a minute." He walked to his truck, came back with some magazines, and handed them to me.

I accepted them. *Guide To Running: For Starters* rested on top.

He pointed to it. "Research I've done shows that if you combined your morning elliptical workout with some running or jogging, you burn twice as much fat, in half the time per workout."

I drew my lower lips through my teeth, assessing his words.

His voice came firm. "At high intensity, the fat literally falls off. Plus, it tones all over the body. You said the weight loss is getting harder. I'm sure this will help, if you embrace it. Think about it, okay?"

I nodded, trying to keep an open mind. "If you say so, I could think about it. I've avoided it all this time. Truth is, I was scared. I guess there's no harm in trying or reading about it at least."

I tucked the magazines over my thigh and pressed my arm on them, rising.

He walked back to the road and entered his truck.

I waved to him as he drove off toward his farm. He waved back before disappearing into the distance and I trotted back to the residence.

CHAPTER 26

*I*nside, I sank into the couch, and threw my head back. Running. Hiking. Plus a date?

God, what do I do?

I took a deep breath to calm myself.

He asked for just one date. But it was a date nonetheless. Probably leading to more. If I was going to turn him down, I needed to do so now. We're already too close to play games.

Plus, he seemed like he'd been through enough stuff, just like me. So I'd hate to cause him pain or heartache.

But something else bothered me. If this moved into something more serious and longer lasting, I could already imagine the headlines: Candace "Wit" Rodriguez Falls Off Stage—Onto A Farm, Into The Arms Of A Farmer.

I shook my head. They'd laugh so hard they'd fall off their chairs!

I rose and walked to the window. *Why am I thinking like this?*

I can't compare him to Ray in status, but he had class, he respected himself, and carried himself well. Where did my relationship with Ray end up with all the status that he had? Moreover, I needed to look beyond the physical.

I went back to the couch and sat.

Almost by design, I stared straight at the art with "Fearless Love" on it. JB's gift.

I realized just how thoughtful he was. He knew what I valued and gave a gift with meaning.

But I'd come here to get my life together, not to fall in love, or get involved.

Restless, I stood up, suddenly needing a change of scenery for clearheaded thought.

I walked over to the sunroom, resting into its soft leather chaise lounge couch. Outside, birds flew in patterns, like during migration.

Winter was coming. This was the time to soak up any warmth left.

I maximized my workouts these days, seizing the sunshine to stay outside longer.

Last week, Mrs. Cantwell and I did our last harvest, saving the final harvest of spinach for this weekend.

It was emotional and fulfilling knowing we planted the seeds together, and harvested the fruits together too. She'd said the garden would lie bare next season while she focused on helping to cultivate the primary farmland.

The sky grew darker, and clouds gathered even more. A rumble grumbled occasionally.

Hmmm. JB was right. He'd predicted that rain could fall.

I'd better cancel my evening walk as I planned my next workout, focused on getting more done this week.

Still, JB's request lingered in my mind.

I knew what I had to do. I had to pray.

* * *

SEVEN THIRTY P.M., and I'd washed my face free of makeup, pulled my hair into a bun, and dressed in a simple belted, long patterned summer dress. I walked to the main house for dinner.

Mrs. Cantwell had set the table. I usually assisted her. However, today I was a few minutes late. She asked me to sit and eat and not worry about helping. With my thoughts occupied, I obliged.

Dr. Cantwell gave a quick prayer of grace to which we echoed, "Amen."

We dug into our food. Each either too hungry to chat or preoccupied—like I was.

"How are things coming?" Dr. Cantwell asked.

I glanced up. "The workouts are fine. For my music, I'm finalizing both songs now. I'll do more when the team arrives closer to the date of the concert."

I scooped brown rice, added mixed vegetable stir-fry to my plate, and oven-roasted grass-fed beef. I set aside an apple and a banana I'd take with me for later. After sipping some water, I began to eat. I was halfway through fast chews and swallows, when I glanced up for some more water.

Both Cantwells stared at me, smiling.

Mrs. Cantwell spoke first. "You wanna talk about it?"

I used the napkin to wipe my mouth, eyes traveling from one to the other.

Then I belched, a little too loudly. "Excuse me." Oh yeah, the food went down a bit too fast! Wait, how… did they know I was worried?

Mrs. Cantwell edged her water glass aside. "The first time you chowed down so fast was the night before your blood work at the clinic. So we know something's obviously bothering you. If you don't want to talk about it, that's okay."

How right she was. I'd been scared then about what the test would say concerning my health, considering my weight and lack of exercise. I'd explained to them that I ate fast when worried. I sipped more water, cleared my throat, and wondered how to present it—delicately.

I took a deep breath and glanced from one to the other. "He asked me out on a hiking date."

Dr. Cantwell picked up his fork and scooped a mouthful of rice and ate.

That's one way to react. But he was never around much so he might have nothing to say.

I turned to Mrs. Cantwell.

"JB," she stated.

I shifted in my seat and lowered my fork to my plate.

Her eyebrows arched, and she smiled, putting down her fork as well. "It's a good thing. Right?"

I didn't respond, still mired in indecision.

Dr. Cantwell shrugged.

Mrs. Cantwell picked up her fork and toyed with it then looked up. "He's a gentleman."

True. Meaning, in Mrs. Cantwell-speak, "He's a farmer but give him a chance after all he's a gentleman."

I swallowed and returned her gaze, intent to be open with how I felt. "He's a farmer." Better to put my one reservation out there.

I noticed that Dr. Cantwell ate more intensely, barely chewing before swallowing.

Mrs. Cantwell pointed to him. "So is my husband. He's a medical doctor, but he loves farming, so do I. It's not a bad thing."

I exhaled, picked up my fork, and dug into my food again. She followed suit.

Afterward, we packed up the dishes, and walked them to the kitchen sink. Mrs. Cantwell and I washed them out and placed them in the dishwasher.

"Do you like him?"

I smiled. "Yes. Of course."

She put the towel in her hand down. "Then realize that almost every man, who God used greatly in early Bible times, was a farmer. Either animal, plant, or both. Abraham, Isaac, who sowed and reaped bountifully, Noah, after the flood. Joseph, who stored grain in barns to save Egypt and beyond. They all planted, and God gave the increase. He blessed them." She spread out the towel.

"It's not about the worldly prestige, or what people will say. It's about God's divine purpose and blessing. I think JB has such blessing. Look at how he has transformed the farm since his arrival. Yes, today farming is looked down upon, but I've yet to see a human being who doesn't need food to survive. What could be more important than the skill of ensuring the continuity of human life on earth? Pray, Candace, but don't dismiss him yet."

I shook out my own towel after wiping my hands.

She turned off the kitchen lights as we left. "Fame and status won't follow you to build your home. You build with the man you choose. That determines whether your home stands. Sometimes, the person God brings us isn't everything we wanted, but they will always be everything we needed. Trust God on this decision, Candace, and you won't regret it. Talk to Him about JB and let Him lead your choice. Either way, know we're praying you through this."

* * *

RUNNING IS ALL ABOUT TIMING. *Of your breath, gait, and stride. Control your breathing. Keep it steady.* I drew in a long breath, shutting my eyes.

I opened them, pulled my foot backward to stretch out my hamstrings. I set it down and repeated for the other leg. Next, I turned my arms forward each the opposite way, to release tension and wake them up, and get them ready to work.

The morning coolness melted on my skin, and vapor soared from my exhale. Early morning temperatures now dropped to high-50s. I repeated the instructions again to myself. Then my plan, "run one mile, walk one mile." Done.

I began jogging, feet pounding away on the tarred road.

By a full minute, I became aware of my breathing. It came in raspy. But I chose not to stop.

No pain, no gain.

I pressed forward and stamped away, one foot in front of the other.

I kept running until I reached the fork on the road. The left road went toward JB's farm.

The right one? I'd never taken it. I narrowed my glance, undecided. Meanwhile, I stooped over,with hands on knees to catch my breath. My water bottle jammed against my ribs, preventing me from bending completely.

Might as well.

I yanked out the bottle, raised my head, and drank, letting it cool my tongue, which was already feeling dry. I dropped the bottle back into its waistband clip.

Straightening, I regulated my breath, and assessed my options.

Which way do I follow? I made a quick left, then turned right. I walked more rightward, crossing the street and entering the right path.

Trees somewhat shaded the way.

"Run to explore," one of JB's magazines had said.

"Exploring," I muttered as I wove deeper into the path, striding briskly.

I checked my sport watch. 1.4 miles run. Not just one!

I smiled. Time to walk one mile.

But... what if I kept running?

I took a deep breath. I wasn't tired. I got a little breathless earlier, but I'd live.

I had to push.

I stared straight ahead, picked up my stride, and resumed running. So much greenery appeared on this path, flanking both sides. The road became less tarred. Foliage ate away at it, exposing natural soil beneath.

Farther inward, it also narrowed, enough to fit only one person comfortably. Low grasses blanketed either side now, no longer tall ones, spotted with brightly colored flowers.

A magnetic sight! I ran until the ground turned fully natural.

No more tar, just sand, weeds, and damp soil. The air smelled fresh, musky sometimes, then more earthy.

Mist rose in pockets around me, deeper within the clustered vegetation than at the edges, emitting a serene ambience.

Surprisingly, the path was well worn. I'd expected differently.

Huge trees flanked my left and right. Tender ones crouched beneath.

Thanks to fall, the leaves bore a mix of green, red, and golden brown—a natural play of colors.

Breathtaking...so much nature. So close to me, yet I only discovered it today.

I continued running, then I sipped some water. It spilled on my chin, but I didn't stop to wipe it.

By my tracker, I'd run another full mile. If the experience of JB's hike would be anything close to this beauty, it'd be well worth it.

Deep longing for a fresh start overwhelmed me.

Why was I so worried about how the world could react to him being a farmer? He was also a stockbroker—former.

I recalled the Scripture I'd read before falling asleep last night, bearing Mrs. Cantwell's words in mind.

Jeremiah 29:11spoke to me, where God promised to give "a future and a hope" to those who trust Him. If God intended me to be with JB, I made up my mind that I'd stop fighting and let God have His way.

The path split in two and a giant oak grew from the center of the split. The path to the left looked bushy, and relatively untrodden.

I stuck to the right path. I quickened when it sloped slightly down-hill, and so caught my breath more easily.

Before me, sunlight warmed a clearing. Not long, I emerged fully into it.

I stopped at the end of the path, now sprayed in full natural light. The morning sun shone above, illuminating water drops on the leaves.

A few yards farther along, a small clear spring whistled running water, pouring out between rock formations. Below, it fed a brook. The flowing water glistened off the sun's rays.

I giggled, tapped a nearby leaf, and the droplet dripped down my arm.

Someone lightly touched my arm. Jolting, I tore my eyes up. I hadn't heard anyone coming.

There he stood, breathless, panting, smiling—and shirtless.

"JB! How did you get here?"

He pressed a hand against his chest, breath heaving, and then stood tall.

"If you wait for the perfect time, it never comes."

His chest rose and fell fast with his breath. I tried hard without success to ignore the ripples of muscles fighting for oxygen before my face.

I didn't know he had a six-pack. He wore loose formal shirts most times. Never anything tight.

There's the farmer, Candace.

I swallowed. I had to catch my thoughts before they ran away with me. I shifted my eyes to his face.

His forehead crinkled. "How did I get here? I ran. Just like you." He pointed toward the path. "I saw you running way ahead."

He patted my shoulder proudly. "You did it. I'm impressed. Good job!"

He pointed at my tracker. "How far?"

I glanced at it. "Two point five miles and counting."

Something rustled behind me, and I spun.

A deer stared at me. I stared back, taking one slow step away. It took two steps forward, still staring.

"Easy." I lifted my hands a bit.

JB came up from behind me and sandwiched himself between the deer and me.

It didn't move.

"Walk back to the path, slowly," he said without turning.

I backed up to the start of the path and stood there.

JB took a step forward. The deer was right in front of him.

I was confused. Usually they run whenever they spot humans. Why was this one aggressive?

JB raised his hands in the air and waved them.

Yet the deer stood rooted.

Then JB widened his stance like a fighter, he let out a shout that shook the leaves, his back arching. The deer turned and fled. It ran until it disappeared from sight.

I'd snuck behind a tree, peering from there.

He walked back, rubbing his palms together. Twisting his head to the side, he chuckled. "Time to run back home. Ready? I'll beat you to it if you let me."

Just like that. As though nothing happened.

I looked from him to where the deer had stood, and back. Then I stood up straight. "Sure. Let's."

He began running as soon as the words left my mouth.

I raced to catch up and chased him into foliage, pushing him against a tree trunk.

He wriggled free and fled, laughing. "You gotta fight fair, Candace! That's hardly fair."

I left him there and ran ahead, then stopped. "You take the lead. I'll come slowly behind, being a newbie."

He nodded. "I'll keep checking behind for you."

I felt that it wouldn't be fair letting him run slower because of me. As I ran along, I rounded the bend where the giant tree split the raw path.

I glanced behind. Something happened back there. I may have gotten my answer from God. I smiled.

Hiking? Check. Date? Check.

CHAPTER 27

*T*here's something about people supporting you that gives you strength.

Then there's something about God supporting you that hands you victory.

I should have known.

A non-runner wouldn't advise you to run.

Yet he never forced it on me. Instead, he offered. He would probably never have told me he ran unless I asked. Such humility!

When I emerged from the path, I saw him across the street. I glanced both ways for traffic then ran toward him, bubbling with pride.

He beamed, raising his hand for a high-five.

I took it though panting still. "I just ran a 5k! Can you imagine?"

"You sure did! You've been putting in work, building your endurance and it shows in your fitness level. No one runs a 5k their first time unless their body is primed for it through other workout. You're stronger than you think."

I checked my tracker—3.9 miles in about one hour ten minutes total, including the distance I ran on the street before entering the path. My lungs burned, but satisfaction cooled my face along with a chill morning breeze.

It was barely nine a.m.

He stood to his feet, his arms spread wide.

We hugged then pulled apart, each sticky with sweat.

"Congratulations, Candace!" He extended his hand, and I shook it.

"Thank you. You know I couldn't have done it without your help. You sent me running."

We began walking, making our way back toward the Cantwell farm.

"Do you run all the time?"

He nodded, using his hand to swat off sweat dripping down his forehead. "Every day. Five miles."

He was going the opposite direction from home, but I wanted his company.

He nudged me with his elbow. "Your body has optimized your fitness from all your hard work these many months. It takes most people several months, even years to go from couch to 5k. But it took you just one day."

I shook my head, still marveling. "I'm glad you came along or I wouldn't have believed it myself. I'd have thought it really didn't happen or feared that I'd collapse if I tried running one more mile."

I still hadn't told him what was now uppermost in my mind, since about a half hour ago. "JB, I'd like to do the hike with you."

He pumped his arm. "Yes! Want to start now?"

I eyed him playfully. "Right. After running a 5k!"

We walked on for a bit.

Tell him now, Candace.

"And yes to the date."

He was quiet.

Then he turned as our steps fell in unison. "Thank you. Your acceptance means a lot to me. What do you say we do it next Saturday before it gets any colder?"

I reached for my water, but the bottle was empty when I shook it. I put it back in its holster.

He stretched behind and gave me his. "I've got a few droplets left. This should get you home."

I accepted it and drank up. "Thank you. Yes, Saturday is fine."

"Sorry for not wearing a shirt. I'll be well clothed next time. I never ran into anyone on the path before until today. My apologies."

I laughed. "Ah well, when you're the lone runner between the two farms, why would you see anyone else?"

He smiled. "Correction, there are now two runners on these farms. You'll run again won't you?"

"I will. Bright and early on Monday."

"See you then."

We'd arrived at the entrance to the Cantwells' farm, but no one was in sight.

Mrs. Cantwell was usually out by now. Then I remembered: garden season was over.

"I suggest we leave early on Saturday. Say, six a.m.?"

On a normal day, that was too early for me, but for a hike? "Sure. Six it is. See ya."

He broke into a broad grin.

There was one thing I hadn't said yet. "Thanks—about the deer." I pointed up where we just came from.

He nodded. "You're quite welcome, Candace. Now you know."

I frowned a little. "Know what?"

He took one step away so I knew he was about to get mischievous. "Now you know deer don't like you, but chickens do."

I pumped a fist in the air, and he dodged, fast-paced walking away.

I turned with a smile and walked to the residence—body aching but with my heart full.

* * *

"Candace, this looks better." Mrs. Cantwell held up a scarfed yellow top with a hood. "What do you think?"

I took it from her, examining it. "Um, I think it's too thick. Maybe it's good for winter. Not for a fall hike. It's pretty though."

She placed it inside our cart regardless. "Maybe the next one then."

This was our third store so far, shopping for the hiking date. We bought hiking gear first, followed by boots. Clothing led us here. I spotted a peach short sleeve shirt with a front zipper.

That looked more like it...

I pulled it off the rack and checked the size. The tag read Medium. Just glancing, I knew it would fit. *About time!* I could hardly believe that I now wore medium size. It took longer than I'd expected to get here, with all my diligent hard work but I was grateful. The fabric felt somewhere in between acrylic and breathable wear. I placed it in our cart.

She held up another. "Oh, look at this one. Isn't it beautiful? You'll look great in this."

She was right. Sometimes I wondered who was more a shopaholic between us. She exuded excitement well above mine every time we came shopping—whether for food, clothes, or anything else.

But she was right. It was pretty and I wanted it. "Yep, I like it. I don't have any red in my gear."

We tossed it in as well. I showed her my preference. "I found one that would work perfectly."

As I showed it to her, she nodded. "Good find. Looks like it would really work. But do you like the front zipper?"

I smiled. "That's the reason I chose it. I can adjust it to my sweat level during the hike."

We strode to an arched fitting room so I could try out the clothing while Mrs. Cantwell waited in the general area.

We'd already chosen some form-fitted long black sweat pants, in addition to other bottom workout gear. We added some new socks too.

After I made final choices, we proceeded to the payment counter, satisfied.

Next and last stop was home.

I put the items away when we arrived home, smiling at the memory of Mrs. Cantwell's reaction to the news that I had accepted the date and hike with JB.

She had thrown her arms around me and squeezed me like an orange. "How wonderful!" she exclaimed loudly. "We got to get you some nice clothes." Hence today's shopping spree.

On our way back, she had a list going, rattling them off her tongue.

"I have to pack you some food. After all, you will get hungry, right? Don't forget some fruit too."

She shared about the time she met Dr. Cantwell. She said he'd been so skinny. Such that on their first date, when she'd asked him if he wanted her pie for dessert, he got offended. She said she'd felt bloated and didn't want to eat another bite, but he would have none of it.

He took it hard and blamed it on his skinny frame. She said much later, she had to explain her reason to him when they became more familiar.

"Today, his BMI is 24.9, and he's saying that's still healthy. I told him, he's one reckless sandwich away from obese. My point is you can never have too much good food on a hike. I'm originally from the South. We're not stingy with food. So, I'll pack some good food for you both."

I said thank you, breakfast would do just fine and I'd be happy to prepare it with her.

"What kind of food does JB like for breakfast?"

I was startled. "Um…we haven't gotten that far."

She frowned, when turning in to the driveway. "What do you both talk about when I see you chat all the time?"

Chuckling, I gathered my purse. "Life."

She shook her head. "Well, somewhere in between life, you find out what the man eats 'cuz the way to a man's heart is his stomach. I'm sure you heard that one before."

"Yes, ma'am. I'll ask him." Playing Southern courtesy.

Sitting on the couch at the residence, I tore price tags off the new clothing. I drifted back to her earlier story.

JB had never complained about my weight nor mentioned my size. He'd only courteously offered support both material and physical, and then cheered me on the day I ran a 5k.

He never disdains me, nor does he disrespect me. He's attentive, smart, and perceptive.

"Did you hear what I just said?"

My eyes flew up.

Mrs. Cantwell stood at the entrance, bags in hand.

I wiped a stray tear.

"Goodness, Candace. Teary-eyed? What's wrong? Are you okay?"

"Yes." A laugh broke through my tear. "He's just such a wonderful person."

She drew me into an embrace, then pulled out and held me at arm's length, smiling. Surely, she saw the storm in my eyes. "You like him."

I couldn't deny it.

"And you're scared it might all be too good to be true because nothing this nice ever happens to you."

Right on point. "Yes! What if it's me who messes this up? Maybe push him away? Or lose focus on my music or my weight loss? What if he becomes more of a distraction than an asset? What then? How do I handle it?" I wiped my eyes with my sleeve.

She held both my hands, drew me to the couch, and we sat face to face. "I had the same fear as you do, when my husband approached me. Three relationships back to back had ended badly. I was scared when he came along. But I took a step of faith."

She raised her forefinger. "Just. One. Step. To trust God. It changed the course of my life. I'll never be happier than I've been with Jim beside me as my husband. Never. Is he perfect? No! But he's perfect for me, as chosen by God."

She pointed at me. "You have to take your step of faith, as God leads you. Believe all things will work out for your good, as Scripture says."

I completed the verse for her.

"Yes!" she exclaimed. "Did you ever know you'd be in Day Spring Farms? Did he? God works His purpose, and none can change it. Don't fear the thousand things that you imagine could go wrong, young one. If something goes wrong along the way, God will make things right for you. Rather, focus on what is going right."

I was so glad someone understood my predicament.

"Now let's focus on getting you ready for this first date and hike. Make it a good one! I want to hear all about it when you come back."

I know she does. Silencing a chuckle, I resumed what I had been doing.

"I never had a hiking date. We're too old to do that now. My knees might go rickety on me."

I couldn't stop a giggle. "I'm sure you'd be fine if you did, Mrs. Cantwell. Thanks for your advice. I appreciate it. It took a huge burden off my shoulders."

She smiled, handing me two bags she'd put down when she'd entered. "You'd forgotten the shoes in the car. I saw them when I went back for my cell phone."

I accepted them. "Oh thank you."

She walked toward the door. "Let me know what the man eats okay?"

I put the shoe bags away. "I will."

As I plunked into the couch exhausted, new workout clothing of every sort surrounded me. My chosen wear used to be chunky jewelry, fancy purses, and cute dresses. Now, sweatshirts, sneakers, and socks conveniently took their place.

It dawned on me that I had changed. A whole lot. I dragged myself to my feet.

Time for my evening walk.

CHAPTER 28

"Today's the day, Candace. Rise and shine! See you soon. :)" JB texted.

I smiled, putting my phone down and raising my feet to slip on my socks, then sliding them straight into my shoes. It was already 5:45 a.m.

Done. I texted him back. "Almost ready. See ya. :)"

I'd woken up a little before five a.m., prayed, did my Scriptural meditation, then showered, got dressed and ready.

I closed my eyes, keeping my Bible on the side desk.

Lord, I commit my day into Your able hands. Lead me, guide me, protect me, and be with me. The steps of the righteous are ordered by the Lord, as You said. Lord, please go with me on this hike. Favor me and keep me safe and alert. I remembered the deer experience.

I've never been on a hike. Help JB and myself as we go on this journey today. If this is Your will, work it out, and make me know it. In Jesus' name I pray, amen.

I rose and collected items I'd placed at the door the night before, to make it easier to pack them.

Next, I strapped on my sport watch. I set it to begin tracking calories burned. Next, in went the food Mrs. Cantwell had brought over in a food warmer fifteen minutes ago.

Glancing around, I checked to ensure that I had everything I needed.

Fitness watch, sunglasses, cellphone, face towels, coconut water, and flashlight. Satisfied, I walked out of the residence and locked the door, leaving the key under the doormat.

Heading to the front of the main home via the flagstone path, I spotted JB pulling up his black Ford F-150 at the driveway. His brake lights cast a red hue to the predawn.

I veered to the main house, knocked, and popped my head in, letting Mrs. Cantwell know I was leaving. She came outside and asked if we had everything. I said yes.

JB alighted and strode toward us. "Good morning!"

We echoed his greeting.

Mrs. Cantwell descended the steps. "Take care of her, JB. You both be careful on those rocks. Call me if you run into any problems. I can't climb, but I can get help."

He patted her arm. "She's safe with me."

I hugged Mrs. Cantwell. "I'll call you once we get there."

She headed back to the house.

JB took the bags from me and loaded them into the truck's back seat.

"Thank you for the food, Mrs. Cantwell." He waved to her.

The aroma must've wafted to his nostrils.

She nodded, reentering the house and shutting the door.

He held the truck door open for me and gave me a hand up its high step.

"Thanks."

He shut the door, walked to his side, and climbed in.

* * *

"Twenty-one miles door to door."

I smiled, snapping my seatbelt loose. "More like door to hike."

A sign displayed Great Falls Tavern Visitor Center.

We parked and I noticed that we were a little early. We'd actually left at 6:05 a.m. and arrived here at 7:18. An hour's drive, thanks to the rainy drizzle we'd encountered more than half the way. At least it cleared up.

I scanned the parking lot. It was pretty packed for this early in the morning. The other cars mostly had families sitting inside—parents with high and middle school aged children. There were a few couples like us, just a guy and a lady sitting and chatting inside their car.

"Why would so many people arrive so early?" I turned to him.

JB shrugged out of his seatbelt. "They probably also didn't know the center opens at nine a.m. I didn't check the time on the website."

I pressed a hand against my headrest, leaning between both seats to reach the bag at the back. Pulling it up, I placed it on the armrest. I sat properly again and adjusted my shirt.

"Perfect time for breakfast. You ready?"

He turned toward me. "Sure. We need energy to hike this mountain. Don't you say?"

I moved the food warmer to my lap. "Yes. Lotta!"

After unzipping the food warmer all round, I lifted the Tupperware labeled breakfast.

Mrs. Cantwell, thank you.

As I twisted its cover open, the aroma of warm oatmeal filtered out first. Wrapped sandwiches containing sprouted wheat bread, fried eggs, olive oil sautéed onions, sliced tomatoes, and basil followed. All topped with lettuce.

JB inhaled noisily. "Mmmmm. Smells good. What do you have in there?"

I eyed him, lifting one sandwich wrap. "You'll see."

He closed his eyes, reaching his hands upward. "Father God, bless the hands that cooked up this delicacy I'm about to devour, amen."

Laughing, I handed him a sandwich, along with a cup of warm oatmeal. "Thank you, CD."

I leaned back. "CD?"

He whispered, "Yes, CD for Candace."

My eyes narrowed. "As in JB for Jabez."

He took a bite of his sandwich. "You got it. Also, CD for the many records and albums you're going to sell come the concert."

I shook my head, biting back a grin. "You believe in me that much, huh?"

"Yep. You sang 'Fearless Love' to me at the hospital. Anyone who can sing like that, got what it takes. So, yes, I believe in your ability."

I sipped some water. "Don't forget I only have two songs as of yet. That's not enough to wow anyone. I need more." I bit into my sandwich and savored its welcome taste. This was good. JB had brought some organic fresh green tea from his farm. Free of sweetener, the natural taste took over. When he asked if I wanted him to bring some he'd recently grown, I said I'd love it. So he did. "I like the tea. Nice natural taste with its own flavor."

"Thank you. I thought you'd like it." He wiped the side of his mouth. "God will give you more songs, Candace. Have no fear. You've already broken through. Once you breakthrough, for as long as you continue seeking His face, working hard on your goal, He'll keep blessing your work."

I sobered up. "Amen."

I was relieved he believed in my talent even though he had nothing to gain from it.

"You know, my brother was pretty impressed with the first song. And Matt is not easily impressed." I laughed, recalling my conversation with him. "He asked how the song came. I said long story."

JB and I stared at each other, and then burst out laughing.

"I could've said, 'Oh, I got it while fainting, and collapsing.'"

He pushed his upper lip forward in a pout, highlighting their full rounded form.

"Or in the middle of the road under a hot sun."

I retracted with a slow nod, hit afresh with the memory of my experience. "Or at the end of *my* road."

He grew quiet as well. "Or at the beginning of a new one."

Our eyes met and held. There was no fear in them. I searched his for a reason why I met such a man as him. His grew wide with appreciation.

"I'm glad we're doing this." He wasn't speaking of the hike, he referenced something more.

"Me too."

"Your tea is getting cold, CD. Drink up."

I frowned. "Can we stick to Candace? CD sounds a bit off. I mean, don't get me wrong, I like JB, but nicknaming might not be your strongest suit."

His arms swung up. He rolled down the window and stuck his head out. "Yes! She likes JB!"

I dragged on his shirt. "Get back in. You're letting the air out!" Laughing while I did so.

He complied and rolled the window back up. "I knew what you meant. I just had to say that for effect."

I ate up the rest of my sandwich after laughing heartily. I'd never seen this side of him before.

I grinned. *This date is starting well.*

* * *

A HALF HOUR LATER, we finished eating. I packed up the wraps and cups and stacked them in a bag, placing it in the back seat.

JB gave me a napkin to use. "Thank you for the meal. It was delicious."

I took it, and wiped my mouth. "You're much welcome. Mrs. Cantwell and I prepared them last night knowing there would be no time to dice lettuce this morning."

He gave a quick tug under his seat, moving it back. "Then you're both great chefs."

And we hadn't called her. Getting out my phone, I dialed her number, pressed the phone to my ear. I leaned sideways to JB and whispered, "I'm calling Mrs. Cantwell." He gave a thumbs-up.

"Yes, it's me, Candace. I wanted to let you know we're here at the Great Falls Hike Trail. We arrived minutes ago and are waiting for them to open at nine. Everything is going fine. Okay, we'll be in touch. Thanks, Candace, again." I hung up. "It went to voicemail."

He twisted, his arm brushing mine as he pulled a folded sheet from the back seat and spread it out on his lap. "We have," he checked his wristwatch, "about one hour before the park opens. We can harness the time. Here. Take a look."

He brought the sheet closer as I leaned over. It looked like both a time planner and a calendar in one with a blank column to the right side, labeled Notes.

He pinned it to the steering wheel with his arm, circling the concert day. "That's our D-Day."

"I'm impressed you'd remember that. Thank you."

He gave me a serious look. "I was thinking we could start planning for your concert now. We control a few things at this end."

"Sure. Like?" I picked up my phone and began a list.

"First and foremost, the land. We need to demarcate the boundaries indicating which is farm use and which is concert use so guests don't trample the crops. Its four months away, so we can work out the designation and mark the boundaries fairly easily."

I glanced up at him. "How much space are we talking about?"

He drew a mock line for boundaries off to the side. "Yours and mine. I mean, both farms. We're doing this together 'cuz I'm practically and by faith expecting a huge turnout. We'll use all land available to us. Hopefully, it'll do."

He was giving me his land to use?

I was speechless!

"I don't know what to say. Thank you. Thanks also for the pressure to write more songs now!"

He pushed hair from his face, his musky body-wash scent wafting over. The gray Nike workout tees he wore shrugged with his movement, revealing his usually hidden six-pack underneath, where it hugged his skin. He was ripped, and obviously exercised more regularly than I'd thought. He coupled his outfit with black-and-white stripped sport bottoms and Adidas sneakers that looked new. He came well prepped. "You're going to write more songs, God helping you.

The rest we can take care of right now. We can't leave it all for your brother to fix. He might not be able to."

JB was right. My brother was already feeling overwhelmed. He was doing the job equivalent of three peoples', thanks to recent short-staffing by John. I heard it in his voice the last time we spoke, which was testy, and he had a short attention span.

"Sounds like a plan."

"Okay, my rough estimate is eighteen acres of land from both farms for use."

I felt I needed to match JB's businesslike focus and agility. "That sounds about right. Half ours—the Cantwells—is farmed. The other half is left fallow. They both agreed we can use that. That's ten acres."

He wrote it. "Then add ten acres from mine since we've expanded to the back of the unoccupied land behind us. I bought five acres there last week."

He raised his head, and tapped his pen on his lips. "So it's settled, we're working with twenty acres of land for the concert, across the road dividing our lands."

He looked up toward the road in thought. "I could move the goat pen farther inward. That will yield sufficient space for prep ground like a mini dressing room, with staging area for concert staff prep and any extra instrumentation."

"I like that. Thank you." I was tapping away on my phone, making notes too.

He threw me a glance. "We might also need to apply for permits from the county. I'll check on that and let you know all right."

Very thoughtful! I didn't remember that piece.

I notated it as well. "What about the weather? Any indication?"

He shrugged. "We can check online." As I wrote again, he chimed. "I'm assuming your brother will supply chairs, equipment, stage construction, etcetera."

On hearing the word *stage*, my heart skipped, and my hand stopped. Last time I stood on one...it didn't go so well. I swallowed hard.

His warm hand closed over mine, reassuring. "You'll be fine this time. Don't worry."

Still, my chest tightened with worry and I felt my brows crease. "Can I just stand on the ground to do it? I mean, I can't fall from there."

"Of course." He gave my hand a firm squeeze. "But no one will see you. They do like to see who's singing. Candace, you won't fall. I'll be there. So will the Cantwells and your brother. Everything will work out. Trust God."

Trust God, I'm told yet again. I wore a faint smile. "Yes, my brother will handle those. Thank you."

JB went back to writing on the planner.

"Oh!" I twisted. "A canopy. For the stage and equipment."

"And direction signs. Enough to go four miles back to the highway."

Good thinking. I wrote it down as both our hands working quick on the notes.

"Don't forget drinking water stations. Mobile restrooms," he proposed. "First aid stations." He bit the end of his pen, thinking.

"One refreshment station serving two hundred free smoothies," I added.

He glanced at me in surprise.

I shrugged, then smiled.

"They'll need two hundred variety barbeque servings to go with that. After all, they're on a farm. We'll make it for the children so parents don't worry about bringing them food."

Now, it was my turn to be surprised.

He shook his head. "I'm doing this free will, so don't say anything more than 'okay.'"

I laughed. "Okay, JB. Okay and thank you."

How many times have I said that in the last half hour? He keeps on giving!

His brow creasing, he glanced at the spread out page, which was already more than half full with notes. "What do you say we start plugging in date and timelines to these things, huh?"

I could only imagine how hard he diligently worked at Wall Street! "Sure, let's do it." With this dedication, he was no-doubt a success, with or without a white-collar career. The man was a hard worker!

Thank You, Lord Jesus!

"You okay? Or you just hate the idea of flowers on stage?"

He caught me staring. "Oh, flowers. Sure. No, that's… that sounds perfect. Flowers. Bright colors though."

He notated it, his gaze falling back to the spread out sheet.

"Volunteers," I gasped. "We'll need them. Lots of them."

He flipped the planner to reverse, having filled the front. Thanks to a half hour of brainstorming. "I suggest we get to work then."

CHAPTER 29

"*H*ere's your guide. Let us know if you need anything." I thanked the park guard and stepped to the side.

Walking down a bit, I stopped, waiting for JB who'd gone to the restroom. I passed the time admiring the white *Boater's Daughter* statues of a man with a fishing net and a lady with a bucket—interactive exhibits for visitors.

"You should try the Billy Goat Trail, if you want. Great view." A lady patted me on the shoulder while I studied the guide. She appeared about middle-aged, but exuberant.

"Did you say, Billy Goat?" Had I heard her correctly? I searched my guide for it.

"Hiked up there three times in the past two years. It gets crowded during weekends, but you're early. Plus there aren't as many people out here today."

I spotted it on the sheet. "Thank you. We'll try it out."

JB approached, drying his hands with a paper towel, and tossed it in the trash bin. He reached me and took our backpack as the lady walked in the other direction. He handed me my waist-clipped water bottle and my phone from the backpack's zipped pocket.

"Ready?"

"The lady suggested we try the Billy Goat Trail."

"I've heard of it. Okay."

I headed to the door, JB leading. "Let's do this."

"Here's the Billy Goat Trail." He traced the path with his fingers. "That direction."

JB flipped his guide around to where we were supposed to commence. "We start...there." He pointed ahead a couple meters.

A good number of people already headed there, so we followed.

To our left, a couple of Asian heritage led a group of six teenagers of different ages into the trail. The couple in front of us—deeply engrossed in their conversation—carried multiple REI headlamps clipped to their backpacks.

Was there a dark alley along the trail? I was glad that I brought flashlights and two strobe lights.

JB allowed me to walk ahead in a narrow curve, while two ladies in matching "Movement" inscribed shirts strode past us. One laughed so loud it sounded shrill.

Soon, we passed the C&O Canal at Lock 19. Then we emerged and turned right at the Billy Goat A Trail along the Potomac River. At the 1.5-mile mark, the intensity of rock hopping increased. My breath grew raspy, and my eyes were struggling to focus a few times.

"We can stop anytime you need a break." JB halted meters ahead and waited for me. He then slowed his stride to match mine.

"I'm okay. Let's keep going." The sun was up but not harsh. Thankfully, the temperature was forgiving, even cool for this time of day.

When we passed Trail Marker 2, it got easier and I was grateful for that. The jagged terrain juxtaposed to the cascade of green.

"Did you see the warning? We should probably slow down."

A warning sign stated, "Many hikers are injured every year on this section of the Billy Goat A Trail."

"We'll be careful." It didn't scare me.

At my dogged response, he fell silent. We stopped under a small curved tree and sipped some water. I also drank a small portable juice packet.

He was sweating pretty good, and his shirt was soaked and stuck to his skin.

"It gets pretty up ahead." A lady with a teenager, probably her son, passed, heading in the direction we came from.

"Thank you!" I shouted, feeling expectant.

A group with her waved to us.

We waved back. My excitement mounted. I wanted to see what was on the other side.

As we proceeded, JB took my hand to guide me from jutting rocks. We were almost two miles in when we reached a beach area.

We held hands firmly, stood side by side, and took in the breath-taking view, while listening to the water lap the shore. Brown sand contrasted green shrubbery on the ground. Blue skies and green trees painted the mountaintops far in the distance with the quiet water flowing in-between. A small tree close by dipped a low branch into the water creating continuous ripples. The sand felt cushy beneath my hiking boots.

JB circled my waist in a side embrace without looking. I rested my head on his shoulder.

As we stood there, I knew a truth in that moment. He loved me— and he was in love with me.

I reached out my free hand and curled it around his waist, like he'd already done mine.

"I like it here."

He kissed my forehead. "Me too."

We gazed into each other's eyes for what seemed like an eternity, sure of what we saw in each, but not saying the words. After all, offi-cially, this was our first date, our first day together. We'd let that suffice.

"A picture?" a man with short beard and a professional camera hung over his neck interrupted. He smiled ear to ear.

We obliged him. "Sure."

I gave him my phone, and JB also gave him his.

We posed, me with a hand to my side, and JB with his arm curved across my shoulder, drawing me in.

We seemed *active* enough.

The man took a couple of snaps, handed back our phones, and we thanked him. He was probably expecting us to use his camera so we could pay him for it but there was no need. Our phones sufficed.

We left the beach area and walked on, shuffling between other hikers coming down where it narrowed. We came to a log bridge over a clear stream filled with large stones. As we crossed, I started to hum.

Then words came, tumbling into my consciousness. Gingerly, I held on until we'd completely crossed.

We were back on the main trail when I sang both lyrics and tune out loud, to JB.

I swung around as his mouth dropped open. "A new song?" We stepped aside.

I nodded, frantically reaching behind to my pocket to pull out my phone.

Then it happened.

The phone slipped off my hand and fell, with its screen meeting the waiting jagged tooth of a rock. I picked it up slowly, with an anxious hand laid on my heart.

Not just for the phone, but for the song I needed to put down before I lost it. I continued to hum the tune, gripping hard onto the words in my mind.

I flipped the phone over. Yep, the screen had cracked in a million places. I couldn't see my own reflection.

I beat down the rising anxiety. *Focus, Candace.* I kept humming.

I dusted off the screen's face with my arm, ready still to type on it.

JB caught my hand. "Stop! You'll cut yourself."

He pulled out his phone, unlocked it, and pressed the Record button, holding it out to me.

"Record on mine." He nodded a go. "Sing. Tune first."

I did. I belted it out like my life depended on it, powered by the moment's urgency. All that came to me, I poured out passionately— tune and lyrics, in gratitude.

MOUNTAIN TOP- LYRICS
VERSE 1:
It stood so high I could not see
Quaking, trembling, knees buckling,
Impossible, no place to turn,
I wearied, fainted, but reached the summit,
Almost gave up, until I saw the sun rise,
Saw the other side,
The flip side of my struggle,
At the peak I overcame,
When I least expected it.

CHORUS:
It's only You,
It's only Jesus,
It's only You,
That led me through,
I can't explain it,
Don't want to explain it, 'cuz it's
Only Jesus(4x)
That brought me to the other side.
'Cuz it's You, Jesus, that got me to the Mountain Top!
VERSE 2:
Now I see the beauty of redemption,
Of restoration,
Now I sing 'bout Your strength that bore me,
Carried me when I was too weak to climb,
'Cuz You knew what was waiting for me,
At the Mountain Top!
CHORUS
VERSE 3:
My Mountain Top is Yours, Lord,
Every day I choose to live as You would,
Never alone, never forsaken,

Ever confident, because I know,

Be it in the valley, or at the Mountain Top,

You are always there with me.

CHORUS

Finished, I exhaled long and we smiled, our faces giddy with excitement.

This was a winning song; and we both knew it.

My best so far. "Thank You, Lord Jesus!" I exclaimed.

"I like 'em all. But this got a zing to it!" JB followed.

"Ah, progress." I couldn't stop smiling. "Oh, the phone."

We'd forgotten my shattered phone. JB put down the backpack and took out a napkin. Collecting the phone from me, he wrapped it up in the napkin, placed it into the backpack, and zipped it up. Slugging it onto his shoulders, he held out his hand to me. I took it, and we kept on hiking.

That was the moment we became a team. One unit, working toward the same goal, going in the same direction—forward. That moment, without any prod, I loved him back.

He stopped about five minutes later, took out his phone, and held it up. "Searching for a network signal."

I looked at him and asked. "Why?"

He began typing. "To send this to your e-mail inbox. In case my phone goes down like yours. You can't lose this song."

I dictated my e-mail address while he typed and hit Send. "It said delivered."

Content, we resumed the rest of the trail, still with our hands joined. His, firmly steadying me when it got too rough, and mine, simply holding on, knowing I was safe with him.

By the sixth mile, the sun was already high in the sky. For shade, we stayed close to any green plant taller than an average child. With my body fully adjusted to the climb, we strode at a leisurely pace.

We turned right onto the Overlook Spur Trail and soon reached an overview of Great Falls. We pressed on, stopping for a minute. Crowds now joined us, but thankfully, we were close to the finish.

JB handed me a bottle of water after I'd run out. He'd taken one of mine before we crossed the log bridge because he couldn't stop to get his out of the backpack. We packed our empty bottles in the backpack, intent to dispose them back at the center.

We made a turn at the Lock 19 Trail and headed back to the starting point. We took another photo by the front Visitor Center where we'd first stopped, then walked to the parking lot, feeling exhausted but also excited and accomplished.

* * *

"Wow—7.9 miles! Done!" We high-fived each other as we drove into the main traffic, heading back to the farm. I reached against the restraints of my seatbelt to adjust the flat shoes I'd changed into.

We'd taken off our hiking boots upon arriving at the truck rather than track dirt inside it. JB pressed High on the air condition, and stirred it to face me more.

I noticed we were working more in unison now.

"Did you enjoy it?" He turned to me.

I laughed. "Of course! You?"

He threw me a glance, brows arched high. "Are you kidding me? I hiked the Great Falls with the most beautiful lady—best. Day. Ever!"

Warmth spread across my cheeks again.

I tried to change the subject. "Have you hiked before?"

He exhaled. "Hmmm. No. Nothing in the magnitude of what we accomplished today. It was a first for both of us." His eyes focused on mine at the red light, as he searched my face. I didn't have to wonder long what he was thinking as heat rose up his neck to his face. "You're beautiful, Candace." He turned back to the road.

Taking my left hand, he squeezed it gently. "I'm happy you had a good time. What do you say we grab lunch somewhere nice since its well past noon." He glanced at his watch.

I checked the time on the truck's dash. Almost one thirty p.m. "Sure. Drive on."

* * *

247

We arrived back at the farm around four p.m. I made my way to the residence. JB had been a gentleman, as he carried my stuff from his truck to the door, setting them down. Then he came back to the truck for me, opening the door and helping me get down.

"Thank you."

He raised his phone toward me. "Now you already got three songs on this device. It's practically yours. Are you sure you don't want to borrow it for a while?"

I shook my head with a lopsided grin. "You hold on to my songs. I know they're safe with you."

He inched up a shoulder, the exhaustion in my body mirrored on his drawn face. "We can schedule, and I could drive you downtown to get another phone."

I didn't want to overburden him. He'd done enough. "Oh no, thank you."

He gave me a big quick hug, and then after a wide smile, strode back to his truck. "See you around, Candace."

I unlocked my door. "See you, JB."

CHAPTER 30

*T*hree months had passed since JB and I took our hike, our first date. Things have moved quickly since then, so has our relationship. With nine more dates under our belt, our bond has grown stronger, and we understood each other better.

I ran twice a week with him, along the same path where we ran into each other weeks back. I still completed my elliptical workouts daily.

It was tough walking when it's so cold, but I forced myself to get out there. I was still fighting for my After with everything I had.

Work on my music progressed at warp speed. I wrote four additional songs, making a total of seven.

Recording equipment arrived one week ago, and I'd put them to good use already. I spent Sundays resting. A few times, I strolled with JB in the evenings, when the weather allowed.

We spent upward of three to four hours on the phone every day.

As a matter of fact, I looked forward to our times together. He usually sent me these cute reminders with a pool-relaxing emoticon when he was about to call.

I smiled whenever I saw it. I replied him with a smile, every time.

No other emoticon felt generic enough. Moreover, I wasn't so much into them.

My new phone even prefilled it in for me, though I disliked the feature. I preferred putting my own thoughts in writing not having a machine do it for me.

He'd begun coordinating with my brother and the Cantwells about concert land allotment. Equipment had also begun arriving.

During Christmas, he gifted me a gold necklace, with a cross and love symbol interwoven as a pendant.

I liked it very much and wore it every day since I saw no need to take it off.

On New Year's Day, at his invitation, we spent the day with his Grandma Patty in Pennsylvania, who couldn't stop thanking JB for transforming the farm into a modern organic farm—something she'd always wanted to do but couldn't.

She looked well and content, but rested more between speech. She blessed us and prayed for us individually.

We returned to Maryland in time to spend the evening with the Cantwells, feasting on barbeques and everything edible without caring one bit about calorie intake. It was the most travel adventure I'd had in a year!

But I was worried.

Stepping up to the weight scale, I stood still to check my current weight, as I did every week. I glanced down after a few moments —183.1.

I balled my fist and chuckled. Ten pounds and one month to go. I got this going for me at least. Since I began incorporating running months ago, the fat literally melted off fast. JB was right—as usual.

I'd increased my intake of protein and snacked on seeds throughout the day, yet I was burning fat and losing weight. On a few occasions I hit plateaus, so I switched up my routine. I either ran more days, or walked longer. Then I rested more and upped the action the next day, or ate little less carbs and more fiber.

The variety kept my body guessing. It left me with no chance for failure.

I'd chosen that I was not climbing onto a stage in anything other than the signature blue dress from Mrs. Cantwell. No. So I was putting in the work and seeing the results.

Granted, from what I saw online, not many people had things going for them the way it was for me. Lots were struggling with full time jobs, husbands, and kids, and some juggled part-time jobs as well —and working out. I had this weight loss and my music as my only goals.

That motivated me. If they could still do it with all they had, I could fight harder. And I did, keeping my eyes set on my goal.

Now, another month ended, and the concert edged closer. I've got to lose these ten pounds. The last ten pounds.

But things have gotten busier for me, with the concert approaching. The busier it got, the tougher it was to stick to my exercise routine. But I still did everything I could. I made up for missed sessions early in the morning, or late at night just before bed.

My fit watch told me how much fat I'd burned in a day. If it was not up to par, I worked harder the following day.

My body felt all the brutal assaults on it. Aches, pains, and soreness came daily. But I was determined, because I knew what I fought for. My After.

I walked to the closet in the bedroom after putting the scale away and as I opened it, the blue dress looked back at me.

Removing the dress, I lowered it. *Try it on.*

I slipped my feet in first, pulled it by its short sleeves upward. I struggled to wiggle it over my hips, but with gentle tugs, it made it up and over my waist. I slipped in my arms next, zipping it up.

I looked up in the mirror at the small-sized dress, running a hand to adjust its sides. It felt as tight as it appeared.

"Ten pounds less," I muttered. And it would fit perfectly.

I'd need a body shaper to hold the excess skin in, but the flaps were now significantly less than they had been, thanks to my consistent weight training and body strength exercises.

Push-ups and burpees, grueling as they were, deserved credit for the toning. They were the hardest to perform, but they worked.

I unzipped the dress, gently slipped out of it, and hung it up. "Thirty more days, baby."

* * *

JB

My phone rang in the middle of my sleep. I looked, with my eyes drooping. It had been a busy day on the farm.

The caller ID showed it was Dan. "Hey, Dan? Is everything all right?" I glanced at the clock. Eleven p.m.

He was quiet. Then he spoke. "Your dad is in the hospital, JB. You need to come. It's bad."

I shrugged off the covers and sat up quickly. "What happened?"

He breathed roughly. "I heard that he fell. Three stories, while working at a site. They took him to the hospital. He was in surgery when I left an hour ago. You're his only family. Though I know he's not the best fellow, but you gotta come down here."

"I'm on my way. Thanks for calling."

As he hung up, I rose and began throwing random items into a bag, getting ready. Not-so-pleasant memories of the man I called "Dad" flooded my mind. He was a rough man. I fought conflicting emotions.

Then my thoughts went to Candace.

I love her so I can't tell her. Especially with not knowing what I'll face in Louisville.

Forgive him.

I ground my teeth. *Lord, how can I?* He caused me so much pain.

Forgive him, son.

I stared long and hard at my reflection in the mirror. The resurgent ache in my heart was clearly obvious in my saddened eyes. I wasn't sure how I would react when I arrived to Kentucky. There's no saying who I'd be when and if I returned to Maryland. If I was unable to forgive Dad, I wouldn't come back to Day Springs Farms, nor to Candace. She'd deserve a better man than I. I rubbed my jaw with finality. No, It was better for her that I didn't tell her.

* * *

CANDACE

It was March 15.

Two days earlier, JB and I took our usual Sunday walk. The weather was frigid cold as expected, and nothing appeared to be out of the ordinary.

We'd talked as we typically did. He teased me about a last line in my latest song. He'd suggested I change one word, *beaut*, because it sounded like *butt* when sung.

We'd ended the day, planning to meet up on the fifteenth, along with Matt, about the concert. It had snowed all week leaving about ten inches of snow on the ground.

When the time came for the nine a.m. meeting, JB didn't show.

I called him and it rang, but there was no response. I left him a voicemail to call me back, saying I was concerned. Then I texted him. Yet, no reply.

"Did he tell you he had something come up?" Matt was busy on his phone, while speaking. After the meeting, we all picked up additional tasks, for more things that needed to be done. He'd hired a new team to sing as backup. Three were volunteers, and one salaried.

I coached them and we'd been practicing for three weeks now.

But today, with JB's unexplained absence, I hardly paid attention to the meeting.

JB had never not shown up, or not returned my phone call. On New Year's Eve, he told me he loved me for the first time. He said he guessed I already knew. Why would he then not make contact if something wasn't right?

"Um—I'm not sure. I'll go up to his farm, to check." I'd informed Matt that JB and I were in a relationship.

He wasn't thrilled and considering JB's status as a farmer, I wasn't surprised. But I'd settled it with God so I wasn't moved. He said that he was simply happy I met someone.

"Okay. I'm heading out to check on the contractors for the stage.

I'll see you later." He pushed off the couch and headed toward his car. I knew what he was thinking. The same thought haunted me.

In fact, it'd haunted me from the start but I had refused to let it worry me.

I went back into the residence and changed from sneakers into flat boots. I put on a light winter jacket and began walking up to his farm. The distance was a mere 1.5 miles, which I typically covered in a breeze. Today, it felt like it took forever.

I met Betsy, the farm's unofficial caretaker, at the milk purchase station. Months ago, JB had built the covered stand into a facility complete with a cashier station, heated indoors, and employed more staff, so that it was no longer a one-table kiosk pitched by the roadside. Betsy was middle aged, sweet but reserved and known to be quite blunt sometimes. She and I exchange pleasantries.

"I'm looking for JB. He was supposed to be at a meeting this morning. Is he okay?"

New white-painted boundary markers surrounded the land, clearly marking where people could not go with red and white colored Do Not Enter signs visible every couple of meters.

Impressive. He invested a lot of effort, time, and resources into preparing for the concert.

Where are you, JB? What aren't you telling me?

"Oh." Betsy bent to lift a gallon of milk onto a buyer's cart. "He had to go back to Kentucky yesterday."

The revelation hit my gut with unexpected force. *What?!* "Permanently?"

Why didn't he call me?

"I don't know." She shrugged and straightened from her task, putting her gloves down. She went outside. I followed. "He asked me to take care of everything here and to make sure you had everything for the concert. He'd said that you'd tell me if you needed anything from us and that I should do it."

I swallowed hard while the pressure in my gut sank lower. This didn't look good. Why would JB leave, and not tell me, not take my calls, and say I should be given *anything* I needed? I needed *him*! My heart longed for his voice, his smile, his presence...

I inhaled deeply, trying to contain the surge of emotions.

Betsy picked up a watering hose then curled her arms, and stood straight. "Now you two were pretty close. I'm surprised he didn't tell you. And you said he missed a meeting this morning?" She dropped the hose, snuffing. "Men!"

I was almost quick to say JB wasn't that kind of man. But something held my tongue from saying so. *Was* I sure? My head whirled. There must be some mistake.

I dialed his number again for the fourth time. It rang then went to voicemail. I pressed it off. I was definitely not leaving another message. The first one was good enough. "I've called him, like right now, texted him, and yet no response. Is he okay?" I blurted.

She huffed. "I know he's alive. He ain't dead. He ain't in the hospital either. Last time I talked to him, he sounded fine."

Her hand flew to her mouth. Wait? She talked to him? "Bet I shouldn't have said that. Sorry. Honestly, I can't tell you anything. You have to ask him yourself. I'm sorry."

Yeah, so was I.

"Thank you, Betsy." My voice trembled.

It was too good to be true, remember?

The fear I'd conquered many months ago, that first night he'd asked me out, rushed at me from inside.

You shouldn't have trusted him or given him a chance. You wouldn't be hurt now. They kept coming. Tears nearly blinded me as I walked away, toward the Cantwell farm.

Too good to be true indeed!

* * *

THERE IS loneliness you can feel deep in your soul. Not that people aren't around you, but because others cannot fill the emptiness left by one who meant so much.

That kind of loneliness, only Jesus can take care of.

At the crack of dawn the following day, I laced up my sneakers and hit the road for a jog, heading toward the path we used to run together. Arriving, I halted at the entrance, and leaned on my knees. My legs felt leaden, and couldn't move. My throat knotted from pleasant memories.

Reality of the previous day hit me as I stared at the path, trees mostly bare of leaves, and shook my head. Who was I kidding? I couldn't enter there. It had been our path—JB's and mine. I couldn't travel it alone. Few tree leaves' alternating green cores and brown tips mirrored my reminiscent thoughts of JB. No. *I'm not going down that road...too many memories of happy times lurked.*

I whisked around to the direction my legs were willing to go, and ran back to the direction I came, while teardrops rolling down my cheeks led the way.

I buried myself into my workouts for the next several days, working out three times a day, listening to Christian radio, and reading my Bible.

Mrs. Cantwell asked me about JB. I said I didn't know and didn't want to talk about him. She backed off.

Matt? He didn't ask. Except how the music was coming. I said fine.

Actually, I hadn't touched it since JB disappeared. I would begin then remember how, where, and with whom I got the songs and who helped me preserve them. And I'd succumb to tears.

I cried more hours a day than I sang, even though I'd promised myself never to cry about a man again. But I knew JB was different. Other times, the songs came out croaky. I couldn't sing straight. I couldn't eat much. I snacked on lettuce, nuts, and everything crunchy all day long. I withdrew, and even skipped meal times here and there.

Every morning I woke up and checked my phone. I'd then put it down, mope around, and clean the house.

After two weeks, there was still nothing from JB. Two days ago, it was tough. I'd started my workout, and then stopped to text Rosa, who'd asked me about JB. I'd told her about him a month ago.

She was excited. In the middle of my text to her, the phone auto-completed my message, adding the smile, typical of my response to JB. I stopped. I couldn't press Send.

My knees wouldn't stop trembling. Then I stopped my workout and collapsed in tears at the base of the elliptical. The next morning, I reminded myself why I was here. If I was unable to practice my songs, I could still work on my fitness.

I simply needed to get my body moving. That much, I was still determined to do.

CHAPTER 31

*W*e'd announced for volunteers at two churches one month earlier. The Living Word Church, where JB attended, and the Miracle Assembly, where the Cantwells and I fellowshipped.

A surprising two hundred people in both youth ministries signed up. We offered them free passes and free tees, in appreciation of their support.

Eighty more indicated they'd be willing to show up. We were amazed!

Every day JB was gone, hope that he'd come back faded.

I'd changed my running and walking route to the opposite direction.

Frankly, it was less torture for my soul. I left his Fearless Love art on the wall, regardless.

But I deleted all his texts.

They were sad reminders of something good I once had. The last time before now when I'd walked near his farm, work was still going on for the concert on his farmland. At least, he hadn't cancelled that. He was a gentleman, I'd give him credit for that. But for running away—no, sneaking away—without as much as a word, he was a coward as far as I was concerned. I had no time for cowardice.

Still, my heart wouldn't let go, hard as I fought to tear him out of it. Love for him had sunk its teeth deeply inside me.

I turned to prayer, and asked God to take it out of me. It was hurting me, not endearing me at all.

Yet nothing changed. I still woke up with the emptiness of knowing what I'd lost.

* * *

MARCH 27.

Today, I had to go into town to place the order for our volunteers' tees, with After, the title of my album, imprinted on each. We planned for four hundred shirts. Although we had two hundred volunteers, we ordered extras in case more people showed up.

"Sis, two thousand people have logged on and signed up for the concert. That's a good number! We're getting somewhere."

I smiled, hearing what he wasn't saying. Sure, 2k was good, but we needed more—like 70k more.

"No worries, Matt. We still have two weeks."

He sighed. "I hope they do."

I walked to his car, turned around, and remembered. I had a dedicated driver, sent by the label to prep for the concert. I only walked to places because I chose to do so, because I still wanted to burn my necessary fat calories.

I strode over to him and entered the burgundy Toyota, supplying him with my destination. The weather was warmer than usual so I removed my jacket and placed it on the seat, left wearing only a long sleeve, fitted wintergreen gown with leather boots. My bracelets became oversized, so I now went without them often.

I threw my head back as he drove.

Thoughts of JB surged to the fore of my mind, our rides to town together, our jokes, laughs, and hugs. I looked out the window where winter still lurked.

JB, where are you? I sighed.

I couldn't believe that I still had to endure this torture. Apparently, he wasn't leaving my mind anytime soon.

When we arrived to the address, I alighted from the car and hopped into the shop, since it was literally off the curb. I pressed the service bell, noticing several customers were already waiting, some busy on their phones. I waited at the front until a man showed up, smiling. "Yes?"

I moved forward. "Hi. I'd called earlier. I'd like to place an order for the shirts, with the design I believe someone e-mailed to you already."

He pressed a button on his PC, then looked up. "Your name please."

"Global Sound Records, please."

He thumbed down a list and stopped. "Ah, yes. Four hundred shirts. Unfortunately, ma'am, they said you are going to be paying. They did not approve the order."

I had to pay for it? John!

"All right. I'll go grab my purse. Give me one minute." I walked to the car to pick up my purse. Grabbing it, I rushed into the store, where the man still waited at the register. I handed him my card. "Here."

He took it, swiped, and handed it back to me. "Just a moment." He began writing out the order and receipt form.

As I turned, someone aimed his phone at me, taking a picture. Oh no! "Candace Rodriguez! Wit? It's Wit!" she shouted.

I stared at her. No one had called me Wit in ages. Moments passed before I sprang into action.

Grabbing the receipt the man handed out, and shouting a quick thank you, I rushed out of the store, making for the car.

Reaching the curb, I stopped, frozen in place. I couldn't move.

There he stood, arms in pockets, waiting.

JB. With his cheeks sunk in, he appeared thin. Our eyes met and held.

I wasn't sure how to react.

"You should get in the car, Candace." He said coolly, and nodded behind me.

I whisked around to see a couple more people were now snapping photos of me.

Much against my wish, I got in one way, and he got in the other door. We both slammed the doors hard.

"Drive!" I shouted to the driver. He veered into the road. I didn't turn.

JB touched my hand, and I withdrew it quickly. "You're not here." I turned to him, eyes steeled. "For the record, you're not in this car."

His breath sounded coarse. "I took a taxi straight from the airport and rerouted it here when I learned you weren't home."

Not.

One.

More.

Word.

My knuckles grew white as I held onto the safety handlebar above my seat, though the car was perfectly stable.

Something else needed stability beyond the car and it was my heart. When I said nothing, we sat apart, in silence all the way back to the farm.

At the farm, I hurried out of the car without looking back. Matt ran toward me from the residence.

Footsteps pounded behind me. JB took my arm and swung me around, facing him, coming between Matt and me.

He gazed into my eyes. A pained look strained his face and he inhaled sharply. "I'm sorry. I'm so sorry, Candace. Please let me explain. It's not what you think."

Hot tears brimmed but instead I shook my fist and yanked my hand away. "I didn't know *what* to think."

Matt withdrew farther.

The tears, borne for weeks, now came free falling. I wiped them as they tumbled. Then I took a calming breath. "I did not know what to think, JB."

His mouth drew into a tight line. "I didn't know what to say if I couldn't tell you the truth."

"Truth about what?!" I pounded my fist repeatedly on his chest, and he stood there and took it. When he pulled me into his arms, my sobs rang in his chest.

"I'm sorry, my sweetheart. I'm sorry I hurt you. I love you very much with all of my heart, and with all of my soul."

But he more than hurt me.

He took my hope with him. Everything I had risked.

I raised my head to meet his gaze. "Where were you?" My voice trembled with each word.

He swallowed. "My dad is into construction. He had an accident at a construction site and fell three stories. He was hospitalized with life-threatening injuries."

I looked away.

That doesn't explain it—at all. "Why didn't you call me then? Or just tell me before you left?"

He released me. "It was complicated. I…"

His face bore a torn look. "I didn't want to drag you into a messy situation between him and me. He…He was not a good man but I needed to forgive him. And I wasn't sure, when I left here, that I would. Memory of the pain he'd caused me hurt deeply. So I decided that if I got there and was unable to forgive him, you deserved someone better, better than me. That's why I didn't tell you or call or return your calls. So you'd be free to move on if I didn't come back. I'm truly sorry."

I stood there, holding my breath, and peering into his eyes, while listening to my hurting heart. I could see he was telling the truth.

"So did you? Forgive him?" I waited. My breath froze over the importance of his answer.

He bent his head, choking back a tear, but his eyes filled with them. "Yes, although it was tough, I did. He passed away that night. One week ago."

Compassion overwhelmed my anger. "I'm sorry for your loss. I really am."

"Thank you."

Though sad for his loss, I hadn't gotten over his shocking exit and silence during the period. I simply wasn't in the mood for further discussion. "I have to go now."

He stood back, appearing not quite ready to move. "Okay. I'll be here later to see you."

I walked toward Matt and JB left for his farm.

However, somewhere, deep inside, I laughed hard at my fear. It had lost—again.

* * *

"CANDACE!" My brother's fingers were typing at lightning speed on his phone, his face wore a huge smile, and his feet tapped the ground.

I spread my winter jacked over my shoulder to keep off the chilly breeze. He pointed at his phone's screen. "See." But I was struggling to focus on what he was showing me, not on what just occurred with JB.

"You've gone viral!"

My eyes grew wide. I shook my head. Gone viral?

Again?

"What?" The word nearly choked me. Had they found something else to ridicule me with? It took me this entire year, to come to a place of healing. I didn't want or care for a rattle.

He brought his phone close, and refreshed his screen.

"Candace, this video was posted a half hour ago. It has been viewed 6,000 times and growing."

I peered at it. "What does it say?"

He expanded it to full screen mode.

"It says, 'Check out the new Candace "Wit" Rodriguez!'"

It showed me on it. At the tee shirt embossment store. Ah! It must've been the girl taking photos of me. She posted a shocked face at the end. But that wasn't what I wanted to see.

"Scroll to the comments, Matt."

He did, and we saw many comments were pouring in.

263

"Wow! Candace looks great! She lost a lot of weight!"

"She is pretty! Check out those legs!"

"She is a superstar! Where on earth is she?"

More were coming. Nothing vilifying…I sighed, and dropped my shoulders in relief.

He raised the phone and tap-danced. "I'm going to resurrect your website, which, by the way, you've abandoned for almost one year now."

I didn't miss the scold in his tone. "I'll post a new announcement of where they can see you on the concert day—in person. Here, of course. I'll let them know you're singing live, they can pay to participate online for a small fee, or come in person and hear you. And they can also preorder your album—right now coming out the following day."

Ever the strategic manager, but I knew he was right, even though I hated to admit it. As much as I'd liked to curl in my shell here and protect my private life on the farm, if I wanted people to show up, I needed to publicize this event completely. And, lest I forget, fulfill my terms to the contract and be free. That was the goal.

Then I could go off to whatever else I wanted to do. "Okay. You can do all that, but say nothing about the weight loss. I still got three pounds to lose."

"Okay, Candace." He sauntered back to the team while I walked into the main house, still heavy-hearted. I met Mrs. Cantwell in the kitchen, hands busy, four stoves steaming with something, with the oven glowing.

I rolled up my sleeves to assist.

"JB is back."

She stopped then smiled. "And?" She waited, oven mitten in hand.

"I don't know. He said he was sorry. Something about needing to forgive his dad. He lost his dad a week ago. He said he forgave him." I exhaled a held breath.

She stooped and pulled the oven open, wincing at the sudden heat pouring out. "Did you forgive him after he apologized?"

I knew where she was going.

I swallowed, picked up a bowl of green beans, and began to snap them, ready to steam. I was slow in answering.

She took notice. "You know, sometimes you might think you know how you'd react in a given situation, until you're in it. Then you totally blow it. Forgiving a parent, or anyone, is not easy. It takes all of who you are. Don't blame him until you hear him out first. Give him the benefit of doubt."

Wait. Was she taking his side?

"Why was it so hard for him to tell me what he said today? 'Hey, Candace, sorry. My dad is sick I need to go see him.' How hard could that be? I called him, I even left him a message. Then I called again and again. After that, I texted him. Clearly, I wasn't worth his response."

I was venting—on the wrong person—and I knew it. But it was going to come out—eventually.

She rose to full height. "Because his dad wasn't the only sick person, Candace. So was he. He needed healing just as desperately as he needed to forgive his father. You can't do one without the other. Spending life with a sorely broken man beyond repair is nothing you want. He went off to find healing—on his own. He was showing you respect, not scorn. You should appreciate that."

I was getting a scoop of my own recipe of quick judgment. She planted a firm hand on her waist. "And since he was gone, how many times did you pray for him? Huh? Not about him, but for him? When you do all that, which no normal person could do—at least not as a first reaction—then you earn the right to condemn another human being." She bent over, now red in the face.

It took me a moment to realize that she probably wasn't talking about me and JB anymore.

I bent low, softening my voice. "Mrs. Cantwell, are you okay? Talk to me." I held her hand.

She was trembling. The mittens fell to the ground, and she crumpled to her knees.

I rose, reached, and turned off the oven, and then knelt to her side. "Tell me. What's going on?"

She sobbed into her blouse. "I'm here trying to help people, fix people while our son is in Boston, struggling to get over his gambling addiction. I've talked to him, taken him to therapy, and prayed. Oh, have I prayed! Yet, he gets worse. Every dollar he doesn't eat, goes into gambling. His wife left him and moved back to her parents' home last night. She called me in tears, telling me that she's pregnant. There will be no money to support the pregnancy. She'll have to bear the responsibility alone. My husband and I have fought over our son's addiction time and time again."

She wiped her eyes. "He left last night and slept in a hotel. He's on a trip now and won't be back until the day before the concert. I don't know what to do. Everything is falling apart." Her sobs shook her entire body.

Now, I understood. Their son must be the reason for the argument I'd walked into months ago. I crawled on the ground and held her in my arms until she quieted.

"Is he a Christian?"

She swiped some tears. "He was. But now, he can't even keep his head straight enough to make a decision."

I raised her to her feet and helped her sit on a stool. I stooped low to look at her bent face. "Can you please invite him to the concert?"

She raised a brow. "Why? He wouldn't come. What can it do for him?"

"Because," I smiled, "I want to introduce him to someone I believe could help him."

A moment passed before she lifted her face. Her eyes brightened. "JB."

I nodded, my smile widening. "You think you can invite him to dinner tonight? Thanks to your scolding, I've forgiven him. I still don't feel like talking to him yet."

She grabbed a napkin. "Sure, I'll invite him. While you're pouting, remember how you felt when he wasn't here and lighten up that face when he arrives."

CHAPTER 32

"*H*ow do you like the mashed potatoes?"

JB inched a nod. "Good. I like them a lot."

What else would he say?

Stop it, Candace!

My thoughts were running rampage, trying to find a reason not to accept him, but my heart and soul fought back.

"How was Kentucky?" she asked.

He shrugged. "Well, it hasn't changed much. Same old."

But he had changed. Though he appeared tired, he did seem more at peace.

"Sorry about your dad. I heard." Poor Mrs. Cantwell, trying everything she could to keep the conversation going.

I, on the other hand, said nothing. I was just eating my raw food cake, I'd made from a recipe online three days earlier, and stocked in the fridge. I was trying hard to lose two more pounds before the concert. *This is delicious!*

"Candace, how are you?"

I choked on the bite halfway through my mouth. I coughed until it cleared.

I hadn't talked to him since he arrived, I was simply watching to see what had changed. As far as I could tell, the man across from me was largely the same man who left.

"Good. Fine. You?" I refused to look at him.

He shifted in his seat, putting the fork down.

"Candace, you have to look at me."

I chewed another mouthful. It tasted like chaff this time but I didn't care. At least it didn't hurt. The table fell silent, all three of us. He reached for my hand and held it until I glanced up. "Don't," his voice quavered, "fight this."

I put down my fork and swallowed. He bowed his head then stood and walked to me. "I love you and I'm so sorry for hurting you! That wasn't my intention. Please forgive me."

The walls crumbled around my heart, one by one. A stray tear rolled down my cheek and he wiped it.

Mrs. Cantwell cleared her throat. "I'm going to the kitchen to check the meat on the grill and gather more fruit for dessert. I'll be back." She winked, reminding me not to forget about her son. I'd promised to talk to JB about him for her. She felt that if it came from me, he'd be more willing to help.

I hadn't been too eager to ask JB for anything especially now, but I wouldn't miss the opportunity to help her son either.

He offered me his other hand. I took it, stood, and we walked over to the living room, leaving our meals.

We sat on the couch, him beside, facing me. "Someday, I'm going to tell you everything. For now, know that you did nothing wrong. You didn't offend me, and I wasn't discounting you by not telling you."

He slid off the couch and knelt beside me, still holding my hand.

"You hurt me badly." I managed through a choked voice.

"I know. I'm very sorry."

I wasn't done. "You knew better, JB. You've shown so much wisdom in times past."

He ran a hand through his hair. "Sweet wine pours from broken pitchers. Wisdom flows from broken lives."

My eyes found his. "I've been walked out on before, and left to figure why things didn't work. When you left, I thought the same thing had happened. Except, that Ray had more guts."

Even now, I could see he was suffering through this, just like me.

"I didn't leave to hurt you. I needed to close a chapter in my past and I needed to do it on my own, with the Lord helping me. I wanted to come back to you whole, and healed not—"

"Broken," I cut in. "I know. I forgive you. But I hated the suspense, and the anxiety. I worried about you. First, I thought something was wrong. Then I thought you were a coward and couldn't stand to break up with me face to face."

I wiped my eyes. "Then after a while, I just didn't know what to think. I prayed to stop loving you. I worked to get you out of my heart, JB. You really hurt me—I'm not going to lie. But since you explained, I understand and have forgiven you. Hopefully, one day you'll tell me what all this was about. For today, I'm glad you forgave your dad. That's most important."

He drew me close and buried his face on my neck. His voice dropped to a whisper. "I love you, Candace Rodriguez. With all of my heart. With all of my soul. I cherish you. I'm yours. With abandon. I will never hurt you again, as much as I can help it."

I curled my hands on his back.

Moments later, a cough behind us separated us. We rose and joined Mrs. Cantwell at the dining room table.

"I've got something here for everyone. Strawberries for you, Candace. Pumpkin pie for you, JB. I love hot chocolate after a bountiful meal."

As we smiled, a heavy weight lifted off my shoulders.

"JB, Mrs. Cantwell would like for you to chat with her son. We're inviting him to the concert. He may have some…money issues he needs help with. I thought with your experience handling money, stock, and such in your former life, you might teach him a few things about the value of money. To help him get things back on track. His wife is pregnant, so they need all the funds coming in, not going out. You think you can help?"

He rubbed his jaw. "I'm surprised that you asked me, but sure. I'd actually helped at a youth center in New York for a few months, mentoring youth about managing funds. I'd be happy to talk to him."

"Great." Mrs. Cantwell lit up. "Thank you, JB. My husband would be thrilled."

We took our share of desserts, and light talk sufficed for the rest of the night.

* * *

I WAS one week away from leaving the farm. It feels surreal. I surveyed the space surrounding me. I'd gotten so used to this place, and so comfortable.

Thank You, Lord, because You're in perfect control.

I'd learned to say that whenever I didn't know where to turn. But I still needed to focus. The concert was seven days away.

JB, who'd been back for a few days now, slid into planning mode with my brother. In a way, logistically, it was as if he never left.

Our relationship remained a little sober, but was warming up.

I still ran in the opposite direction of the road to keep a clear head, but we spent every evening together the last three days, catching up.

I focused on my preparation for the concert, and he gave me the much-needed room, yet stayed supportive. I planned to return to New York City the day following the concert. I was going to tell JB today when we met up.

My brother was handling the logistics for releasing my album, *After*, with all nine songs, the day after the concert.

I asked why he didn't do everything on the same day, but he insisted so I backed down.

Our volunteers' shirts had arrived. The stage was fully built on JB's farm, and the stands for free meat and smoothies went up near the borders for both farms.

At last count, Matt said sixty thousand people had now signed up online to hear me sing live. We needed seventy thousand for both the in-person attendance and online participation. We'd almost hit the number with days to spare.

My album's preorder was now number three on the Billboard 200 charts, projected to debut at number one on the release day.

People hash-tagged my concert on social media, saying they couldn't wait—most out of curiosity just to see me, I guessed.

I was back into my music swing practicing every day—preparing, and praying for it. My focus was to get through the concert day in tiptop shape, both for the music and, well, physically.

Lord, please help me, I prayed.

* * *

April 10.

When you're on a farm, your shoes get dirty quickly—even if you are about to perform live before 5,500 new fans in-person, and 100,000 logged on online.

"Welcome everyone! We're pleased to have you here! Great turnout today." Matt MC-ed, his voice vibrating through the mounted speaker above the dressing lounge.

"Testing. Testing." A tech guy, standing next to me, double-checked my earpiece.

The wooden floor of the newly constructed dressing room atop the goats' pen farmland sounded like a drum beneath, a strong one. The excitement outside was unmistakable. I could feel it in the shouts of the crowd—just like in New York, the day I fell.

I stepped over some cloth stage-cover materials, waiting to be cleared by volunteers. Fantastic people worked nonstop the last twenty-four hours. They all insisted I slept while they worked at midnight last night, so I'd be ready to perform today.

I stood in front of the full-length mirror and examined the rare blue vintage dress.

A perfect fit.

I fit into the dream dress! I chuckled. I was so excited when I taped off the goal weight loss of 177 pounds from the elliptical machine this morning. Look at me.

Twelve months later, a completely transformed individual, in heart, mind, soul, spirit, and body. Grown in Christ.

And in love with a remarkable man.

With faith built to withstand circumstances.

About to be contract debt-free of 2 million dollars and living my new life.

This is my After!

I made it!

Every hurt, pain, sacrifice, and hard work was worth the feeling of this moment.

I treasured it.

"Candace?" a familiar voice shouted. "No way!"

John Akum.

I turned slowly.

His mouth slung agape. His eyes ran from my head to toe then back to my face. He pointed to me and sputtered.

"Saying something, John?"

He swallowed, glancing around nervously, and caught himself. "You, um, look good."

He had to repeat it.

I bent slightly, hand to my ears. "What did you say?"

He leaned in. "You look good, Candace!"

There. He said it, and it came out of him like he was spewing bitter pills. His face contorted, saying he wanted to be far from here.

"Thank you, John." I smiled. "Please grab a seat on stage. I hope you enjoy the concert." I flipped around and toyed with the pin on the dress until he exited.

A winning smile spread over my face.

Mrs. Cantwell appeared in the mirror beside me. Her hands flew to her mouth. "You're beautiful! Look at you!"

I moved from the mirror and hugged her, tears brimming. I forced them back.

It took the makeup artists one hour to get me done. I wouldn't undo their hard work.

"Mrs. Cantwell, I want you to know that I'm grateful to you, your husband, and in fact, your entire family! You fed me every day while I focused on my workout and music. You took care of me like a mother. I couldn't have done this without you, JB, Matt—all of you made me the person standing here today. Thank you."

I laughed, heavy with emotion. "I appreciate everyone who supported me. The four of you, plus Eric in NY who said he believed in my ability to reach my goals. You all made this happen." I waved a hand from head to toe.

She clasped my arms eagerly and shook her head. "No, Candace. God made this happen. Do you know what you did for me? Connecting me to JB who's already helped my son start turning his life around within one week? Reuniting his home with his wife? You saved my family as much as we saved your goals. We helped each other. That's what being a Christian is all about. We're ultimately one family in Christ. I'm glad we served some use to you. Now you go out there and don't make all this hard work be for nothing. Shine!" She shoved me forward playfully.

I exited the dressing room, strode outside, and walked toward the stage's back entrance, my black heels clicking.

I counted my blessings, with each step.

Pounds lost—177! I chuckled.

A new music album.

Nine new songs.

A man who loves me.

A new family.

A stronger faith.

A new life.

New fans—105,500 people—waiting to hear me sing. People I didn't have at this time last year.

A bright outlook on life.

Higher Hope. Greater Faith. Fearless Love.

I climbed the steps up the backstage and entered as Matt yielded the microphone. He stopped when he saw me and gasped, then smiled broadly.

Even he had not seen this dress, or me dressed up, for months. He leaned over and whispered, "Do us proud!"

I walked up to the stage, and the crowd went wild.

People spanned the length and breadth as far as I could see.

In that moment, I felt small.

How could all these people be here to see me? To support me and my music?

Thank You, Lord! This could only be You.

So many mounted screens surrounded me, I couldn't count them. My eyes swept the crowd end to end. I couldn't possibly see the farthest person. They disappeared into the tree cover along the path where JB and I used to run.

Lord, I'm not this important. I'm just one girl.

Mrs. Cantwell once told me, "It takes one person to change the world. The world is listening. What will you sing, Candace?"

* * *

CAMERAS CLICKED AWAY.

I smiled, then I waved to the crowd. Cheers erupted.

"Hi, thank you everyone for coming! It means so much to me to have your support. May God bless you all!"

I closed my eyes for a moment, focusing on Jesus.

My praise is of Him and to Him. I opened my lips.

"I hold on to love, Fearless Love, I cling on to hope, Endless Hope, I dig in the fight, the fight of faith, the fight of freedom, the fight of love, Fearless Love."

The crowd's wild roar swallowed my voice, and overpowered mine. I was forced to stop.

I stepped forward, mic in hand, and bowed, gesturing gratitude with my hands, but they all raised their phones and hand cameras, and took photos of me instead.

I chose to oblige them so they could focus on the music. I spread my arms out wide, twisting and turning 360 degrees and back again.

The whistles, shouts, clapping, and applause—thundered throughout overwhelmingly.

After a full fifteen minutes, things quieted down enough for me to continue. I was speechless.

In my heart rang out, "Jesus, may You be glorified here today."

I began humming "Fearless Love" again into the mic.

I hummed it twice, and gained the huge crowd's focus and attention.

Then I began to sing again. This time, without interruptions.

CHAPTER 33

* * *

*T*he media trucks parked at the far corner as reporters sat close to the front, recording every movement, and every sound.

I got through the first three songs easily.

The chill began to affect me a little so I wrapped a scarf around my neck to protect my throat muscles. Then I asked them to begin clapping.

I leaned closer to the mic.

"When God takes you through the valleys of life before raising you to the mountaintop, it's so that when you stand atop that mountain, you lose fear of the valley—because you've already been there, and won. Here is 'Mountain Top.'"

I belted out the words like sweet honey on my tongue.

At the end of the song, I asked them to personalize it, 'Jesus brought *me* through to the other side.' They complied eagerly.

Hearing thousands of people worshiping God with me, and not simply my own voice—was glorious!

JB met my eyes, but I tore mine away to stay focused. I did see him

276

whisper something to my brother. I focused on each song, letting it flood my heart.

Once the crowd caught each tune, they sang along, as words were displayed on the screen.

The atmosphere felt so heavenly.

There was hardly any difference between the crowd and me.

We sang to God in unison, united in worship. I'd never felt such collective presence of God, with many hearts beating as one.

After I sang the final song, my blood pumped with elation through every vein. They cheered as I bowed one more time, walked forward, and shook a few hands close to the stage.

When I straightened and prepared to leave Matt came up to me and whispered, "They would like to hear about the weight loss part. We have the flyers and sheets you asked for, ready to give out."

I'd forgotten. I nodded, and walked back to the center of the stage. "I'm guessing you'd all like to hear about my weight loss."

The crowd erupted again, applauding. Reporters edged closer, zooming in their lenses.

"I've lost a total of 177 pounds in eleven and half months. I'm now wearing a size 8 dress no longer a size 25. I do have loose skin underneath this pretty dress, and you can see some stretch marks so be sure that I worked hard."

A good number laughed. Applause followed. Someone at the back end shouted, "I love you, Candace!"

I waved again, staying focused. "I achieved this through changing my diet and incorporating daily exercise, and completely by the grace of God. I'm not a weight loss expert, but I put in a lot of hard work, right here, on this farm, for the past year. And this is my After, not just for weight loss, but for every area of my life—spiritual, emotional, and physical—all has changed in the past year."

Applause rang through again. Loud whistles followed.

I pressed to get to my final point. "The road to your After is paved with grit, second guessing yourself, falling many times, getting back up, and keeping on going. It's never easy, but if you don't give up, you will arrive."

I dipped my head slightly toward the backstage area. "I was given so much hope by my hosts, other special people here, and some who are not here today. These people are all my family now. They were all crucial to my success. So I say thank you, Dr. and Dr. Mrs. Cantwell!"

I wiped a stubborn tear. I had restrained from mentioning JB since I wasn't sure he'd want the spotlight.

"If you'd like to learn from my experience, please fill out the sheets you'll soon get, and drop them in the blue bins at the end of these farms. And we will reach out to you." I had to help others. I couldn't keep this gift to myself. "Thank you all!"

* * *

WHEN I DUCKED BACKSTAGE AGAIN, my brother hurried to me, phone in hand. I slipped out of my shoes and changed into flat boots to stay warm, and then wrapping a blanket around my shoulders.

"What? Another viral video? I think I've had enough, Matt!"

"Hah." He smiled. "No, you want to see this, Candace. Really."

He pressed a key and flipped the video to face me.

I shrugged and tried to stay my disaffection for videos.

A cry caught in my throat when I saw who it was. JB.

He held up a direction sign, like those we'd made for the concert, but this one was different. It read: "Candace Rodriguez, will you be my wife?"

I gasped. JB now appeared from behind a curtain, followed by the Cantwells, their son, his wife, and Grandma Patty.

JB knelt on one knee and popped a ring. "Candace, these past couple of months have been a wild ride—for both of us. There've been good times, great times, and not so great times, but we've weathered it all. I'm asking you, with all of my heart, please, Candace, will you marry me?"

I burst into tears and laughter all at the same time. "Yes! JB, yes!"

He slipped the ring onto my ring finger, rose to his feet, and hugged me.

He let go and peered right into my eyes. "I love you, Candace. Today, and forever."

Cheers broke out. Mrs. Cantwell drew close and hugged me, congratulating me. So did everyone else in the room.

Today's concert? My best. One. Ever!

* * *

"They want you to come back."

I frowned. "Who?"

Matt stayed silent momentarily. "The NFL."

Oh, the event where I'd fallen one year ago.

I swallowed. Being slimmer didn't remove the phobia for places where you'd fallen.

"Your new fame has blown everyone's expectations. They want you to sing at the Super Bowl next year, if you please. Also, the label wants to discuss the possibility of starting an inspirational label with us. If you're interested, that is."

I shook my head, not giving it a second thought. "Let's say yes to the NFL, it's nice of them to invite me again. But no for the record's request."

Matt frowned. "I thought that was what you wanted."

"Yes, it was when I was desperate. Now I realize that I can't run my career on the support of only one member of their leadership. Tell them I appreciate their offer, but no thank you."

"If you say so."

I tipped my gaze his way, curious. "Have we paid their two million yet?"

"We're processing the payments now. Two mil cold cash—well, figuratively. They'll get their money via wire transfer in one month after we've gained physical payment. Oh, Candace, they cancelled tomorrow's meeting, because they said it's no longer necessary since you don't owe a dime. And there's something else."

Uh-oh. I inched up, anxious. "What, Matt?"

He smiled. "Everything made from the day after the concert,

including album sales, is yours. That's what I'd negotiated. They didn't expect that you'd succeed in raising two mil so they took the deal. Now, it worked out in your favor. You're now a very rich lady, Candace. Upward of one million dollars and counting from album sales alone!"

Stunned, I hugged him. "You were quite smart to do that for me! For us."

He shrugged. "Hey, I wasn't even sure you'd make half the two mil even if you dragged everyone you could convince out here. But I was hopeful."

He scrolled through his phone, like he always did. He looked up again, smiling wide.

"Candace? Your album, *After*, is now number one on the Billboard 200 charts! My inbox is blowing up. We just received requests for some cash-backed endorsement deals."

I still had an issue to confirm. "Since you're still leaving, who will be my new manager?" Someone shuffled behind me. "That would be me, Ms. Candace."

I turned and covered my mouth. "Wow!"

Dennis Alders, award-winning Christian recording artist, approached me. He'd aged, and was now in his seventies, but he still bore a sharp gait. His towering presence filled the room.

He extended his hand, and I shook it firm. "My voice might not be what it used to be, but I can sure help a young talent like you, and shepherd you."

Oh my! My heart trilled. "Thank you. Yes, of course!"

CHAPTER 34

* * *

I rose early. Today was special. Dressed in a simple angelic-white flowing silk wedding gown, with a veil on my head secured by a tiara, I was ready. My heart fluttered as I clutched my bridal bouquet of white roses. I checked the white pearl drop earrings on my ears and glanced at the mirror for the light makeup.

"Have you added up the guest list yet, Mika?" Mrs. Cantwell shouted toward the other room.

I was back at the Day Spring farms, to marry JB in a quiet, private ceremony, two years from the time we met.

The past year was a whirlwind of busyness for both of us. Had we not spent time together during our low moment, we would not have had the time now, during prosperity to do so.

Our schedules were both fully booked up to a year ahead. JB's farm was doing so well, that he'd gone international.

He bought two more farms in New York where we planned to live. He told me service requests came all the way from Spain last night. Rosa, my friend, in Italy custom-ordered dairy for her special customers once a month.

I could never have predicted any of this. No one could. Mrs. Cantwell came up to me and stood, the way she had at the concert. "You're a dashing bride, Candace! JB will be stunned speechless."

We were having our wedding a few days before my event in New York—the same one where I had fallen two years ago, that started all of this. Close friends and family from both sides gathered as we stood face to face in the February cold wind.

The minister began. "Do you, Jabez Patrickson, take Candace Rodriguez, to be your wife…?"

JB grinned broadly, eyes trained on me. "I do!"

I repeated the vows.

"Ladies and gentlemen, I present to you Mr. and Mrs. Patrickson! JB, you may kiss your bride!"

Cheers erupted as JB kissed me long for our first kiss, holding me in a tight embrace.

JB and I changed after posing for pictures. We then boarded a rented private jet to fly us to our honeymoon, to be interrupted only with my performance in New York.

Rosa was expecting us. She'd persuaded us before the wedding, to honeymoon at Nemi, the town near Rome where she lived. She reminded me how much I'd always talked in college about having my honeymoon in a cliff town with cobbled streets and beautiful sunsets.

"Nemi is perfect for you! As your maid of honor, I insist. I've got enough wild strawberries and tea to make you happy." She'd pressed. "Plus, I can't wait to see you again and show off how good you look."

JB and I looked up Nemi and loved the pictures so we booked it as our destination.

Rosa was thrilled. She said she'd like to prepare a post-wedding get-together for us with her favorite customers, then she asked if I would sing one of my new songs to them.

I said, "Sure."

As we boarded our flight to Nemi, Italy, I turned to JB, clad in all-white suit and tie. "I'm looking forward to Nemi."

He leaned over and kissed me. "I'm looking forward to spending time with my wife."

I brushed aside some stray hair and smiled. *New York City can wait. I have a husband to attend to!*

* * *

"OH SAY CAN YOU SEE..." It was the month of March. I sang the anthem all the way to the end.

The stage didn't fall in. I stood tall. It was amazing. I felt free, and honored—at the same place where I'd so publicly fallen about two years ago.

The crowd cheered. They didn't boo. And I waved at the end.

I had one thing, in addition to the song, to share with those fifty thousand people gathered. I leaned into the mic.

"No matter what happens in your life, by the grace of God, if you believe it, there's always an after!"

They cheered.

"I'm here with my husband, a natural organic foods animal farmer and former Wall Street trader. I am very proud of him."

As I was about to leave the stage, people congratulated me.

One lady grunted at the side, "That's all the job they could find after they squandered our retirement."

The elderly man seated beside her nudged her side and shook his head. "Stop it, Gene. You and I can't even do what he's doing, running a farm. We're too old for that stuff. And who said he's one of those who ate our money?"

She frowned.

Just as I said to the NFL Chairman standing next to them, "Thank you for asking me back! It's been my honor!"

The entire forum rose in unison, applauding, cheering, and whistling, with cameras flashing as I walked off stage.

I joined hands with JB who waited patiently at the base as we took steps full of hope toward our future.

* * *

JB SWEPT me an admiring glance as we boarded the plane, headed back to our honeymoon. "You are the most gorgeous creature."

Warmth crept to my cheeks. "Thank you. But—there's something else I have been waiting to hear."

He eyed me quizzically. Then his eyebrows rose. "Oh. About me and my dad. I'd promised to tell you what happened between me and my dad."

I smiled. "If you don't mind. I'm not going anywhere." I didn't want him to fear anything.

"Okay. From the beginning?"

"Preferably. We've got a long flight ahead of us."

He adjusted his seat back, and helped me with mine. "All right, then. I hope you can handle it."

I opened my ears and heart. "Trust God."

THE END

Thank you for reading **AFTER**! Enjoy a free sample of **JABEZ** (AFTER Series Book 1.5) below. Grab books 2 & 3 here.

AFTER 2

After Series (Book 3)

* * *

WILL HE SUCCEED OR FAIL?

"THE ONLY STOCK YOU'LL EVER SELL IS CHIK'N STOCK."

Jabez Patrickson heard those gut-wrenching words dripping with sarcasm from his father at a tender age and knew the odds were strongly stacked against him. Not only will his father not support his goal to become a NY Stockbroker, he would stand against any chance of his succeeding. JB set his heart on his goal. But several odds stood in his way—lack of money, insufficient education, and moral support. Will he make it to the NY Stock Exchange as a stockbroker or will his dream be squashed before it begins? Will Louisville construction worker be the only job ever on his resume? Or with divine intervention, can he surmount the impossible odds to reach his dream? Be a part of his audience as he tells Candace his story for the first time.

Jabez is a follow-up to Book 1, After. Reading After would improve your understanding of this story, though it's not required to enjoy it.

JABEZ is a novella in the **AFTER** Christian Inspirational Series, Book 1.5 . Read JABEZ here

AFTER SERIES- IN ORDER

BOOK 1-<u>AFTER</u>

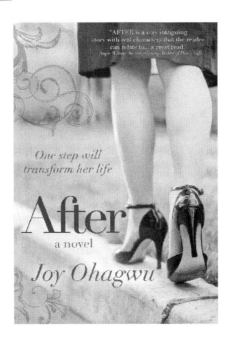

BOOK 1.5-JABEZ

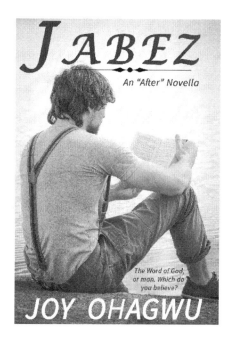

BOOK TWO-AFTER 2

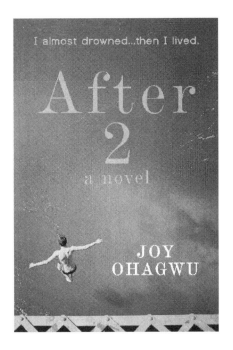

After Series (Book 3)

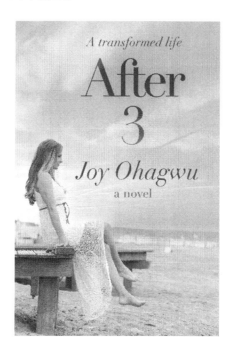

VISIT <u>JOY OHAGWU'S AMAZON AUTHOR PAGE</u> TO LEARN MORE. THANK YOU!

Important Note—If you enjoyed JB and Candace's story, encourage more readers by sharing your positive feedback when prompted to leave a review, letting others know you loved it. Thank you!

A REALLY COOL OPPORTUNITY

* * *

Join my VIP readers club to be the first to know as soon as my books are available for purchase here: http://www.joyohagwu.com/announcements.html

Want to know when my next book releases?
And to grab :
* a free ebook (limited time offer)
* Release day giveaways
*Discounted prices
* And so much more!
Hit YES below and you're in!
See you on the inside!

THEN JOIN MY VIP READERS CLUB

FOLLOW AUTHOR JOY OHAGWU

* * *

You can visit and follow my Amazon Author page with one click and enjoy my other available titles.

You can also follow me on

BOOKBUB

FACEBOOK

TWITTER

God bless you!

BIBLIOGRAPHY OF MY BOOKS

* * *

You can visit and follow my Amazon Author page with one click. And select your next read from my available titles.

RED-The New Rulebook Series #1
SNOWY PEAKS-The New Rulebook Series #2
THE WEDDING-The New Rulebook Series #3

VANISHED-The New Rulebook Series #4
RESCUED- The New Rulebook Series #5
DELIVERED- The New Rulebook Series #6
FREEDOM- The New Rulebook Series #7
REST- The New Rulebook Series #8
SUNSHINE- The New Rulebook Series #9

BIBLIOGRAPHY OF MY BOOKS 2

* * *

UNCOMMON GROUND- Pleasant Hearts Series (Book 1)
UNBOUND HOPE- Pleasant Hearts Series (Book 2)
UNVEILED TRUTH- Pleasant Hearts Series (Book 3)
UNSHAKEN LOVE (Pleasant Hearts Series Book 4)
DECOY- Elliot-Kings Series (Book 1)

The New Rulebook Series Boxed Set- (Books 1-3)
The New Rulebook Series Boxed Set- (Books 4-6)
The New Rulebook Series Boxed Set- (Books 7-9)

Christian Inspirational Titles:

After Series (Book 1)
Jabez (After Series Novella)
After Series (Book 2)
After Series (Book 3)

DISCOUNTED PREORDERS (Limited Time Only)

-After 3
  -Unshaken Love

FROM THE AUTHOR

Thank you for purchasing After! It is my pleasure to share this story with you. I pray you enjoy Candace and JB's story, as much as I did writing it! This novel is entirely a work of fiction. In this book, I have altered date and location of the actual XLVIII Super Bowl for fictional purposes.

Read AFTER 2 here.

NOTE TO THE READER

* * *

Thank you so much for buying **AFTER**, First book of this Inspirational Series Series! I am so thankful that you chose this book out of others to enjoy. Please consider leaving a review after reading. Continue with Blossom's story in AFTER Book 2 here.

God bless you!

ACKNOWLEDGMENTS

* * *

Thank You, Holy Spirit, for all it took to get this book completed. Long writing days and nights, while nursing brutal allergies and pressing forward with unrelenting focus in the midst of competing demands. They were well worth it. Thank You for the songs never sang before, You gave me, lyrics and tunes included. May they glorify You, O God! Thank You, Lord Jesus, for saving me. I remind myself every day that I am saved by grace through faith, and all I boast of, is You and Your unending love for me. It gives me pleasure to sit at Your feet daily and learn. Please hold on to me to the very end.

I'm very grateful to my family for their support and to my editor, Deirdre Lockhart, of Brilliant Cut Editing. Thank you for your hard work! I'm proud of our gold-standard product. My fellow authors at ACFW, I could not have done this without your support! Of course, my sincere thanks to Paper & Sage, to Christa, for the beautiful cover. Everyone loves it! May God bless you all.

To my readers, I feel honored that you are enjoying my books! With every download, you give me more strength to continue writing.

I'm so encouraged by your positive feedback. May they continue. I pray the Lord Himself blesses you with every word you read. Thank you for choosing After! We're in this together, so please buckle in and let's go.

DESCRIPTION

(Culled from Paperback)

* * *

Sixty thousand people watched as Candace Rodriguez literally fell off the stage while performing the national anthem, wrecking more than her self-esteem. Is her music career over? Now, weighing 350 pounds and jilted by her fiancé after the shame of her public fall, can she find another chance at true love? Will her new Christian faith anchor her future hopes?

Former highbrow stock trader, "JB" Patrickson has had enough of life making mockery of his best laid-out future plans. His father insisted he'd never make it more than selling "chickn" stock in Kentucky. Proving him wrong, JB succeeded at the NY Stock Exchange, becoming one of the best US traders…until the market crashed in 2008. Seven years later and mired in debt, he can't shake the urge that God is leading him down a different path. The path of accepting his grandmother's request to come help manage her farm, couple hundred miles away, despite his little to nothing knowledge about farming. Has he fallen low enough to toil with his hands to eke out a single meal? What future could God plan for him on a farm?

Twenty years after returning to the US from a fulfilling medical mission in Asia, Dr. and Dr. Mrs. Cantwell gratefully send off two sons to college, purchase a flourishing twenty-acre farm, and prepare to settle into their empty nest stage. But what will they do if God leads one more life into their path, one needing stitches of the soul not of the body? Can they answer His call to service, or will overlooked pain from the past threaten the fragile peace they'd so desperately coaxed into existence to survive together?

Find out how these lives intersect at the Day Spring Farms, and watch what God can do to turn brokenness and shattered dreams into masterpieces.

AFTER, an inspirational Novel by Contemporary Christian Fiction Author, Joy Ohagwu, is poised to spotlight the strength in transformation, courage in love and hope in times of despair.

JOIN MY VIP READERS CLUB (AND GET A FREE EBOOK HERE)

* * *

Join my VIP readers club to be the first to know as soon as my books are available for purchase here: http://www.joyohagwu.com/announcements.html or click on the next image >>>

Want to know when my next book releases?
And to grab:
* a free ebook (limited time offer)
* Release day giveaways
*Discounted prices
* And so much more!
Hit YES below and you're in!
See you on the inside!

THEN JOIN MY VIP READERS BY CLICKING ON THE IMAGE

After

By
Joy Ohagwu
Copyright Second Edition © 2016
Life Fountain Books

All glory to God
Printed in the United States of America

❀ Created with Vellum